CONQUEST OF THE PLANET OF THE GEEKS

Sex, Drugs & Superheroes II

David Reddish

Digital Fabulists

DIGITAL FABULISTS
PUBLISHING FOR THE FUTURE

ALSO BY DAVID REDDISH

published by digital fabulists

*Sex, Drugs & Superheroes: A Savage Journey Into a
Wretched Hive of Scum and Supervillainy*

The Passion of Sergius & Bacchus

Sex Drugs & Superheroes III: The Wrath of Comic-Con

ISBN-13: 978-0692566428
ISBN-10: 0692566422

Cover design by: Michael Szalapski
Printed in the United States of America

For my grandparents.

CONTENTS

PROLOGUE

Garmanbozia

F uck, get hard!

I stood over the toilet, staring down at my flaccid member, hanging indifferent between my legs like the trunk of a geriatric elephant. I knew full well if I couldn't take full advantage of my morning erection, I'd have to wait at least another day before I could get one again. I tired of the waiting. No amount of stimulation—visual, tactile or mental—could restore life to my manhood.

After several minutes of more coaxing, stroking, yanking, slapping, tugging, humping and, well, anything else I could think of, I conceded my defeat. Useless again. I slammed the toilet lid shut and flushed, my eyes drifting to the rank of orange pill bottles now crowding my Claratin and daily vitamins. I needed the Claratin to survive the wretched smog of Los Angeles, and now I needed its prescription neighbors to function too: Klonopin for anxiety, Ambien for sleep and the Wonder Twins: Lexapro and Abilify. Or at least the Lexapro and Abilify purported to do wonders for people with my... condition...and for some, maybe they did. But after almost a year on my superhero meds, I had yet to experience anything I'd classify as "wonder." Plenty of other descriptors came to mind —alienating, stifling, dehumanizing—but never wonder. As it was, between the headaches, dizzy spells, nausea and flaccidity, said medication made me barely function at best.

Barely.

Still, even the most basic function in daily life trumped the alternative, which, for the record, was no function at all, as I'd learned in the hardest way possible. I had to remind myself every morning of the days in bed, the blackout shades expelling all natural light from the apartment, the crying fits, the bottomless pit of darkness which consumed me, rendering me helpless to escape, robbing me of the hope of ever feeling joy again. Yes, I had bad days, and I gave them no more than a passing thought in the beginning, which is why it took a near-intervention from my roommate before I called my doctor.

No, Leak-Win, sleepin' sixteen hours a day isn't noh-mal. That's tsuris. It's a problem.

I could hear her rusty-gate Yiddish-accented words echoing in my head. I reached down and tapped one white Lexapro and one teal Abilify pill from each bottle and tossed them into my mouth, puckering at the powdery bitterness against my tongue.

Crying foah days isn't noh-mal.

I juggled the pills around with my tongue, watching myself in the mirror with disgust.

Sayin' you'd be bettah off dead isn't...

I swallowed both pills dry, chasing them with Claratin and my vitamins. I stared at my naked, emaciated body in the mirror—the pasty white skin devoid of the now-unaffordable expense of tanning lotion, the glimmer of my piercings at my left nipple and belly button, the latter sporting a skull in a glass ball within the divot of my navel, a USB drive hanging from a lanyard around my neck, and my eyes, so dilated and glassy that the once-shining green irises I'd so prided myself on had all but vanished.

Leak-Win, I think you have bipolah disordah.

I recall staring down at the diminutive frame of my spinsterish physician, her lips drawn into an affected frown of sympathy. I felt so helpless, so violated. "I would be better off dead, then," I grumbled to her. That made her reach for her prescription pad.

Not that I blamed her. My friends did the right thing by urging me to see her, and her treatment regimen offered hope for people with my…condition. It also offered a broad array of nasty side effects, both physical and mental. I hadn't written so much as a word since the day I started the meds.

I glanced at myself in the mirror one last time. *This is living?* I wondered.

I switched off the bathroom light, burying my face in a towel hanging on the back of the door. I pulled the fluffy terrycloth up over my ears, held it there, and closed my eyes. The towel smelled of faint bleach—the staple odor of hotel linens. I stood there breathing the fumes, barricading myself from the world, with only the recirculated wisp of air conditioning filtering into the room from a vent above the door to caress my spiny, naked back. God, I couldn't. I just couldn't, or—

"Liquin!"

The familiar voice forced the towel from my face as I opened my eyes in the darkness. Had I left the lights on, no doubt I would have caught a glance of my own bemused expression— eyelids half closed, mouth stretched the length of my face as if chocking back some poison. I had to get moving.

"Liquin!" the voice insisted again. "Are you taking a bath with the toaster again?"

"No!" I barked, reaching in the dark for my boxers. I pulled them on, feeling around for the button fly to make sure I had them on the right way. "Did they give us a toaster with the room?"

"That's good," the voice continued from just beyond the door. I threw it open, squinting in the refracted daylight of the hotel room, my disgusted expression unchanged. "Because, you know, they have safety cutoffs on the power outlets for a reason."

Before me stood the glowing form of The Admiral, my roommate of the day, her characteristic smile phosphorescent white, her almond eyes complimenting her butterscotch skin, smooth and flawless and jet black Latina hair highlighted with shimmering auburn tresses. She seemed to radiate energy no matter where she went, no matter what the circumstance. She wore an *X-Men* t-shirt, altered and fitted to show off her curvaceous torso, designer jeans and her trademark fedora. She cocked her pelvis and rested a hand on her hip, showing off her apple-shaped ass bulging under the denim. I scoffed a half-assed laugh, stepping past her, into the disaster bunker that had been our hotel room the night before.

Roxanne Rodriguez and I had lapped the same social circles for years. I always knew to say hello to her, to wave or exchange a friendly hug, but I never really knew her that well. Then, in a chance meeting at the DMV of all places, she and I had the get-to-know-you conversation that had eluded us for so long. Her own enrollment alongside my dear friend Kate at the Hollywood Film, Television and Drama School of Los Angeles, sealed our steadfast friendship. Roxanne swept into my life like a hurricane of energy, brightening my days with laughter and conversation, offering genuine compassion and support as my biggest cheerleader. Movie nights with Kate and her boyfriend Windsor, fueled by bottles of red wine, became regular events, as we'd trade horror stories of dating sprawled in our pajamas on my couch. Roxanne made for a guiding light as my life darkened. I often wondered how I'd ever lived without her—she was the big sister I'd never had.

"I'm not going to kill myself the day of Comic-Con, my good Admiral," I assured her. "At least, not until we check into the other hotel. That way the housekeeping staff can clean up my cadaver and they won't come after you for a tip. The room won't be in your name." Not that I'd given any thought to the possibility.

"Ew!" squealed The Admiral. "You better leave money for tip, little brother," she said, following me across the bedroom. "I'm not paying for that shit!"

"I'll keep that in mind," I moaned, rummaging into my suitcase. I selected a nondescript pair of jeans and a distressed yellow t-shirt upon which I'd spray painted the words "TWILIGHT SUCKS." I tossed the shirt to the edge of my bed and pulled on my pants.

"Dude, you're not even ready to go yet!" The Admiral reprimanded me as she noticed my still-open suitcase.

"I'm an expert, I know what I'm doing," I said devoid of passion, as if spieling tired sound bites.

"But what are you wearing for the weekend? Where's all the paperwork? What about the First Aid Kit?!"

"God, Roxanne!" I whined, pulling on my shirt. "It's set. Everything is ready. You're going to be fine. It's all fine."

"Liquin!" she growled. "It's Comic-Con. Your reason for living. Act excited! Spin up the FTL drive!"

"Yes, Admiral," I obliged, collapsing onto the stiff, bleached sheets of the unmade hotel bed. Roxanne frowned, but the sound of her ringtone—a bizarre mash-up of Metallica's *Enter Sandman* and Lady Gaga's *Telephone*—prompted her to retreat to her side of the room.

"Retract the flight pods! Recall the fighters! Stand by for hyperlight jump!" she called, wading through the clutter of the room to find her phone. Without missing a beat, I watched her answer the call: "You got Roxanne! *Darling!* Hey..."

Roxanne worked as the assistant to a Hollywood Legend and received calls around the clock for this-or-that, some request for autographed merchandise, errands to run, invitations to Hollywood parties, and just about anything else. Her ability to manage such a broad fleet of demands had earned her the nickname of "The Admiral" from me. Well that, and her ability to wrangle and date several men at once.

I wallowed in my angst another moment or two, listening to The Admiral spout Hollywood platitudes like boiling water from a geyser. She had a point: if I had a reason to keep on living despite my continued failure as a screenwriter, it had to be Comic-Con. I relented from my moping and started to pull myself together. I pulled on my "TWILIGHT SUCKS" t-shirt, selected a few other random geek-tastic fashion bits from my suitcase, and started to zip it shut—

"First-Aid!" Roxanne called from across the room. I stuck my head up like a periscope over the edge of the bed to see her still on the phone, but with a wild grimace on her face and two thumbs extended up, signaling her readiness for a good time. I dug through my suitcase, rolling my eyes in annoyance, and pulled the First Aid kit from the bottom of my luggage and popped it open to let Roxanne give a final survey of the contents of the retro-travel box. A bottle of scotch, a gram of high-quality medical marijuana, Vitamin B12, Vitamin C powder, laxatives, anti-gas pills, painkillers (regular and prescription), Ambien, antacids, a bottle of rum and a few stray pills of Cialis made their homes into the tiny compartments of the kit. One last supply—a bottle of vodka which, I had earlier discovered, stood too tall to fit in the last open bottle-slot of the kit. Undeterred, I'd transferred the booze from the oversized glass bottle into an empty shampoo bottle from my home recycle bin. As I glanced at the "Coconut Follicle Moisturizer" label, I strained to remember: Had I thought to rinse the shampoo bottle first?

"You're marvelous" The Admiral purred with muted excitement as she sashayed over to embrace me, Bluetooth still attached to her ear.

"I sure hope so," I grumbled, resituating the garments in my suitcase to make room for the First Aid kit. Consolidation of space...always a necessity at Comic-Con.

"Did you pack your meds?" The Admiral asked, her tone somewhere between that of an affectionate grandmother and an emasculating Nurse Ratched. I glared up into her chestnut eyes and ivory smile, feeling like I'd just inhaled a gallon of lemon juice. Without another word, I went straight to the bathroom, threw my pill bottles into my shaving bag along with my toothbrush and hair products and went back to my suitcase, dropping the blue faux-leather toiletry bag on top of the rest of my luggage and slammed closed the lid of my suitcase, zipping it shut with an annoyed yank.

"Stop it," The Admiral ordered.

"What?" I grunted, playing dumb.

"Don't do this…"

"Do what, Roxanne!?" I threw up my arms in feigned exasperation.

"Don't act like this! You're better than this!"

"Am I? Am I really?"

The Admiral relented a moment with a frustrated scowl. She gripped me by both shoulders, pausing a moment to adjust her fedora and remove her Bluetooth as she did so.

"You are Liquin Sonos, crypto-insurrectionist author, screenwriter—"

"Wannabe screenwriter," I injected.

"And executive geek who has finished one Hell of a good script!"

"Which nobody will even look at," I added. "I still hate my life."

I threw myself down on the bed again, face up, staring at the popcorn ceiling above us. I reached up under my shirt and palmed the USB drive, its sole contents the master file for *Leopard Messiah,* my scriptural "masterpiece." Since finishing it I wore it like some religious charm around my neck, keeping it close to the heart I'd poured into it.

Roxanne moaned and rubbed her forehead. We'd done this dozens of times before, and each stand-off always ended in a draw, with both of us exasperated, me hating everything, and The Admiral wondering how I could believe such awful things about myself. Dare I even suggest the possibility that maybe I was *correct* in hating myself!?

"It will get better, Liquin, you know that," The Admiral soothed with tenderness in her voice, sitting down on the bed next to me. "This weekend could change everything! Monty Doyle will be there, and you're going to meet him, and he's going to take you on as his new wunderkind client!"

"You seriously think Monty Doyle will spend more than five seconds looking at me before he dismisses me as a nobody?" I grumbled.

"I wouldn't have set this up if I thought otherwise," Roxanne pressed me. "Now come on!"

I sat up in bed, my skull limp on my neck, rocking about with a sarcastic glare. "You arranged for us to meet," I reminded Roxanne, "not to have a *meeting.* This is Hollywood—there's a distinction!"

"Still," Roxanne urged.

"Still there is no assurance of anything," I countered. "I appreciate you getting me in to that party but it doesn't mean anything!"

The Admiral flinched, a slight pain evident in her face before she hid it again behind the shining smile and eyes. "One day you'll thank me."

"For cleaning up my corpse, or for jump-starting my career," I nagged. "Either way..." I paused a moment, forcing a smile to my face, letting my genuine gratitude show through. I really did appreciate her effort, but if the past two years of rejections heralded any indication, this weekend's meeting would prove little more than another missed opportunity for which I would want to take a bath with my blender. That's where *Neodämmerung* came in—my master plan, my last stand, my reckoning, my chance to bet it all and win and finally stop all the crazy, all the fighting, all the pain—

"Liquin, please..." The Admiral let out a soft plea, shaking me back to the present. I shut my eyes in shame. "Please can you just try to have a good time?"

I sighed and rubbed the bridge of my nose between my eyes. "Alright," I said in a soft volume. Despite my half-hearted response, Roxanne leapt to her feet with glee. Maybe she knew that she wouldn't get any more excitement out of me, at least not until we reached the Con.

"Come ooooon then!" The Admiral sang. "Let's get moving! Executive geeks!"

I threw on my backpack and followed her out the door, dragging my suitcase behind me. The Admiral had an elastic spring to her walk, always full of vigor and excitement. I didn't know how she did it.

Dear God in Heaven, how did this happen? I thought I'd won the game, but I'd discovered I'd just survived my first turn. I had to wonder how many chances I got. Just two years prior I'd had the time of my life at Comic-Con. I found my creative inspiration, affirmed my friendships, and from the people I loved so much, discovered that *maybe* I could love myself a little. Boy did that wear out fast. Within a year I'd finished my magnum opus and couldn't find a single fucking person in the business to read it. I'd taken to keeping all my rejection letters, letting them pile up like death threats against Martin Scorsese in his *Last Temptation of Christ* period. They almost outnumbered the pages in the script, and that was without even getting a response from some of the agents I'd contacted. And then...

Then the spells started—nights sitting in the bathtub in the dark, a hot washcloth over my face, or whole weekends spent in bed, only getting up to urinate or take Ambien. I'd come home from subbing at some elementary school bawling like one of the bullied kids or cut out after half a drink bar hopping with friends. Everything *hurt*. My weight plummeted from a robust 135lbs. to under 120. I hated eating. I hated breathing. Sometimes I thought it was all some horrid dream, but the constant pain reminded me—I was still alive.

My friends put the brakes on me after I told them how I spent my lunch hour at school sitting in a locked, darkened closet brooding. Between that and my bathtub act, they convinced me to get some counseling. I didn't object. By that time, I'd been keeping my toaster in my bathroom just in case I needed to check out whilst wallowing in my dirty water. My eventual therapist, the tiny spinsterish rusty gate-voiced Jewish woman, diagnosed me as bipolar almost immediately, though where the mania came in, I couldn't figure out. Maybe she heard about some of my Comic-Con antics.

So then, after a year on Lexapro and Abilify, I'd lost my bathtub antics, my libido, and my income. Oh yes—a janitor found me in the closet one afternoon. While I never received an official discharge from LA County Schools, they never asked me to sub again. I couldn't blame them; after all, who wants a teacher in the closet in 2010?

All the more reason for the *Neodämmerung*. I had burned myself out. I'd exhausted my options. I didn't know what to do anymore, and no matter where I turned, nobody would help me. Hell, nobody would even fucking *listen* to my problems, or even offer sympathy for what I was fucking going through! Nobody fucking cared when I needed it, not when I was close and begging right in front of them. That would change though. I'd found the way.

The Admiral and I made our way out of the Hyatt, and out onto Harbor Blvd. where the Con traffic had already begun to compile. She ranted on about her excitement to see the Con, to finally experience all the crazy geeky insanity. Of course, it all came second nature to her, not to mention free: the Legend booked a free room at the Hyatt on her behalf, and her famous associations got her a free Professional badge. Even with all the Legend connections, Roxanne still couldn't get us a room for the whole of the Con, but at least we had a place to stay an extra night; it would enable me to get a jump on Preview Night, the special pre-show for professionals and 4-day attendees to walk the open Exhibit hall and experience the Con at its most pristine. It also allowed them to get a jump on all the Con-exclusives—the posters, the action figures and God knew what else.

As we approached the geometric architecture of the Convention Center—the rectangular base adorned by a cylinder of rose windows tunneling through the front of the building with concrete isosceles triangles jutting upward into the atmosphere, tickling the overcast sky above. I yawned. Why couldn't I get excited? Comic-Con was my home! The only place I felt normal! All I wanted to do was go lay in bed somewhere with the covers pulled over my head in a state of utter catatonia. What the fuck troubled me so?

Oh, right, the Lexapro and Abilify. The drugs didn't just

keep me from getting plummeting depressed, they kept me from getting too excited also. Hooray for pharmaceuticals!

The Admiral and I made our way to the professional entry line which snaked down half the length of the building. I had never seen it so long, but given that preview night catered more to the Pro-crowd anyway, I suppose it should not have come as a surprise. The Hall Nazis, already out in full force and dressed in their standard red polo shirts covering their muscled, Naval cadet bodies barked and yelled, commanding all of us to stay in line. As one particularly dreadful one passed us, rabid as R. Lee Ermy on speed, I first noticed the guy behind us.

Towering, gaunt, with spiky jet-black hair sculpted with putty and a torn up Pink Floyd shirt held together by industrial staples, his pale blue eyes shined like those of a Fremen, striking enough to capture my attention away from the Admiral. He had a torn up backpack, adorned with magic marker graffiti slung over his shoulders, black cargo pants, and a pair of bowling shoes to accent his wardrobe.

"Nice shirt," I blurted. The Admiral, still ranting about some business venture, halted her pontificating to notice the hipster shipwreck standing behind us. The hipster-Fremen-shipwreck looked up at me and smiled, his blue eyes glowing with perfect smoothness.

"What's up dude?! Thank you!" the hipster said. He threw back his shoulders, adjusting his posture into a more erect and healthy pose, tucking his thumbs beneath the two straps of his backpack.

The Admiral stepped forward and held out her hand. "Roxanne Rodriguez," she said, pumping the hand of the hipster. Dear Lord, did she always have to act like she was at some business mixer? I mean, yes, she'd come to Con for business, and yes, the Hollywood industry had a huge foothold at the Con but...well...it wasn't *that* douchy yet. Was it?

"Raz-Ar," the hipster growled with a smile, making no effort to even acknowledge Roxanne's outstretched hand.

"What?" Roxanne blurted in confusion.

"Raz-Arrrrr" the hipster repeated, still ignoring Roxanne's extended palm. He seemed to hold the last syllable for emphasis, sounding like a misfit pirate. "Sorry," he said after a beat. "Raz-Ar doesn't shake hands. It's a thing."

"Around here I can't blame you," I injected. "Avoid the Con crud!"

"Yeah," said Raz-Ar. "Raz-Ar doesn't want to get sick." The Admiral shot me a sideways look of confusion, not knowing what to make of this oddity before us. I just smiled.

"Raz-Ar...that's an unusual name," I observed.

"Raz-Ar likes it," the guy smiled. By then I could no longer ignore his constant speaking in the third person. Under any other circumstance, I'd have written him off as a freak. But at Comic-Con, and with shimmering eyes like his, something made him intriguing.

"Like you have any room to criticize odd names," the Admiral chided me. I scowled and glanced at her.

"I'm Liquin," I introduced. I started to extend my hand, but then pulled back, remembering. Much to my surprise, before I could even mask my forgetfulness, Raz-Ar grabbed my palm in his own, shaking it with vigor. The Admiral snickered under her breath.

"Raz-Ar likes your name too," he said with a smile. "What made you pick it?" In that moment, before I could answer, I first noticed the scars on his arms; perfect lines from palm to elbow, some thin and almost invisible, others broad, thick and deep purple, all bisecting the horizontal length of his arm like speed bumps and pot holes on the freeway. He had to have dozens of them and, I guessed, he'd carved them himself.

"Sorry, what?" I said, distracted.

"He wants to know why you picked your weird-ass name," the Admiral uttered, voice cool.

"Ah, that," I acknowledged. "I didn't pick it, my parents did. It's my birth name."

"Sweet!" Raz-Ar moaned. "Raz-Ar likes."

"They never explained where it came from," I added, "though

once my dad told me that when he was young, people would huff some paint thinner called Liquin to get high. I hate to think that's where it came from, but..."

"Maybe they were huffing it when you were conceived," Roxanne teased.

"Could be," I ceded. "The most I know for sure is that Mom says they were lying in bed one day, staring up at the ceiling, and there I was. Or at least my name, anyway." I shrugged to punctuate my story.

"Raz-Ar likes," he repeated. "What brings you to Con? Are you Pro?"

"Yeah," the Admiral said without modesty. "I'm assistant to a rock star. He wanted me to come check things out."

"Oh," Raz-Ar grunted, indifferent. "What about Liquin?"

"I'm a writer," I answered. "Scripts mainly."

"He's brilliant," the Admiral added. I rolled my eyes.

"Sweet dude!" Raz-Ar said, nodding his head with palpable enthusiasm. "Raz-Ar writes too! Short stories and poems and whatever. And Raz-Ar draws a bit."

"A man of varied talents," the Admiral said as she pulled me by the arm. "Nice meeting you!" I spun around to realize we'd made it all the way to the entry hall. I dug into my backpack, producing my bar code for admission and smiled one last time at Raz-Ar before rounding the bend through the door inside to the registration booths.

"He was interesting," I said, not quite knowing what to think of the man.

"He was way into you," the Admiral snickered. "Which is why I had to rescue you."

"Why's that? He was cute!"

"You saw his arms," Roxanne pressed. "The last thing you need is a suicidal guy in your life, especially given your own condition." She might have had a point, though even the Admiral didn't know about *Neodämmerung.* Nobody did.

I frowned again, as I approached an open registration agent and scanned my barcode. She presented me with my Pro-Badge lanyard, which I immediately draped around my neck, and then tried to push the usual Comic-Con door freebies on me—the swag bag, the free comic issues, the schedule book. I accepted the final item, shoving it in my backpack, but declined the others. When the Admiral and I regrouped, she having donned her own badge, I noticed she'd ditched the swag too. We took a quick detour to the nearby bag check where I dropped my luggage, sighing with relief at my liberation. I turned around and evaluated the churning crowd, pensive a moment.

"Oh God, I'm so not ready for this," I moaned. I rubbed my temples, tense with stress. The Admiral looked at me a moment, scrutinizing my face, before grabbing me by the hand and tugging me through the Convention Center lobby. "Now what?" I badgered.

"Bathroom break," the Admiral chimed, pushing me into a nearby men's room, already crowded with attendees, many of whom bunched up near the mirror, checking their elaborate costumes for perfection. Before I could even think about peeing, Roxanne appeared behind me, pushed me into an empty stall and followed me inside, locking the door behind us.

"Dude, what the fuck!?" I exclaimed, sure that the Hall Nazis would be on us in seconds. The two of us shacking up in a filthy Convention bathroom stall?! What could be sexier?

"I'm not letting you do this," the Admiral declared, rifling through her jacket pockets.

"Do what? Shack up with cutter boy back there?"

"The dude was a freak," the Admiral continued, "but I really don't care what you do with your dick so long as you do *something* with it. This isn't you." Before I could ask her what she meant, the Admiral produced a large prescription drug bottle, sans label, filled with pills of various sizes and colors.

"I'm not sure I like where this is going," I admitted.

"You are Liquin Sonos," the Admiral observed. "Crypto homo insurrectionist writer and Comic-Con Paladin. This is your home, and I want you to have a good time!" She popped open the bottle and dumped a few pills in her hand, muttering to herself… "No, no, no…"

"What are those?" I asked.

"This one is Vitamin-B12," the Admiral said, handing me an ovular, gold pill. "And this is Percodin," passing me a white, chalky capsule with numbers engraved in the side. "And this is Adrenochrome." She handed me a red gel-cap and smirked.

"And I'm supposed to take these now?"

"Yes!" the Admiral charged. "Buy the ticket, take the ride, like Dr. Thompson always said! Like you always used to say before you got all…"

"Depressed?" I finished.

"I was going to say lame," the Admiral retorted. "But depressed will do."

"You know the good Dr. Thompson shot himself in the head when he got depressed, right? Maybe you could think of a better point of comparison?"

"Hunter was much older than you," Roxanne countered. "If he were here right now, what advice would he give you?"

"Dude, this is hard core stuff," I said glancing at the three pills in my hand. "Percodin is a crazy painkiller and Adrenochrome… where did you even get that?"

"I work with rock stars. Now bottoms up!" the Admiral ordered.

"Adrenochrome is illegal. It's extracted from human kidneys! And I don't even know what it'll do. What if I have a bad trip?"

"It doesn't have to come from human kidneys. There are ways, trust me. And this trip is going to suck balls if you don't start tripping right now! You won't hallucinate, you'll just…" The Admiral clenched her jaw, hesitating. "Oh, just take it! Hurry, before security shows up!"

"Dear God," I grunted, anxious at the thought of getting detained by security and having my Con attendance stripped for life. I shot a glance at the Admiral, then at the pills. I sighed. "Fuck everything," I moaned, tossing all three pills into my mouth and swallowing them dry.

"Very good," Roxanne said in triumph. She threw open the

stall door, went to a sink and rinsed her hands, ignoring all the strange looks from the other bathroom goers as I exited the stall behind her.

"It's a special cocktail the Boss taught me," she explained. "It's called Fuckitall." I cracked a smile, though I knew my eyes brimmed with cynicism.

"Will they make me sick to my stomach? Because the last thing I need is to be hurling all through the convention hall." I followed the Admiral out of the stall, ignoring the sideways looks from the geeks watching us, wondering how we'd fornicated in a bathroom stall without making any orgasmic noise. I stopped at the sink a moment to rinse my hands, smiling at the woebegone geek, dressed as Dr. Who, giving me a glare of disgust.

"Fuckitall is perfectly stomach friendly," the Admiral began. "No puking from..." I lost the sound of her voice as she exited the bathroom, her words falling into the noise of the brewing Con. I grabbed a paper towel to dab my hands, and chased after the Admiral. I found her outside the bathroom entry, hands on her hips, tapping her left foot in annoyance.

"Stay close, I don't want to lose you!" Roxanne chided. I scowled and rolled my eyes.

"Didn't you just call me a Con Paladin earlier? Don't you think I know what I'm doing!?"

"I know you do, Liquin, though you seem to be off your game as of late." The Admiral bowed her head, gaze fired off from under her brow like a bull about to charge. Actually, given the craziness and crowding of the Con, the Running of the Bulls didn't seem a far cry. And it probably smelled better.

"Yeah, well," I growled, "it's fucking Comic-Con, you're here, I'm here, our friends are on their way, and above all..." I took a step toward the Admiral, raising my right palm as if to take some grand oath...

"I am still the best at what I do!"

With that, my vision blurred, my balance slipped, and I toppled forward into the Admiral's arms. She teetered backward, supporting my weight, trying to steady me back to my feet. My neck went limp, dropping my head against her shoulder like dead weight, my nose squished against her collar bone.

"So it begins," I heard her mutter.

With all my might, I raised my head, trying to reclaim my bearings. The shapes and details of the world around me dripped and melted into a collage of colored blotches moving about through my vision. Lines and angles vanished. I felt like I was standing in a living oil painting, a great gelatinous amoeba of light and noise pulsing with primitive life.

"You smell nice!" I blurted, my voice high-pitched and tight. My mouth stretched into a tight smirk as Roxanne steadied my face between her hands. My gaze fixed on the two pools of pale copper light in her eye sockets.

"Right here," Roxanne said, holding two fingers just below her glowing irises. "Just remember, stay focused."

"What have you done to me Admiral?" I sighed, rubbing my face.

"Don't ask questions Liquin. Just go with the flow." Roxanne grabbed me by the arm, leading me through the pulsing color of the Convention Hall Lobby. I looked down at my feet, which seemed to sink into the carpet below with each step, the color sticking to my shoes each time I lifted like cake batter.

"Are we still in the bathroom? Is the Con flooding?" I yelled. Roxanne yanked me by the arm in reprimand.

"Keep it down!" she seethed. "It's the Fuckitall. It makes things confusing. It's the fucking point!"

"Dear lord," I muttered, batting my eyes, trying to get some kind of focus from my vision. "When are the others getting here?"

"You know this," Roxanne grumbled. "You issued the itinerary."

"That's right, I..."

And then, total darkness. Like, complete and total darkness. I felt cold, as if lying naked in front of an open window in

December at my parents' house in the Midwestern corn fields. I shifted, feeling some scratchy texture against my bare skin across my whole body. I had the most peculiar taste in my mouth—chalky, yet minty—and my tongue felt numb.

...Reasons to stay alive...

Stick it in and find out.

I am the lizard queen!

Strange flickers of light and color flashed into my head—blue, red-orange, fluid and rippling like the surface of a disturbed pond. My eye muscles throbbed and felt tight. Then...

"I have been, and always shall be, your friend."

His towering and taught form appeared like the spectre of Marley before Scrooge, somehow comprised of blue and white light against a dim and shifting background, his body draped in white gauze, translucent enough to hint at the tan skin beneath. His blond hair glimmered, almost metallic in some near halo. A flowing monastic robe of burnt sienna hung over his outline, and his eyes glowed with blue-within-blue purity.

"Adam?" I gasped, feeling disembodied and displaced.

"It will take more than strength to survive what's coming," Adam intoned, voice reverberating like a cathedral bell.

"Dude, did I just O.D.?" I asked. "Am I dead? Are you?"

"No," Adam smiled. "We're in Santa Fe station, platform 9 ¾."

"Santa Fe station doesn't have a platform 9 ¾!" I barked back. "It has like two! And anyway we're inside!"

I'd said it without even realizing...the Spanish mission-style architecture of Santa Fe station, its brown tile and varnished wood polished lit by the dim hue of candles bunched in great candelabras about the main concourse. The rest of the furniture —the benches, the ticket kiosks—had all gone missing, replaced only by the torches and thick red, velvet curtains that draped over the arcing glass windows.

"The beginning is the end is the beginning," Adam rang again. "Reflections show us not who we are; rather, who we could be." He took a step toward me, resting a hand on my shoulder. "Remember."

I reached up to feel my face, at once recognizing the odd surface covering my body as a sheet, enshrouding me head to toe, the ends presumably tucked under the end of the mattress.

A strange *thunk* caught my attention, prompting me to sit up against the taught pressure of the sheet, pulling it from its tuck points and letting it fall over my body. I struggled out from under it into a darkened hotel room—one I didn't recognize but for the standard hotel room configuration: two beds, dresser and armoire, table and chair in the corner. In the near-pitch black I pulled the sheet from off my body as I rose to my feet, realizing I was completely naked in the process. Well, at least it wasn't a bathtub full of ice.

I fumbled around, feeling my way through the room, looking for some concealed light switch when I heard another *thunk*. I stretched out my arms, making my way forward toward the noise when my right hand caught on the coarse surface of a wall covered in cheap paper. I inched forward, forward, until I came to the cool metal touch of the door frame. I glanced down to see only darkness…no light from inside the bathroom. At least, I assumed it was the bathroom.

Dear God, what had the Admiral got me into now? What if I'd been abducted to Tijuana or something! I'd have to spend the rest of my life—not to mention COMIC-CON—in white slavery! Assuming a Mexican kidnapping cartel could get more than five pesos for my emaciated, fugly ass…

I felt around for the door handle, and hearing movement beyond, I applied the slightest pressure to the grip. It gave way beneath my touch, indicating the unsealed lock. I took a deep breath, clenched my teeth, and threw open the door!

The portal flung ajar with a blast of hot, moist air, bright light pouring out, the intensity flash-blinding me. All I could make out before I'd squinted my eyelids closed was the vague form of some hulking figure…with two giant horns coming out of its head, surrounded by a grey haze, a mixture of steam and smoke.

I yelled in shock from the surprise and from my aching retinas, staggering a backwards. From inside the bathroom, there came a shrill, shrieking howl like that of a frenzied raven. I yelled again as backed slam into the sliding closet doors, the cool of mirrored glass kissing my bare skin, one hand covering my sore eyes, the other gripping for some support. The horned figure shrieked again, this time louder, followed by the sound of metal against marble and porcelain against...well I didn't know, but it sure was *loud.*

I fell to the ground, the tender skin of my ass cheeks grinding across the carpet. I hollered from the stinging rug burn, meeting again with a desperate yell from my assailant. I heard a great crash as I blinked my eyes open, trying to let my irises adjust to the bright fluorescent light, followed by the tapping of tiny plastic and metal objects against the tile floor.

As my vision returned, I met with the vision of a frantic, slack-jawed image of Brigham Truman, my dear friend and illustrious talent agent, scared out of his wits, surrounded by the strewn carnage of toiletries strewn about the room, clawing at the wall, his eyes and mouth wide as a something out of a Munch painting. On his head, a multi-pronged purple crown rested, providing an ironic juxtaposition to his Shelly Duvall-in-*The Shining*-level hysteria.

"Here's Johnny," I croaked, one hand on my burning posterior, the other still shielding my eyes. "Don't look at my doodle!" I added as an afterthought, rolling onto my side.

Brigham gasped and choked, one hand fanning his face, the other locked to his chest, clutching for his imaginary pearls. He let out one final shriek, popping out of his throat like a cawing bird.

"You're letting all the smoke out!" Brigham howled. "Get your naked ass in here!"

One hand over my crotch, the other over my wang, I scooted and sidewinded my way into the bathroom, Brigham slamming the door behind me. As he tucked a wadded towel on the floor back under the door crack, I reached up and grabbed another off the rod hanging over the toilet, wrapping my lower extremities.

"Shit," he uttered. "I haven't been scared like that since

Gorillas in the Mist." I stared at him, blank. He clutched for his pearls again, as he always did—a sort of nervous tic or pose to suggest dignity, I never could decide which. Brigham frowned, his eyes narrowing to slits. "I hate gorillas. They scare the hell out of me."

"Dear God Brigs," I uttered, heart rate slowing. "What the Hell are you doing? Where are we?"

Brigham crawled over the floor, collecting the various pill bottles, beauty products and other Lord-Knows-What strewn over the tile. He looked up at me, his trademark Kissinger glasses fogged from the steam.

"I'm trying to get stoned without smelling up the room or getting evicted!" he said with slight offense. Hands full of bathroom supplies, he went about rearranging them on the counter top. I rubbed my eyes one last time, sitting down on the commode, trying to process all the crazy. Without looking up, Brigham passed me hash pipe of red and gold Pyrex glass, already loaded with charred, ground marijuana. "That's my Gryffindor pipe," he added, passing me a lighter.

I put the pipe to my lips, flicking the lighter to flame, then paused a moment.

"Wait a second, what the Hell am I doing?!" I moaned, extinguishing the lighter and moving the pipe from my lips. "I just had a blackout of the past...what time is it?" Brigham spun around and took a seat on top of the counter next to the sink, looking at his watch.

"Ten," Brigham declared. "At night."

"Ok, so I lost...how many hours is that?" I wondered aloud. "Fucking Adrenochrome."

"Roxanne gave you Adrenochrome?" Brigham interrogated in alarm.

"Yeah..." I chimed in innocence.

"Great," Brigham croaked. "Yeah, smoke that." I obeyed his command, taking a deep puff from the pipe and passing it back to him. I coughed hard and deep from the sting of the smoke, but only once. Breathing deep the steam soothed my lungs as the numbing THC flooded my body and I relaxed, feeling the cool porcelain of the toilet tank against my back. Brigham took a hit of his own, exhaling the smoke through his nostrils. Between the smoke, the steam, and his fogged glasses, he looked like something out of a Buñuel film.

"Why the smugness?" I asked, rotating my neck back and forth from shoulder to shoulder, enjoying the weed-fueled relaxation.

"Have you ever taken Adrenochrome?" Brigham prodded, taking another hit from the pipe. "*Expecto Patronum!*" he declared, suddenly distracted by the threads of smoke in the air.

"Um, what's the deal with Adrenochrome, and why should I be worried?"

"Don't worry," Brigham hawed. "But you're going to be having one hell of a weekend!"

"Terrific," I sighed. I looked down at my exposed chest, the USB drive hanging from my neck, sweat beads erupting from my pores. A moment of reality struck me, and I sat upright, firing off a glare at my illustrious companion. "Ok, wait a tic, where are we, where's the Admiral, and most importantly where are my clothes?"

"Girrrrrl," Brigham purred, rising from the counter and turning off the shower. "The Admiral is at dinner with some writer friend. *We...*" He threw open the bathroom door and switched on a light, illuminating the hallway and room beyond. I followed him, holding my towel around my waist with my right hand.

"We are at the Bayfront Hilton," Brigham presented, arms outstretched into a sizable and tasteful room. He walked over to the window, hidden behind curtains. "It is, as you should recall, the newest slice of elegance here in the Gaslamp District, and as you can see..." Brigham threw open the curtains with all the flourish of a gameshow model, "we've a Hell of a view." The open curtains revealed the colored lights of San Diego, its majestic skyline off to the right and the studded boats afloat in the bay to the left. Dividing them, still looking like a Kryptonian city, the Convention Center glowed through its angular architecture, still swarmed with Convention-goers as they spilled out into the streets.

I took a breath of wonder, my jaw slackened as I stepped to Brigham's side, looking out over the city, letting my towel slip a bit from my waist. I jarred myself from my awe, catching my loin cloth as it dipped below my hips, exposing my pubic line. Brigham snickered.

"Well, you're right," I said. "That's pretty amazing. Now can I please have a pair of shorts?"

"Prude," Brigham spat, moseying back to the bathroom. "Top drawer!"

I opened the top drawer of the bureau that supported the room's TV set to find my clothes arranged to perfection and folded with utmost care. I selected a pair of camouflage boxers, slipped them on, then dug deeper to find my pants and "Twilight Sucks" t-shirt. "I did all this while I was stoned on Adrenochrome!?" I queried. "I don't even fold this well sober!"

"Maybe that's your problem, girl," Brigham fired back from the bathroom.

I sat down on the edge of the bed and rubbed my face, just in time to hear a scratching at the room door, as if someone tried to open it. Brigham poked his head out from inside the bathroom, looking for the source of the noise, before letting out one of his trademark shrieks of panic.

"They've found us! The jig is up!" Brigham ducked back into the bathroom and slammed the door, just as the door to our room slid open to reveal Roxanne, now dressed in a Harley Quinn t-shirt and wearing a cardboard facsimile of the purple crown of Galactus, with several flimsy, cardboard antlers flapping back and forth at the sides, meant to represent the techno prongs of the Marvel deity's headpiece.

"Heyyy baby!" Roxanne crowed at me, closing the door behind her. "Feeling better?"

"I wouldn't say better, exactly," I muttered, "but at least I'm semi-lucid."

"Is that Roxanne?" Brigham called from the bathroom. I could see a shaft of light appear opposite the door to the bathroom, suggesting that my illustrious friend had opened it to take a peek.

"Yes dear," Roxanne soothed. Brigham shrieked, throwing open the bathroom door, running into the bedroom and leaping into Roxanne's arms like an excited toddler. She smiled, wincing her eyes in genuine delight. Brigham released her, took a step back, and admired her form a split-second before letting out a scream.

"*Where* did you get that Galactus crown!?" Brigham erupted, hand to his chest as if to clutch a set of imaginary pearls about his neck.

"They were passing them out at one of the booths," Roxanne explained. "Some promotional thing for a new Galactus toy, I think." She took the crown off and handed it to Brigham. "Here, you can have it."

Brigham squealed with joy, hugging Roxanne again and donning the headpiece. "It's fabulous!" he exclaimed. "You're *fabulous* Roxanne!"

"I try," Roxanne declared. "Did Liquin not tell you about them?"

"Are you kidding?" Brigham scoffed. "He's only become lucid in the past few minutes." He turned to me. "Still trying to process the Adrenachrome hole in your memory, am I right?"

"Something like that," I ceded. "No idea what I did this afternoon after I took the Fuckitall." I hesitated a moment. "Well, except for something about a lizard queen."

"Oh my," Brigham uttered, clutching for his pearls. Roxanne laughed.

"Yeah, that was you," the Admiral charged with glee. "You screamed that as we were checking in here at the Bayfront."

"Oh God," I blurted, burying my face in my hands.

"You had the fear," Roxanne went on. "You turned to me and said that you thought the desk agent was actually a carnivorous salamander. When she asked how your day was going, you screamed 'I am the lizard queen!'." I groaned with embarrassment. "Needless to say," Roxanne added, "that got her attention."

"I can't believe she let us stay," I moaned.

"It's Comic-Con," Brigham reminded me. "Shit like that happens all the time."

A mechanical vibrating in my pocket wrestled my attention away. I drew my cell phone from out of my pants and gasped with excitement as I read the caller I.D.

"Hello Kate darling!" I greeted with exhilaration. I looked up to see the Admiral and Brigham both smile with joy.

"Liquin," Kate croaked into the phone. I could hear strain and fatigue in her voice. "Come downstairs, hon. We're here. We have stuff to carry up."

"Be right down, my dear." I hung up the phone and looked around for my shoes before ducking out into the hall. Brigham and the Admiral followed without instruction, their intuition signaling what we needed to do. Halfway down the corridor, a thought struck me.

"Brigham dear," I mused. "Four of us in the room...I don't suppose we have enough towels?"

"Good point," Brigham said. The three of us gazed down to the far end of the hall where a maid had parked her housekeeping cart outside a room. In the silence, we heard the squeal of a vacuum cleaner.

"Take what you can, just don't get caught!" I declared, patting Brigham on the shoulder as he took of down the hall, running on his tip-toes, looking like a Scooby-Doo character. The Admiral and I exchanged a look and a snicker as we continued on to the elevator bay.

"Let me know if you need to sleep in our closet," I said to Roxanne as we boarded the elevator.

"I think I have it covered," she replied. "I'll be bedroom hopping, but I should have a place every night." A moment of silence passed between us as we listened to the motors of the lift lowering us to the lobby floor. "You sure you'll be ok?" Roxanne asked, voice tender.

I looked at her and frowned. "Guess we'll find out."

The elevator doors parted to reveal the cavernous lobby of the newly-opened Bayfront Hotel, the interior shining with white marble floors and wood-panel walls, vaulting upward to a cathedral ceiling. Great curtains of tiny sliver beads hung from the rafters, along with ultramodern light fixtures of blue and orange hand-blown glass. The whole place felt like a mix of Hollywood and a beach resort, in part because of the gaggle of convention attendees milling about, their badges on dangling from lanyards around their necks. I sighed, cracking a grin of satisfaction: we'd scored with this reservation. Located adjacent to the Con and brand-spanking new, the Bayfront wasn't just the hottest property at the Con, it also attracted a good chunk of the Hollywood crowd, both to stay or just to mingle because of its proximity. In other words, we were bunking with the cool kids.

Windsor Kane, my dear animator friend/brother geek had pulled his SUV up to the loading zone in the cul du sac just outside of hotel registration and already began to unload massive suitcases to the curb. Dressed in his standard black t-shirt and jeans, dark-rimmed glasses resting high on his nose, he looked just as he always did.

"Hello Straightness!" I greeted with outstretched arms, walking out to meet him. Windsor looked up and ran a hand through his jet black mop of hair and smiled.

"Helloooooo chief!" he replied, his voice rumbling with a magnificent, low timbre, like a bass drum. He and I exchanged a quick hug, and I could smell the faint odor of tobacco concealed beneath his Estee Lauder cologne. I sighed, knowing what that would portend...

Straightness greeted the Admiral with another hug before he let out a grunt. "Jesus God," he spat. "This fucking traffic! It never gets better. God I need a cigarette..."

"Like heck you do!" The voice, even in such annoyed tone, made me smile. Kate Schuster emerged from the back seat of Windsor's SUV, one arm carrying a large camera bag, the other a hard plastic case for lights. I rushed over to help her, taking the light box from her and lifting it down to the curb. "You already had two on the way down here!"

"Lay off me, woman!" Windsor called back, taking his backpack from the trunk of the car and slinging it over his shoulders before closing the door.

I watched Kate's face for some sign of humor, but saw none. Her blue eyes shimmered like ice as she pulled her neck-length hair back under her ears and straightened her *Firefly* shirt over her athletic form. She glared at Windsor a moment, then turned and greeted me in a whisper.

"Hey Starbuck," I said, embracing her in a greeting. "Rough ride?"

"I'm ready to kill him," Kate muttered, "but what else is new?" She reached down and lifted the camera bag on top of a roll-away suitcase, extending the handle to steady the extra load. I reached for the light case, but Kate snatched the grip before I could. "It's ok," she affirmed. "They roll, I got it. What's the room number?"

"Nineteen-seventy-seven," I told her. "Brigham is up there."

"Good," Kate said, charging inside without a word to Straightness. "One drink, then I'm passing out."

I glanced over at Windsor to catch his reaction. He watched Starbuck mosey off and shook his head, taking his suitcase from the curb and following her inside. I stood there in thought a moment, Roxanne stepping to my flank as I let out a sigh.

"More good news," I groused, shaking my head with disapproval.

"Hey," Roxanne said, rubbing my back. "You take care of you. Let Han and Leia fight it out on their own time. The important thing is, we're all here together, with you. You're going to go out there tomorrow and rock this Comic-Con, and you're going to rock your meeting with Monty Doyle, and you will be God Emperor Geek!"

"Time will tell," I said, embracing her again. "And that's the best you're getting out of me tonight." I let go of her, forced a smile, and left her standing there on the curb without another word. She knew how to get back to her hotel, and arguing with her or belaboring the point any further would have been a waste of energy for both of us. She might anger over my curt manner with her, but it was for the best.

I cut back through the hotel lobby, but decided to avoid Starbuck and Straightness for the time being. Instead, I headed for an escalator that took me to sea level, then took a stroll outside along a stone patio overlooking San Diego Bay. I had the impulse to go pour a drink or load my hitter and medicate myself to numb the pain, but I couldn't find what good it would do. High above, the moon hid behind the haze of a cloud, and the roar of the traffic from the Gaslamp District and the nearby Coronado Bridge melded into a hum of white noise. At Comic-Con, Geek Mecca, a place overcrowded with the community I loved so much, I found myself alone.

I leaned over a guard rail, looking down at the blackness of the water, just thinking. I shut my eyes, trying to balance my thoughts on the rhythm of the water, the churning dark. I wanted it to absorb me, to grant me solace and serenity and just *shut the world up!* I wanted fucking peace! I thought about hurling myself into the cold ocean water, just letting myself sink like Virginia Woolf. That did wonders for her career…I could see the *Hollywood Reporter* headline: "Cast of *Avengers* assembles at Comic-Con; unknown geek writer drowns self."

Who'd be capitalizing on who?

My mind lit on the Hole song "Reasons to be Beautiful, "a rock anthem which, urban legend held, Courtney Love had written in response to the suicide of her husband, Kurt Cobain. I didn't know the truth behind the scuttlebutt, only that nothing in the lyrics suggested another meaning to the song.

"Ten good reasons to stay alive," I sang to myself. *"Ten good reasons that I can't find."*

So fucking true. What reasons did I have to live? What had earned me the right to the polluted, carcinogenic air I breathed? Why did I keep going? I had no career, no boyfriend, and I would be sick—sick in my head—for the rest of my life. I'd spoken at length with my doctor about my bipolar disorder, and even her spinster grace, who always tried to hard to sugar coat or mask grim reality with "attitude" or "positive thinking" or some other bumper sticker platitude, didn't even hold back. My condition would deteriorate for the rest of my life. My mental stability would further erode, treatment would become more difficult, and most frightening of all, the deep, dark rabbit hole of depression would go deeper, and even with the proper therapy and medication, I would sink further down, never to fully escape again.

The USB! My thoughts lit on the phrase. I felt confident that it remained safe and tucked away in my backpack, though I would need to double check to satisfy my own anxieties. I'd worked on it a week, recording myself, and laying out all my final instructions for how to complete *Neodämmerung*. I would put Kate in charge, and I knew she wouldn't let me down. I trusted her like a sister, like something even greater, as if part of my very soul. Starbuck would feel angry, no doubt, but she would see it was for the best. I reached up and felt the thumb drive still hanging around my neck—the other piece of the plan. Everything would fall into place by Sunday, no matter what Monty Doyle would say, even if he promised immediate payment and representation.

I hung my head again, shamed by the flicker of hope that the thought of Monty brought me. Why did I fucking bother? It wouldn't change anything. *Neodämmerung* was my final recourse. And it would work, I knew that.

A frigid chill blew in from the water, making me shiver and drawing my attention away from my own self-pity. My teeth chattered and the skin of my bare arms turned to gooseflesh. I hugged them in close to my body, rubbing them together and trying to keep warm. Another icy blast of wind rippled the distressed cotton of my t-shirt over my back. As I turned to head back inside the Bayfront, I heard a dull rumble like thunder in the distance. But it couldn't have been thunder—it was July in

San Diego; it never rained!

I paused and, like Lot's wife, turned back to look at the lights of the adjacent Convention Center, moonless sky, and black water. I sniffed, a drip forming in my sinuses, a feeling of deep foreboding welling in my stomach.

"I'm still the best at what I do," I said aloud to nobody in particular.

Wasn't I?

THURSDAY

Spectre of the Past

O vernight our room at the Bayfront had morphed from contemporary style to cave dwelling. I awoke sore and irritated, writhing over the lumps of the supposedly brand-new mattress. How could a hotel less than a year old have a mattress that felt like a bed of nails so soon?

I popped up from under the sheets into the cavern of the room. No light seeped in from behind the curtains, or from any of the room appliances. The sound of running water only added to the cave atmosphere, no doubt a result of one of my compatriots bathing in the early hours. For that, I felt gratitude. Comic-Con needed a collective bath even more than it needed more hotel or exhibit space.

I folded my arms over my bare chest in an effort to combat the arctic blast of the A/C. As I felt around in the dark for a light switch or the climate control panel, the bathroom door yawned open, and Kate appeared, dressed only in her lingerie, her hair dripping wet and slicked back against her cranium.

"Morning Liquin," she chirped. "I was just about to get you up. I already sent Windsor on to hold us a place in line for Hall H."

"It's freezing in here!" I blurted in response. Kate switched on the light to the room, revealing a stack of hotel glasses piled next to the TV set. I glanced at the goblets, then over to Kate, expectant.

"Brigham's work," Kate explained. "He wanted to make sure we had enough supplies."

"Yeah," I added. "I told him to get extra towels for you and Windsor..."

"Oh he did," Kate said, slipping into her jeans. "Be careful which drawers you open." I cocked an eyebrow at her. Kate smiled, her blue eyes wide. "He really didn't want to get caught."

"Fair enough," I conceded. I pulled open a drawer to grab a clean set of pants and shirt, and met instead with a pile of washcloths stuffed so thick and heavy in the drawer that I could barely get it open. Underneath, all my clothes still rested in perfect order, now imbued with the smell of fresh linen. I couldn't complain. I selected a pair of dark blue designer jeans and another distressed t-shirt, this one bleached, torn, and adorned with safety pins about the neck. On the chest, I'd spray-stenciled the words "Joan Jett" as a tribute to one of my favorite rock goddesses.

Since my diagnosis, and since finishing my script, I had taken to designing everyday punk style clothes to reflect my state of mind and soul. My work ranged from strange jackets or cabana shirts made from vintage bed sheets to punk/garage band style shirts indicative of my anger, despair, and general lunacy. I'd even managed to sell a few pieces to friends to pick up some extra cash. Even if my work sucked, even if I died young, at least people would always call me stylish.

"God," I moaned in cranky agony as I finished dressing. I went over and threw open the curtains, expecting a blast of SoCal sunshine, but instead met with only more gloom. From our window we could see the clotting line on the grassy knoll beside the convention center for Hall H with the quaint backdrop of the Gaslamp District, but the crowd seemed huddled somehow, and well...depressed. A wall of ashen clouds blocked out any sunlight from above, and a slight blur over the picturesque image of the Con suggested rain. RAIN! In JULY! In

CALIFORNIA!

Was it possible for God to commit a sin? Or did He just hate us that much?

I grunted, letting my neck muscles go slack and resting my head against the window pane.

"I know," Kate said, toweling the moisture from her hair. "The weather sucks."

"Yes. Yes it does," I agreed, not bothering to lift my head. "It does nothing for my mood."

"I know," Kate said again. Another moment of silence fell between us.

"Not to worry," I sighed at last, digging through the layer of towels in my drawer again. "As Con Paladin, I am still prepared for all possible contingencies." From the very bottom of my clothing stack, I produced a black fleece hoodie, lined with red satin and baring a "Gryffindor" patch over the left breast. "Hogwarts fashion," I declared, sipping it up to my chest.

"Cute!" Kate exclaimed, pulling on a Robin t-shirt—the same shirt she'd worn at her very first Comic-Con two years before.

"What a difference two years makes," I cooed, smile on my face. "I remember when you were terrified to even show up to this thing."

"I'm now enlightened!" Kate chimed, stepping into the bathroom to brush her teeth.

"No kidding," I grunted, following her to the bathroom door, leaning against the doorframe. "How are preparations for the thesis film?"

"Script is ready," Kate said through the brushstrokes. "Puck has the sound equipment, and we're due to shoot tonight and tomorrow." She paused a moment and frowned, before amending, "weather permitting."

"And Straightness is going to do it?" Kate chortled at my question.

"He says so, though I still have my apprehensions," Kate admitted, punctuating her statement with a burly wad of white spit into the basin. "He's been rehearsing, but his coordination isn't the best. I'm afraid someone really will lose a limb." I laughed.

"You mean to say the guy has a problem with…" I cleared my throat. "His swordplay skills?" Kate smacked closed her blush compact and tossed it on the bathroom counter, where it landed with a *clack.*

"Only the pre-choreographed moves," she replied. "Like so many performers, he's better when he's spontaneous."

"Oh my!" I exclaimed. Kate switched off the bathroom light and pressed by me through the door to put on her shoes.

"It's the secret to a two year relationship," she added.

"*Ooooh my!*" I repeated again in a purr. I turned the bathroom light back on, checking myself in the mirror. I had a bit of stubble about my face, but didn't mind. At Comic-Con, that early in the day, I didn't give a damn. I did, however apply a light slathering of gel to my hair, transforming it from bed head to sassy spike.

"He's that good in the sack?" I called out to Kate. She marched back to the bathroom, leaning in and catching my eye-contact through my reflection in the mirror.

"Liquin, he's also the best at what he does!"

I paused in shock a moment, staring back at her through the mirror before busting out into hysterical laughter.

"That's fucking awesome," I declared. "I'm jealous! Not of Windsor, er, you I mean, but of the good sex. It's been ages for me!" I thought again about the Lexapro and sighed, trying to push the thought from my mind. Another thought struck me. "Don't you worry about his insulin pump?"

"At first," Kate confessed. "But Windsor gets so into it…and for that matter, so do I…that I've learned not to mind. The first time I knocked it out of him I cringed, expecting blood to gush everywhere or him to faint or slip into a coma or something. Before I could even react he said…" She paused.

"What!?" I pressed her.

"Lord," Kate said, rolling her eyes, holding a hand to her forehead. "If you tell him I told you this…"

"Kate, it's me," I injected.

"Ok fine, but you've been warned. He said..." Her voice dropped in a faint imitation of Straightness's tone. "Fuck it! I want to die inside you!"

I froze, my eyes wide as skillets, tilting my head back in alarm and clenching my jaw.

"Ok, maybe I didn't need to know that."

"Uh huh," Kate murmured. "To the Con?"

"Right, cheers, Comic-Con! Here we go!" I shot back into the bedroom, grabbed my backpack from a corner of the dresser and pressed on right for the door. She was right. Knowing Windsor's dirty talk would make it a bit harder to look him in the eye when next I saw him. Fortunate for me, Windsor never looked anyone in the eye, except for maybe Kate, though even pondering that gave me the willies in my state of mind.

I halted in the doorframe, propping the door with my hip, rummaging through my backpack to double check. I felt around in one of the small knapsack pouches for the smooth plastic cube that would save my ass. At last my fingers gripped it, and I pulled it out just to make sure: yes, I had the USB, the word *Neodämmerung* scrawled in black marker on a tiny label. I held it there, the light of the LED bulbs in the hall casting a shimmering glow in the plastic.

"What's that?" Kate inquired, a hint of suspicion in her voice.

"Nothing," I told her, slipping the USB back into my backpack, walking past her in the hall. "Just making sure. Shall we?" Kate followed me, and I took care not to look at her until we boarded the elevator. I knew she wouldn't press me with further questions if I played it cool.

We made our way downstairs, stopping for a quick yogurt parfait and latte from a makeshift Starbucks cart in the hotel lobby, which amounted to little more than a glorified Sunday morning after-church coffee hour cuisine, at outrageous prices of course. Still, after experiencing as many Comic-Cons as I had, I'd learned to accept a certain level of price gouging; it just came with the territory, even if the profiteering did get worse every year.

Thank heaven Kate and I did cough up the extra cash for donkey-piss flavored coffee, too. Outside, we met with a damp, icy chill, at least as far as Southern California summer chills go. The temperature had dropped to well below sixty degrees Fahrenheit, and Kate and I both tensed our shoulder muscles as we stepped out into the courtyard. I coughed and scowled, feeling the pressure change in my sinus cavities. Not a good sign...

Outside the Convention Center, a makeshift shanty town like something out of Depression-Era Chicago, or possibly *The Day After* had exploded overnight. An odd blending of banquet tents, camping gear, cardboard boxes, lawn furniture and sleeping bags, the shortage of hotel rooms and overcrowding of the Con panels had at last manifested. Attendees would rather live like the homeless than miss out on the spoils of the Convention. I shook my head as I pondered: at what point would Con City become a year-round phenomena?

"Shit," I muttered. Kate whipped out her phone, pecking the keys with a frantic pace. Her turquoise eyes darted upward, scanning the crowd. "See him?" I asked.

Kate's face rested blank with focus. Without a word, she strode onward towards the massive, snaking cue of huddled masses cloistered beneath the plastic and canvas awnings. Like a bloodhound on the hunt, she pointed, reaching out a finger at some indistinguishable point in the crowd, leading me along, stepping over wet and frigid patrons, many of whom glared at us with acidic disgust as we worked our way toward the front of the line.

Straightness sat with legs folded on the ground in a plain black hooded sweatshirt, hood raised to protect his head, and his laptop open, resting atop his knees. A black t-shirt draped from his head to the top of the screen like a loose tarp sought to protect his bespectacled face and the screen of his computer.

"Morning Starbuck, morning chief!" Windsor greeted us, pecking away at the keys without looking up. "Jesus God, this rain!"

"I know," I moaned. "It does so much for my fucking mood."

"Did you get me coffee?" Straightness blurted, eye twitching in a nervous tic. Kate and I looked at each other, then at him, blank stares in our faces.

"Did you not get *yourself* coffee this morning already?" Kate uttered, drawing out every word in annoyance. Straightness held up an empty paper cup, shaking it back and forth to signal he'd drank it empty. Kate threw back her head and rolled her eyes.

"I'll get it," I offered. Kate grabbed me by the arm.

"No, I'll do it. You owe me Windsor!" Kate released me and made her way back through the squatting crowd toward the hotel.

"Starbuck, have I told you today that I love you?!" Straightness yelled after her. As she shrank into the distance, Kate swatted at the air in futility.

"Everyone loves Starbuck," a voice from the crowd shouted back. I looked at Straightness and smiled.

"They do have a point," I observed. "How are things going with you two anyway? Are you ready for the shoot?"

"I'm not liking the idea of filming in the rain, chief," Windsor said, eyes still locked on his computer screen. "But I'll do it for the lady."

"You'll do a short combat film but won't get your own coffee?" I needled him. "What the Hell is that?"

"Dude, it's raining! And I've been holding your spot for hours!"

"Ok, you have a point," I confessed. "Kate didn't seem too happy about it though."

"She's fine," Straightness dismissed. I took a sip from my coffee, scanning his pale, Italian complexion. Our conversation barely seemed to register. "She's just stressed about the shoot. The good news is I only have to do stunts if one of the performers doesn't show. Otherwise, I'm crew." He looked back down at his laptop, typing again.

"What are you working on?" I asked, trying to move the conversation forward and taking another sip from my coffee.

"I'm emailing another animator friend of mine. The guy just opened a school for animators out east." Windsor bit his thumbnail as his eyes darted back and forth over the screen, as if proofreading something of great importance.

"So…you're…" I probed him.

"Excited for the Disney panel!" Windsor fired back, shutting his laptop and slipping it into a beat-up messenger bag. "*TRON 2*! Can you believe it!?"

"I'm excited to see footage, then I'll decide if I'm excited for the movie to actually be happening," I said. "Though I am intrigued by the rumor that Jeff Bridges plays himself at his current age, and then a de-aged character so he looks like he did in 1983. Either way, Disney is marketing the fuck out of it. They're hoping for a hit."

"Never did get over losing Harry Potter to Warner's, did they?" Straightness mused.

"Who would?" I admitted.

A few minutes later, Kate returned with a cup of overpriced, swill-tainted coffee, squatted down next to her boyfriend, and handed it to Windsor.

"Thanks BooBoo," Straightness chirped, leaning in for a kiss. When Kate didn't reciprocate, Windsor pecked her on the cheek, but never seemed phased by her indifference. She looked at me and sighed.

"So is the Disney panel first?" Kate asked, sounding tired.

"Dreamworks/Universal," Windsor answered. "I plan to live tweet the whole thing!"

"I'm sure that will prove indispensable to the world at large," I scoffed. Kate giggled.

"Hey! Twitter is the new blogging! The new useless sound bites that define a pop culture conversation!" Windsor contended. "You should do it Liquin!"

"God, nobody wants to listen to my pointless pecking," I spat.

"You mean tweeting," Kate amended.

"Whatever," I grunted. "Twitter isn't the way to get ahead in this business."

"I'm not so sure, chief. Like I just entered a contest for *Avatar*. The winner gets to go to some cast and crew party." Windsor sipped his coffee and reached out for Kate's hand. She made no effort to return his grip, but didn't resist when his palm finally found hers.

"Yeah. Let me know how that turns out," I chuckled.

A flutter of noise startled the crowd, pulling our attention toward the Convention Center. Those waiting in cue rose to their feet, the wave tracing its way to the rear of the line. As it met our position, we stood too, following the long rope-lanes of the cue into Hall H. It took almost ten minutes just to get from the courtyard to the building, and the whole set-up reminded me of the ride cues at Disneyland, or possibly the line for the electric chair at Sing-Sing. Well, I imagined, anyway…

Just before we approached the main door to the Convention lobby, a familiar pair of shrieks captured our attention. Windsor, Kate and I turned to see Brigham and Roxanne, locked hand in hand, racing down the side walk curb of the Convention Center, weaving through the scattering of attendees and crowd control barkers straight for us.

"EJO!" Brigham declared, prefaced by one of his trademark shrieks. He wore full length cargo pants and a *The Girl with the Dragon Tattoo* t-shirt. At his side, Roxanne doubled over in laughter, dressed in Tibetan prayer beads, black jeans, and leather vest over a black and pink Supergirl thermal…rather like Lucinda Williams by way of geek girl.

"Wait for us!" Roxanne howled, ignoring the disgusted stares of the people in line behind us. "Jesus Christ!" she panted.

"EJO!" Brigham declared between gasps. "E…J…O! I'm gonna die!"

"Come on," I grunted, as we integrated Roxanne and Brigham into the line. "What's with you two?"

"Late night," Brigham wailed, clutching for his pearls.

"Early morning!" Roxanne corrected, grabbing Brigham by

the arm. They both burst out laughing again.

"We'll tell you later," Brigham assured us, extending a limp wrist as if to tame our doubts.

"What's with the EJO?" Kate inquired, her face a vision of skepticism.

"Edward James Olmos!" Brigham erupted in a you-oughtta-know blurt.

"It's like saying 'Oh my God,' and abbreviating to OMG," Roxanne explained.

"But it's Comic-Con..." Brigham interceded.

"So EJO!" Roxanne giggled.

"Have you two been hitting the sauce this early?" Straightness asked as we entered the dark, refrigerated cavern of Hall H. "And if so, care to share?"

"Psssh, no booze this early!" Brigham slurred. "Percodin on the other hand..." He and Roxanne screamed with laughter again. Kate and I looked at each other, sharing a silent *groan* between us. Straightness just looked at our two cackling geek companions, his lips pursed in a perplexed pucker.

Hall H opened, as it always did, as a mouth lined with black velvet curtains and stacked with rows of metal folding chairs like lines of teeth of some great Lovecraftian beast. The only illumination came from the digital screens staggered above the three sections of chairs, four each at regular intervals throughout the Hall. On the far wall from the entry, the main stage glowed like some religious altar, a great digital projection screen framed by wallpaper of the Comic-Con logo in a staggered pattern. Below the screen, a podium, chairs and folding tables waited in silence for their panelists.

"So what, Edward James Olmos is like, what, God now?" Kate asked in bemusement. She stopped a few feet into the Hall, as did the rest of us, to collect a pair of special digital 3-D glasses for the panel footage. She scanned the room, walking down the center aisle looking for good seats.

"Statement of the obvi!" Roxanne declared, running up alongside Kate.

"Totes obvi," Brigham parroted.

"Just because he was on *Battlestar Galactica?*" Windsor pressed.

"And *Blade Runner*," Brigham reminded us. "And...um..." He looked at Roxanne. She just turned and shrugged with a grin. "And who gives a frak. He's EJO!"

"He also won an Emmy for *Miami Vice*," Straightness added.

"Which is oh, so geeky," Kate groaned with a smirk.

"And that movie about the Menendez Brothers," I interjected.

"Aaaaand, we're done," Brigham declared.

"LIQUIIIIIIIIIIIIN!"

"Dear God!" I spat, looking around. I didn't need to see the source to know the voice.

"KAAAAAAAAATE!"

"Knew it was coming," Kate said in a half-hum. The five of us lit our vision on what looked like a human bowling ball standing a few rows ahead on one of the folding chairs—round, but solid as a rock. His flailing arms matched his chattering personality, but the man still had charm.

"Hello Puck dear," I chimed as the five of us met our solicited.

"Still plenty of seats, guys! Thank me later!"

The five of us fought our way over to Puck, who danced a giddy jig as we walked up. I couldn't help but smile and embrace him at first opportunity.

"It's Con!" Puck squealed as I wrapped my arms around his bulbous body.

"Still the lifesaver," I uttered. "Or at least, the seat saver!"

"Hey Puck," Kate greeted as he and I parted our embrace. They exchanged a brief but genuine hug.

"Are you excited?" Puck asked, his own enthusiasm barely veiled.

"I'm exhausted," Kate groaned, dropping into her seat. "Everything ready for Saturday?" I sat down between her and Puck, listening to their conversation ping-pong. Straightness plopped down next to Kate perusing his Con schedule, and Roxanne and Brigham next to him, the two of them engaged in some snickering conversation.

"Totally, except Frank is sick with the Con crud. He should be fine by then."

"If not, Windsor, you're stepping in," Kate declared. Windsor looked up from his Con schedule, his nervous tick twitching under his eye.

"Wait, what am I doing?" Straightness asked, eyes darting back and forth between Puck and Kate.

"The big saber battle for our short film. We'll need you to do the stunts," Puck explained. Windsor's eyes narrowed.

"Right on. Remind me, who am I dueling? he asked, voice low and musical.

"It's minimal," Puck said. "You're dueling Ragnar Wortham."

I sat straight up in my seat, heart pounding, blood cold as ice water in my wrists. My jaw clenched, and my fists balled. I looked over at Kate, who immediately sunk her face into her palm. Straightness curled his lips into a cartoonish frown, eyes darting about, not knowing where to look. Roxanne's jaw dropped.

"Good CHRIST!" Brigham screamed, hand to his invisible pearls in a Tallulah Bankhead gesture, his reaction never to be outdone.

"Oh. Right," Puck murmured. He puckered his lips in an inaudible whistle, looking away from me. I didn't move.

"Hi, I'm Roxanne," the Admiral said, leaning over the group toward Puck. "I don't think we've met…Puck, is it? Some people are bad about introductions…" She looked at me, I could tell through my periphery. I didn't move. Kate looked up at her and frowned. She and I both knew Roxanne was just trying to diffuse the situation, but it was too late.

"Ragnar Wortham?" I blurted, as if to spit acid. *Ragnar*?"

"Here we go," Brigham muttered.

"Ragnar!" I grunted again.

"Liquin," Kate started, her palm outstretched to try and clam me. "I know you and Ragnar have history…"

"Yeah," Puck cut in. "Isn't there some history about…" My

gaze darted to his face like some predatory bird about to pounce. Puck recoiled, melting into a demure slouch. "Oh shit," he grumbled.

"You're putting that *son* of a *bitch* in your thesis film?" I hissed.

"Maybe we should talk about this later!" Roxanne chimed in. "Liquin?!" She forced a Cheshire smile across her face as she nodded, trying to calm my ire.

"You know, he has some redeeming qualities," Straightness offered.

"You. Are. Not. Helping!" Brigham, Kate and Puck mumbled in unison.

"Ok," Straightness muttered. "I'll just...I...Oh."

"I don't fucking believe this," I moaned.

"Later!" Roxanne pleaded again. "What's first on the schedule?"

Windsor fumbled through the schedule, slapping the pages, until he lit on the correct day and time.

"Today's Thursday, right? Hall H?" he posed in a rhetorical tone, still trying to clear the air after my meltdown. "Something called *Megamind*. Looks like a Will Farrell movie."

All six of us groaned. I mean, we had nothing against Will Farrell in principle, but the promise of seeing him did not drag us from bed so early that morning. We lined up for geekdom, and somehow one of America's lowest-brow comics didn't seem to cut it, even in a superhero parody, which is exactly what *Megamind* turned out to be. Farrell showed up dressed as the titular character—an animated character—face painted blue and wearing a spandex uniform. The man also wore a large, blue, plastic prosthetic head to expand the size of his cranium. The panel consisted of the kind of PR wanking that had come to plague the Convention—softball questions and vanity posing. To his credit, Farrell did manage to entertain us with his mugging, and his onstage companion, the loveable Tina Fey, added a good deal to an otherwise mundane presentation. When the moderator finally opened the floor—the floor 6,500-

capacity Hall H—the first question came from some unassuming guy, who, to our head scratching, stopped mid question, tore off his shirt, and started screaming like a madman.

"MEGAMIND!" he yelled, tearing his outer shirt from his body to reveal a *Megamind* t-shirt beneath. He flailed his arms and charged head first down the aisle from the microphones, across the side aisle, and out of the building.

I smacked my lips in disapproval.

"Studio plant?" Straightness asked.

"Damn right," I said, venom welling in my stomach again.

"How can you tell?" Puck wheezed.

"They're just now debuting the trailer for the fucking thing," I spat. "How is anyone going to have a fucking *Megamind* t-shirt already?"

"Good point," Puck nodded, crossing his arms.

"For that matter," Brigham injected, "how much do you think they had to pay Farrell to show up in that garb? His poor agent!"

"Agent my ass," I hissed. "He's gotta be getting a cut."

"I see the point though," Kate piped in, thoughtful. "I mean, nobody would have done this a few years ago. Can you imagine, like, Heath Ledger and Christian Bale showing up in costume, in character at a Con?"

"Good point, Boo-boo," Straightness said, wrapping an arm around Kate.

"The age we live in," I uttered.

The studio plant didn't bother me—well, ok, it did. I absolutely hated that Comic-Con, the love fest of geekdom, the Woodstock of all things nerd-tastic, had degenerated into a marketing and public relations blitz. But even more than the shameless Hollywood posing and pandering, the mention of Ragnar Wortham boiled my ire.

Ragnar and I had history, and all my friends knew it. Hell, everyone in Los Angeles probably knew it, given our Davis-Crawford style feud which had dragged on for almost a decade. Ragnar had once called me a friend—a best friend even, and I'd returned the sentiment. Funny and sad how much things change. He hated me now, with a passion, and had vowed to ruin my life if he ever had opportunity. I didn't know what had pissed him off—well, I did, and it was stupid, but it wasn't something I regretted. I'd done the right thing. That's why he hated me so. Not that I felt better about matters.

I don't think I moved, even to breathe, for the rest of the panel. As the *Megamind* crew left the stage and the lights came up, I felt Kate lay a tender hand on the scruff of my neck. I shot her a disapproving look, but didn't recoil.

"You know what that's for," she whispered to me. I gave her another sideways glance.

"Ragnar? Really?" I hissed back. She stared right past my rage, her perfect blue eyes bypassing all my veneers, right into my soul.

"It solves a lot of problems. I'll tell you later." I looked away from her, back up at the giant digital projection screen hanging just ahead of us. "Trust me."

I didn't say anything, but tipped my head over my shoulder, down to rest atop hers. I could get angry over just about anything, but not at Kate, even when she might have deserved it. As I lay my head atop her own, I glanced to my left at Puck, who'd remained silent quite out of character. I noticed him glance over without moving his head, no doubt to see if he too would incur my wrath over his association with my nemesis. I decided it best to hold my tongue, at least for the moment.

"Is *TRON* next?" I said, lifting my head from Kate's and stifling a cough. I felt an odd tickle in the back of my throat, and a strange weight on my forehead. My eyes throbbed a moment, then all of the disturbances subsided. I looked over at Straightness.

"This should be it, chief," he said. I noticed him and Kate take each other's hand, their fingers intertwining. Down the row, the Admiral and Illustrious Brigham whispered to each other, snickering with laughter. My eyes narrowed, sensing some covert activity between my two compatriots.

"What's got you snickering?" I asked.

"Molly darling!" Brigham chimed back, his face turning a bright shade of red. Roxanne gave him a gentle smack, to which Brigham responded with a guffawing laugh. Roxanne shook her head, repressing her own laughter, as she looked over at me with a Gwynplaine smile and half shrug.

"Should I know Molly?" Kate whispered, just loud enough so both Straightness and I could hear her. Windsor and I exchange a quick look.

"No, Starbuck," I answered, patting her leg.

"MDMA," Straightness uttered in his timpani rumble. "It's like mild Ecstasy."

"Lord," Kate groaned, planting a palm to her forehead in exasperation.

I sighed as the lights went down, and the panel for *TRON: Legacy* took to the stage. Jeff Bridges, still charming and sexy even in slovenly, unkempt middle age, drew most of the attention away from the plastic but arresting Olivia Wilde, the pretty but pretty boring Garret Hedlund, and the look-at-me-I'm-a-hotshot director, Joe Kozinski. Also joining them on stage, Executive Producer Sean Bailey sat posing for press photos and not doing much else.

"Why is the Executive Producer here?" I heard the Admiral squawk down the row.

"Part of the act," Puck called after her. "Showing he's important."

"That's why it's *show* business," I added. "Gotta show you're important!"

"You mean he doesn't have any function in this panel at all?" Windsor inquired in sarcasm.

"He's the smoke eater!" Brigham squawked. "He's part of the circus!" Kate looked at Windsor, then at me, then leaned over to Brigham.

"Is that like a fire eater?" Kate wondered aloud, her words slow and deliberate, as if expecting a snarky response.

"Sorta," Brigham called back. "Except fire eaters have talent. Smoke eaters just blow smoke up their own asses."

The rest of us broke into laugher, attracting the attention of the other attendees in the surrounding rows. We all had the same reaction—avoiding eye contact with all of them like shamed children. Even our mea-culpa posturing didn't stop our giggles.

What amazed me should have scared the Hell out of every studio publicist in Hall H. Bridges dominated the panel. The moderator kept trying to pull the focus onto Hedlund, Wilde and Kozinski, but none of them had the wit or appeal of the veteran actor. By the time the moderator opened the conversation up to questions on the floor it seemed like the whole crowd had forgotten about the pretty or pretty important people on the stage, and only asked questions to Bridges. That didn't bode well for the film—Flynn, Bridges character, wasn't the lead, it was the star part. Hedlund and Wilde would have to carry the bulk of the drama, and if they couldn't distinguish themselves as young, hot actors on a near-bare stage, I knew they'd have real trouble when surrounded by overpowering special effects.

From the corner of my eye, I saw Brigham hand something small to Roxanne, who passed it to Straightness, who passed it to Kate, who grunted as she handed it to me. I watched Kate roll her eyes and shake her head as I beheld the small gelatin capsule in my hand. Inside, I could see golden powder sparkling in the dim light of the Hall. Without a second thought, I pitched it into my mouth and swallowed it dry.

Brigham had just passed me, the quasi-suicidal, bipolar plate of hot mess, a dose of MDMA. And I'd taken without hesitation. Of course I knew a drug like MDMA posed dangers, and of course I knew my chemical imbalance would only make the effects of the drug more accentuated. But, I was at Comic-Con for God's sake, watching Hollywood douchery ruin what should have been a great program. I needed help!

The panel concluded in an unexpected way, with Kozinski showing off some early IMAX 3-D footage from the film which looked amazing, and having the whole crowd get up out of their seats to record some ADR sound effects for arena scenes in the film. To his credit, I'd never seen anyone do anything like that before, and for all the anal-smoking, it ended the panel on a great, high note. If nothing else, when I got home, I could tell everyone I would be in *TRON: Legacy*. If I survived the weekend.

As the panel let out and we rose to our feet, I felt a strange current of heat wipe over my body. I steadied myself against my chair, light headed, black and fuzzy spots dancing in my vision. I could hear my heart thudding in my chest. The veins in my forehead throbbed. I took a deep breath, my clarity of vision returning, and stroked my temples with the back of my hand.

"Is it just me or is it hot in here?" I yakked, still unsure of myself. I looked up at Kate who cocked an eyebrow as Straightness laid a hand on her shoulder, pulling her along after Roxanne and Brigham, who'd already made their way to the exit.

"I know dude! I think it's hot!" Puck chattered after me. "I mean, everyone always says it's cold in these friggin' things, but I always break a sweat! I have no idea why. I don't get it, I mean…"

"Puck dear," I said, wrapping my arm around him, feeling the moisture seeping through the thin preshrunk cotton of his t-shirt. I opened my mouth to offer a snide remark and caught a whiff of his sausage-like aroma. I wouldn't call it an odor; Puck always seemed hygienic, even if he did sweat all the time. I paused a moment, rethinking my strategy, my heart still thundering beneath my ribs. "Puck, you're a great guy for getting us seats," I declared as we exited Hall H. We dropped our 3-D glasses in a recycle bin in the main lobby before exiting into the overcast and chilly weather outside. I hugged Puck closer, leeching off his body heat. "Not everyone is as cool as you my boy. And it's fucking cold out here!"

I took a step back from Puck as the six of us regrouped, an island in the crowd as it dumped from Hall H and flowed back around to the front of the Convention Center and into the Exhibit Hall.

"I fucking love you man!" Puck said, grabbing me and hugging me close again. I gasped as his bear grip squeezed the air from my body, then found myself hugging him back, an odd smirk of genuine joy and appreciation on my face. Since when did I ever do that??

"Thanks," I wheezed through his death clutch. He released me and I gasped for air, doubling over and stumbling backward into the Admiral and Brigham. Both of them burst out laughing. Roxanne leaned over and pasted a wet kiss from her voluptuous lips on my cheek, giggling while she did. Brigham held my hand with one of his own, the other resting on his breastbone, fingering his imaginary pearls. I glanced up at Kate, her arms folded in faux disapproval, and Straightness, who bit his lower lip trying not to laugh.

"You ok dude?" Puck asked.

"It's just hot!" I said again. "Well, actually it's kinda nice out here..."

"We're walking the floor," Kate declared, taking Winsor by the hand. "We'll catch up with you guys when..." She paused, then shook her head, laughing. "Later."

"Me too guys. Gotta get my Con Exclusive action figures! I hear they have a prototype variant this year!" Puck spun around like a ricocheted billiard ball, then took off running after Kate. A few steps ahead, I saw him trot up alongside she and Windsor, his body language signaling an intense conversation. With Puck, everything always was.

I looked back over at Roxanne as she waved farewell to our compatriots, and noticed the oversized, polarized 3-D glasses on her face from the presentation.

"You know those don't work outside Hall H, right? That's why you were supposed to return them!"

"Oh, I know dear," the Admiral soothed. "But they're just fabulous! And I dunno, everything looks 3-D to me!"

"Fabulous," Brigham repeated.

"Oh you would," I prodded, turning to Brigham. "You, who wore a crown..." I paused, taken aback. "What the Hell?!"

Brigham, as usual, had managed to derail my thought process, this time by wearing a pair of sunglasses—I mean, I guess that's how I'd classify them—with standard frames, but in place of lenses, featured a long, black strip of polarized plastic that concealed the entire upper half of his face. At a glance, it resembled one of those odd digital black bars that tabloid magazines used to cover up the identities of random passers-by in paparazzi photos.

"Anonymity glasses, girl," Brigham spouted with pride. "I'm an upstanding member of the industry; no need to embarrass myself!"

"Can you even see through those?" I squawked.

"Oh totes!" I can see the Admiral is wearing her pilfered 3-D glasses, you're wearing a look of disdain, and that guy dressed as Deadpool over there isn't wearing underwear!"

Our eyes all darted—well, my eyes anyway; I had to guess about the other two—to a Cosplayer dressed in black and red spandex, head to toe, as the Marvel character Deadpool. He glanced up at us, scratched at the phallic bulge between his legs, and walked back toward the Convention Center.

"He totally just did that on purpose," Roxanne groaned.

"Totes," Brigham concurred.

"Ok, what are we doing?" I took a deep breath, still a bit light headed and overheated, despite the plunging temperatures and damp air overlooking the Bay.

"Lunching," Roxanne declared, seizing my arm and yanking me along. Brigham hooked my other arm, the caboose in our drug-addled train. She weaved through the crowd, across the busway in front of the Convention Center, and down to Harbor Drive where we had to wait to cross over into the greater San Diego Gaslamp District. That was the first time we saw the protesters...

"Holy shit," I uttered, pulling both my companions close. In the small garden walk just adjacent to the Convention Center, where Fifth Avenue and Harbor Drive meet, a modest cabal of demonstrators yelled through bullhorns, trying to capture the attention of the crowd. In their hands they'd erected cruel signs of yellow and black with slogans that read "GAYS BURN IN HELL," "DIE FAG DIE," "JESUS HATES GAYS" and the like. The breath escaped my body as if a bulldozer had steamrolled my diaphragm. I'd seen chaos, even wickedness at Comic-Con, but never hatred, never anything so black and malignant as a mob of bigots.

"Why are they even here?" Roxanne wondered in exasperation.

"Cocksucker. Motherfucker!" Brigham murmured. I held his arm extra tight, staring past the oblong rectangle of tinted plastic over his face, knowing without evens seeing any detail that his eyes screamed in agony, his long-buried pain that he tried to so hard to conceal with laughter and love and pills and booze and anything else seeped once again to the surface.

"Brigs?" I asked, trying to sound as nurturing as possible. He shook his head, his lower lip twisting with anger and sorrow.

"I fucking grew up with this shit," words staccato, as if uttered by castanets. "I've seen my parents, my sisters, people I know pull this fucking bigot bullshit at rallies, at pride festivals, fucking everywhere. I've seen them outside the Trevor Project when I was a fucking volunteer at a fucking *suicide hotline* for *fucking kids!* I do not need to see this shit again."

"Come on," Roxanne ordered, yanking us along. "Fucking bigots!" she screamed at the protesters. "Jesus fucking hates you, you know that!?"

I'm not sure the protesters heard her or that I even agreed with what she said, but it sure made me feel better.

The next thing I knew we'd wandered into a large urban eatery where the hostess had seated us under some giant clockwork mechanism, no doubt meant to act as a decoration more than serve some practical function. Nevertheless, I felt as if I'd wandered into some magnificent steampunk café, a shark-ish smile widening across my face. Roxanne, seated to my right, looked over at me through her 3-D glasses, leaned up to me, and planted another kiss on my cheek. I smiled even wider, shrugging up my shoulders like a bashful child. When the waiter came to take our order, I looked around, having already forgotten my surroundings.

"Where the fuck are we anyway?" I blurted. Brigham slapped a menu against his forehead, hiding his face.

"The Spaghetti Factory my love," Roxanne said through giggles. From the look of Brigham's arms poking out from behind his menu, vibrating up and down like a jackhammer, I could tell he tried to stifle his laughter too.

"Oh, are we drinking!?" I chimed in with glee.

"YES!" Brigham exploded, his voice unusually resonant and glottal. "Scotch on the rocks!"

"Glass of Pinot Noir," Roxanne added.

"Um…" All at once I felt confused, overwhelmed by the venue and my options.

"Gin martini, two olives," Brigham suggested.

"Gin martini, two olives!" I repeated with giddy relish. I looked up at the waiter and smirked, meeting with his perplexed and skeptical look.

"Any gin?" he asked, a bit sheepish.

"House gin is fine," I told him. Across the table, Brigham coughed and cleared his throat. I looked at him, expectant.

"You mean Bombay," Brigham clarified. "House gin indeed."

"House gin," I said again.

"You cannot drink house gin!" Brigham bellowed.

"I'm not paying top shelf prices!" I barked back.

"No house gin!"

"Then you're buying!"

"I'm not paying for your ass!"

"Gentlemen!" Roxanne silenced us. "There's no shame in house gin." She looked back and forth between us like a chiding mother. Brigham frowned and I smirked.

"House gin, two olives," I declared. The waiter made a note on his pad, then lingered a moment.

"Yeeeeeeees?" Roxanne piped through a toothy smile.

"What's with the glasses?" our waiter asked. "Is that part of the Con, or…" He trailed off, uncertain where to go with his statement. I furled my brow, confused a moment, before I again noticed the odd glasses worn by my companions. Whatever or not the MDMA had made me into a happier person, I didn't know, but I sure managed to lose track of myself, along with everything else.

Roxanne and Brigham exchanged a look, then stared back up at the waiter.

"They're fabulous!" Roxanne grinned.

"And illustrious!" Brigham furthered, smile even wider than Roxanne's. "We're trying not to get noticed!"

"Trying *not* to?!" grunted the exasperated waiter. A beat of silence followed, Roxanne and Brigham unsure what to say.

"It's Comic-Con!" I broke in, capturing the attention of the table. "Think about it!" I had no idea what I was saying or what it was supposed to mean, but at least it sounded good. Politicians did the same thing all the fucking time, and it worked for them!

"Yes!" Roxanne agreed, pointing a finger at me.

"Yeah!" Brigham added, puckering his lips in naughty defiance.

"Yeah," the waiter sighed, walking off into the restaurant to put in our drink order.

"Hmmm," I purred, wallowing in my own self-satisfaction.

"Nice guy," Roxanne mused, unfolding her napkin into her lap.

"Should we really be drinking alcohol with..." I paused. "Ya, know, with the Molly?"

"YES!" Brigham snarled, cocking his head back a moment, hand to his chest. Roxanne looked over at me, bowing her head in sarcasm.

"It'll be fine, Liquin," Roxanne said. "Now where's my wine?"

"You just ordered it," I reminded her.

"That's no excuse! I need my wine!"

"Girl has a point," Brigham added.

When our drinks arrived I downed my martini like a camel, and felt nothing of the numbing effects of alcohol in my system. Still, I knew better than to try and overpower one drug with another. Comic-Con offered enough chaos without a rolling bipolar drunkard raving through the crowd in his boxers, or, knowing me, less.

By the time our food arrived I'd lost my appetite, but I forced myself to eat a bit anyway. I found myself preoccupied by the grape-sized beads of sweat forming on Brigham's forehead, or the Tinkerbell-like glitter on Roxanne's face. As they ranted on about boys, dating, sex, Hillary Clinton, sailors, Hall Nazis, penises, shoes, and God knows what else, I realized I'd started fanning myself about halfway through my martini, and hadn't stopped for damn near an hour.

"Is it hot in here to you?" I blurted. "I mean, it's fucking cold outside! Do they have the heat on in here or something? Are you hot? I'm hot! Like, HOT!" Another grim realization struck me. "And my God, am I talking too much?"

Roxanne and Brigham stared at me a beat, before exploding in laughter. Brigham's face turned red as a candied apple, and Roxanne kept snorting between guffaws. My gaze teetered back and forth between them, waiting for some explanation. I frowned, one hand to my chin, balancing my elbow against the table as I drummed the fingers of my free hand. Then, another realization...

"It's the MDMA, right?" Brigham and the Admiral burst into laughter again.

The three of us walked back to the Con arm in arm after lunch, down the crowded sprawl of Fifth Avenue, past the barkers—that annoying group of promotional envoys that tries to get attendees to buy, see, attend, or do whatever the fuck else—across the railroad tracks and into the Convention Center Lobby.

"Full disclosure," the Admiral said. "Do you remember any of this from last night?"

"We actually went into the Exhibit Hall?" I questioned, my eyes narrowing in suspicion. My response triggered yet another inevitable laugh from Roxanne, who, by this time, had curled her smile back so far the entire world could see her wisdom teeth.

"Do you remember anything?" she asked.

"Um, just some song lyrics," I confessed. "Someone saying 'stick it in,' and screaming about the lizard queen…"

"Yeah, that was him trying to check in to the Bayfront," the Admiral grimaced at Brigham, who pursed his lips in silent judgment.

"Oh my!" Brigham interjected.

"And I had that weird vision of Adam," I added, half anticipating what would happen next. True to form, Roxanne and Brigham froze in their tracks, grabbing me by the arm, anchoring me with them.

"Adam!" Brigham bellowed. "Not him again…"

"Hang on!" Roxanne urged. "Pow wow time!" With that, she yanked both of us into the nearest men's room, pushed us both into a stall (thank God there wasn't a line) and locked the door behind us.

"What a lovely smell you've discovered," Brigham retched, glowering down at the filthy tile beneath our feet. In an act of divine mercy, the toilet itself looked pretty clean. Not that I double checked or anything…

"What about Adam?!" Roxanne growled, suddenly severe. "Is he here? Have you been talking to him?"

"Of course I do, he's a friend!" I spat back. "He's at some wedding or something this weekend."

"Guy's wedding," Brigham clarified. I looked at him a long moment, regret burning in my stomach.

"Yeah, Guy, his business partner. It's his wedding." I looked at Roxanne, her rich brown eyes glassy and empathetic.

"This is *your* Guy?" Roxanne demanded. "Your Guy that you dated, that you met at Comic-Con a few years back?"

"Not *my* Guy," I rebutted. "But yes, him. He's still a friend too and I would totally be at his wedding right now if it weren't Con weekend."

"Are…" Roxanne cooed. "Are you ok?"

"Yes, I'm fine!" I hissed back. "It's life, right? We couldn't make it work because of the distance!" I sighed. "And I'm a raging psychopath!"

"Will you fucking stop it," Brigham groaned.

Just then, a light knock on the stall door captured our attention.

"I'm busy!" Roxanne hollered without hesitation or regret. The knocking ceased.

"Look, it's fine," I contended. "I'm fine, it's fine, Adam and Guy are fine, it's all fine. It's not fine, however, that we're doing this in a men's room stall!"

"Amen," Brigham said.

"What did Adam say?" Roxanne pressed.

"I dunno, it was a drug hallucination! Something about... some challenge coming and how I always had to remember reflections aren't what they seem or something..." As I recounted my vision, I reached up under my shirt to feel the USB drive still hanging about my neck, the memory chip which contained the master file for *Leopard Messiah*. I sighed heavy.

"I'm meeting with Monty Doyle on Saturday, ohmygod..." I uttered, dropping my face into my hands.

"Yes, you are," Brigham prodded. "So get it together!"

"You don't need to think about that right now," Roxanne soothed. "One day at a time. Enjoy the Con." She pulled my hands away from my face, holding them tight in her own. She hunched down to make eye contact with me, pulling me back into the present. She probably sensed I stood on the razor's edge of another bipolar rabbit hole-depression crash, and given how the MDMA altered my senses, she may have been right.

Either way, I didn't have a crash in the bathroom, and Roxanne and Brigham did keep me from, at the very least, getting trapped up into my thoughts. But what the Hell was that hallucination of Adam about anyway? He and I had affirmed our friendship, and any temptation to have frivolous sex went out the window during our heart to heart. And anyway, that was two years before! Why was I having visions of him now dressed like Alec Guinness?

I couldn't dwell much on my Adam fixation, which, in

retrospect, probably served me better than had I walked around brooding the rest of the day. Instead, Brigham, Roxanne and I locked arms again, and entered into the massive Exhibit Hall for the first time...or at least, the first time I would remember that year.

And I was home again. The cavern-like exhibit hall with it's unfinished, rafter ceilings, dangling banners of yellow and blue, great statues, displays and sales booths and aisle upon aisle of attendees crowded together, climbing over one another trying to see their favorite exhibits. I tipped my head back, reveling in the atmosphere, holding my friends tight to me. No matter what, the unbelievable rush of walking into that Convention Hall, energized and full of wonder, never got old.

We'd entered the Exhibit Hall midway at Hall E; the sort of center for toy marketing blitz. All the major toy and collectable companies had set up massive booths displaying their upcoming toy releases and gone all out in putting together their booths: giant Transformer statues guarded the Hasbro booth. A life-sized Jabba the Hutt lounged around Kenner, and Mattel had built a giant Castle Greyskull walk-through exhibit, which made me squeal like a five year old as soon as I saw it. I charged through the crowd, plowing over children, the elderly and cosplayers galore to the entry of Greyskull, camera in hand. By the time Brigham and Roxanne caught up with me, I'd demanded five snapshots from some poor booth attendant who probably signed up to work at the Con thinking he'd have something to qualify him for his Screen Actors Guild card.

"These aren't the droids you're looking for. Move along!" Brigham declared. Roxanne snatched the camera from the unfortunate Mattel employee with a seductive and flirtatious smile, as Brigham locked on to me and pulled me along. I wrested from his grip, taking the camera from Roxanne and proceeded to stop and swoon at every glass case displaying some new toy. By the time I'd made it to the third case, the shrieking laughter of my companions caught my attention.

"What!? They're making new He-Man toys!" I whined,

offended by their judgment. The Admiral and the Illustrious One laughed even harder, Brigham fanning his ruddy face and Roxanne buying her own countenance in Brigham's shoulder. "What?!" I begged again. "He-Man is my favorite!"

"Big surprise there," Brigham grunted. "A muscle guy in a leather harness that hangs out with a dude named Fisto!"

"Not like that!" I rebutted. "I have great memories of watching He-Man as a kid. I'd get home from school right as the show would come on, and I'd have popcorn and play with my toys! It was great!"

"Mmmm-hmmm" Brigham hummed with sarcasm.

"Dude, it's a happy memory!" I snarled. "Don't cheapen it; I don't have a whole lot of those to draw on!" I sighed. "I'm not very good at being happy." Brigham looked at me through his thick, Henry Kissinger glasses, the size of his blue eyes inflated by the concave lenses. He blinked once, and smiled.

"You're better at it than you think," he declared.

"How's that?" I groaned, fully expecting more ridicule.

"You are lit *up!*" Roxanne squawked. "I've never seen you like this."

"What!?" I urged again, this time with a playful tone. "It's He-Man!" I reached up and fanned my face, feeling overheated. I realized right away the oddness of my gesture...the Exhibit Hall temperature was usually kept somewhere in the arctic range. Strange that it should get so warm, especially given the overcast weather outside.

"It's endearing," Brigham assured me. "Revel in it!"

I put my hands on my hips, cocking my head to the side, raising an eyebrow, letting my posture convey my don't-make-fun-of-me-you-son-of-a-bitch attitude.

"I know what you want to do," Brigham teased. "You should."

"What?" I spat.

"Do it! Go! Go on!" Brigham nudged. My eyes darted back and forth between he and Roxanne, as I waited for further elaboration.

"What?" Roxanne pressed Brigham, also confused. Brigham

frowned.

"Spring in your step," Brigham said. "Do a little...*strut?!*"

"Oooooohhh," I growled with orgasmic basso.

"Do it. Do it. Do it," Brigham chanted in perfect rhythm. I felt my pelvis start to groove and thrust. "Strut it. Strut it. Strut it!"

I spun around on my heel and let my feet kick out, arms outstretched in front of my, cocking my head back and forth like a chicken. For some reason, people got out of the way as I walked toward them. I didn't object.

"Strut! And strut it! And strut it!" Brigham drilled, walking behind me, his volume amplified with each declaration. No doubt he'd noticed the parting crowd and decided to take advantage of my sway.

"And WERK!" Roxanne called out, joining in the revelry.

"And STRUT!" Brigham alternated with her. As they yelled louder and louder with reckless abandon, I started to hear nearby snickers. Still, knowing a lucky Comic-Con opportunity when I saw one, I ignored my audience and kept the pace.

"And WERK!"

"And STRUT!"

"And YOU get a car! And YOU get a car! And YOU get a car!" I rattled off for no apparent reason. Hey, my friends had started a good beat! "You get a car and YOU get a car and YOUUUU get a car and..."

I froze, gasping like wheezing donkey. High on a top shelf of rod stainless steel coated in black plastic, I spotted Count Dooku's lightsaber from the *Star Wars* film series.

"EJOaDookuSaber!" I slurred, jumping up and down like a toddler, stabbing my pointer finger into the air. Roxanne and Brigham, still in their "incognito" glasses, looked about for the object of my attention.

"Girrrrrrrl," Brigham purred.

"Oh my God, you have to!" Roxanne blurted, running from Brigham's side to my own.

"It's $200! I can't afford that! I'm a starving artist!" I exploded, overwhelmed by my defeat.

"But how rare is it? You should get it if you want it!" Roxanne insisted.

"You want a Prequel Prop?" Brigham groaned.

"Do *not* start with me on that debate, Brigs!"

"Interested?" The question came from a dashing Sales Hunk, dressed in a black polo-uniform, his pectorals bulging beneath the knit fabric. Despite great skin, perfect teeth, and groomed jet-black hair, I still placed him at about 45 years old. Still, I wouldn't have kicked him out of bed.

"Hellooooo," Roxanne sang, her wisdom teeth again revealed in a vast rictus. Apparently, she wouldn't kick him out of bed either. She puffed out her chest, her breasts standing at militant attention, resting her hands at the small of her back to accentuate her perfect ass. "I'm interested in your lightsaber!"

"Shit," Brigham said, planting his face deep in the palm of his hand.

"Yeah, it's rare," the Sales Hunk said.

"Does that mean it's pink inside?" Roxanne asked. Even I rolled my eyes at that one.

"Red," the Sales Hunk answered, trying not to laugh. The look on his face suggested utter confusion if amusement, as if he couldn't quite believe that yes, this woman was serious.

"Mmmmm," the Admiral hummed, her smile enveloping most of her face. "Can I get a discount?"

"For you, $175."

"Frak me!" I blurted. I without any thought to my companions, I started down the aisle for the exit.

"Don't you want to see him take it out?" Roxanne called after me. I swatted at the air in a futile *shoo* gesture, mimicking Kate from that morning.

"Can't talk, coming down," I muttered to myself. By then, the MDMA had started to wear off, I could tell; the air around me felt freezing. No doubt the Illustrious One and the Admiral would soon feel the same way. I exited the Exhibit Hall in a huff, pushing through a crowd of Cosplayers dressed as the cast of *Dragonball Z.* As I headed through the lobby, I had second thoughts: why not buy the damned saber? I'd get to enjoy it for a few days, at least! Still, I reasoned with a sigh, what little funds I had would need to go to good use for the *Neodämmerung.* Better that I conserved what little I had for the weekend.

Outside the Convention Center, the temperature had fallen, or at least it felt to me as if it did. Rain had begun to fall again, and the cool moisture mixed with the diesel exhaust of the Con shuttle buses parked at the curb. A shallow cough erupted from my core, and I felt a slight tickle at the back of my throat. I hugged myself for warmth, running a finger at the bottom of my nose to wipe collecting water as I started off back to the Bayfront.

By the time I arrived in the lobby, a full stock of phlegm had drained into my nasal cavity and down the back of my throat, and my tonsils had begun to swell and ache. The elevator I called was thankfully empty, save for the oversized poster-stickers advertising *True Blood* complete with naked images of the cast. I leaned my head back against the wall as the elevator car ascended, trying to rest, but unable to tear my eyes away from naked Alexander Sarsgaard. I suppose even at my least libidinous, I still had some humanity left.

Back in the room, I found Kate wrapped in a white terrycloth bathrobe embroidered with the Bayfront logo, sitting alone on her bed, making some notes in a black and white composition notebook. She'd left the curtains full-open to the view of the Con, and even in the dim light from outside, her blue eyes sparkled with life.

"Hey Starbuck," I said as I entered, dropping my backpack next to the dresser and collapsing face first onto the bed I shared with Brigham. "I feel terrible."

"Yeah, not feeling so hot myself," Kate replied making a final note on a page and dropping the notebook into her lap. She turned to me. "It's the weather. Allergies. It's why I came back."

"Same here. And I'm tired as fuck." I rolled onto my back. From outside, a clamor of horns rose over the Con, capturing both our attention for a moment before dismissing the noise with a grunt.

"How was the floor?"

"You mean you haven't even been down there yet?" I squawked. "What did you do after the panel this morning?"

"Windsor and I went to another panel, then I came here." I detected some hidden angst buried in her tone. I rolled onto my side, examining Kate's face a moment, trying to ignore the irritation of my sinuses and remind her that even at my most medicated and miserable, I was still her Liquin. "I had work to do," she added, wary of my stare.

"What's really going on, Starbuck?" Kate ran a hand back over her head, pulling her shoulder-length tresses back and suppressing a frown.

"He's on my nerves. I love him, but..." Kate shrugged, sighed and looked up at me, keeping her cool. "Well, you know as well as anyone how he can be."

"Yes, I do." I admitted with a chuckle. "But he's gotten better."

"He has, and he hasn't. I don't know. Lord..." Kate sighed again, collapsing onto her left side, legs still folded Indian-style beneath her, head landing on a pillow as she stared over at me. "This whole thing with the animation academy has me thinking."

"You're afraid he'll leave?"

"No, not just that. I'm almost done with school. When I am I'll have crazy debt and no job prospects, even if our little movie is great. It just makes me wonder if Windsor and I are what each other need. What if I want to leave?"

The very mention of the possibility that either Starbuck or Straightness or worst of all, both might depart Los Angeles leaving me to my own flaws and vices made my stomach hurt. I balled myself on the bed into the fetal position and tried to conceal my own anxieties. Kate didn't need any of those at the moment.

"You have a choice to make I suppose, but then, that's just kind of how life is. The first step toward a decision is knowing you must make one."

"You're right, I know," Kate uttered. "That doesn't make it an easy choice, and that doesn't mean any of them lead to happiness."

"I know."

"I mean," Kate went on. "You inspired me so much. So did coming to Con that first time. And Windsor…he is great, despite his many idiosyncrasies." Kate smiled. "*Many* idiosyncrasies," she repeated.

"Then you need to evaluate your options." I sat up on the bed. "By the way, I wish I could offer myself this wisdom, but somehow my mutant power for blowhard drivel only allows me to spout it at others, never at myself."

"Stop," Kate urged, sitting up to face me. "You know how good you are."

"Psssh," I spat.

"The way I see it, Windsor and I can stay together, and one or both of us can gamble on the career financial success of the other, or we can split, and then…" Kate paused, shrugging her shoulders to her ears. "Then, come what may." I nodded, silent.

"God, I'm fucking freezing!" I stood up, kicking off my shoes and opening a drawer in search of warmer clothes.

"Try the closet," Kate suggested, looking back down at her notebook. I complied with her suggestion, opening the storage closet and finding the clothes rack loaded with six other terry bathrobes.

"What the Hell?" I giggled, taking a robe from a hook.

"The Illustrious One," Kate purred. "He doesn't want to run out of anything."

"That's just good planning," I said as I threw the robe over my back. "I wonder how many trips this took him. And for that matter, how didn't he get caught?"

Just then, the room door flew open again, and Roxanne and Brigham stumbled into the room, both dripping wet and wearing their unfortunate eyeglasses, looking as though they'd emerged from the mouth of Hell.

"Oh good, you found the robes," Brigham moaned, nudging

me out of the way and snatching a robe from the closet.

"Thank GOD!" Roxanne exploded, diving into the tiny storage space, yanking a robe from a hook, throwing it over her head, and collapsing on to the empty bed. Kate watched in awe as Brigham bundled himself in the white cloth and slid into bed next to the Admiral.

"I guess that explains the extra," I mused to Kate. She cracked a grin. "What the Hell happened to you two?"

"YOU ABANDONED US!" Brigham shrieked, a lump of white cotton on the bed.

"YES!" Roxanne howled, her cry muffled by the thick robe covering her head.

"We were lost and coming down and we were somewhere and you weren't there and then we couldn't remember where we were!" Brigham whined.

"YES!" Roxanne cheered again.

"I told you," I started. "I was coming back here."

"I was negotiating that lightsaber for you with the hot dude," Roxanne reminded me.

"She would have slept with him for a discount, too!" Brigham added. "I would have slept with him!"

"I showed a boob!" Roxanne declared, sitting up for a split second, head emerging from under her robe, before dropping back to the mattress, concealing herself in the folds again. I looked at Kate and frowned, rolling my eyes and sitting down next to her on the bed.

"YES!" Brigham trumpeted.

"Lord," Kate muttered. Roxanne shot back to her upright posture again.

"And then I asked the guy for a marker and some cardboard and made a sign that said 'honk if you're horny' and carried it around!" Roxanne chirped, proud.

"YES!" Brigham belted again.

"And then I carried it outside and got all the bus drivers honking on the curb!"

"She did!" Brigham meowed, snapping upright with a

lascivious grin.

"Was your boob still hanging out at that point?" Kate asked, teeming with sarcasm.

"Just a bit," Roxanne smiled.

"Just a little nip," Brigham added.

"And where is said sign now?" Kate asked, incredulous.

"Gave it to a kid dressed as Beast Boy. Think he was five or so…" Roxanne rolled over.

"Ok, I need a drink," Kate said, tossing her notebook aside and walking over to the First Aid kit, arranged next to the TV on the dresser. She opened the case, took out the scotch, poured a heaping shot into a nearby goblet, which may or may not have been used, and slurped a long sip.

"And I need a shower," I declared, rising. "But first…" I joined Kate at the First Aid kit. I took the scotch bottle, opened it again, and downed a long swig, coughing a bit as I swallowed. "That's better." I replaced the bottle in the First Aid kit, went into the bathroom, and turned the hot water on in the shower at full temperature.

I writhed a bit against the hot water as I entered; the bathroom had grown quite cold, probably due to the tile and granite countertops. I adjusted the water temperature at the control knob, then sank to the floor, resting my chin on my knees, hugging my legs close. I closed my eyes, waiting for the steam to loosen all the crud in my sinus. I sighed.

Kate had a point, one which, because of my self-absorbed misery, I'd somehow managed to not consider. What if she did have to leave? Who would I talk to then? Yes, I had Windsor —though he might leave too—and Brigham, and Roxanne, and Puck, but…

Well, I'd noticed something as my twenties progressed. The great community, the surrogate family of friends, lovers and general comrades that I'd worked so hard to build and cement since arriving in Los Angeles had fragmented. We still loved each other, and we still hung out, but not like we used to. It seemed like I knew what everyone did at any given hour of any day thanks to Twitter and Facebook and the like, but somehow I felt more isolated than ever, as if those "networking" sites and smartphone apps only provided the illusion of togetherness and community. In reality, they actually fragmented everyone even more than before. Other than my folks, I couldn't remember the last time I'd spoken to someone on the phone; every communication now seemed to come via impersonal text —messages or bubbles on some chat program. It only made me feel more alone.

I thought to myself about aging. At the end of that July, I'd turn 30, ostensibly ending my Saturn Return. I never put much stock in old astrological terms or predictions, but I'd heard about the Saturn Return—the three year period between ages 27 to 30 —in a movie once, and found some frightening statistics about the number of artists who died in that window: Kurt Cobain, Jimi Hendrix, Janis Joplin, River Phoenix, Jim Morrison, and so many more. Would I become one of them? If I did, would it insure my legacy? Gore Vidal once observed that death is a great career move for artists.

I sat up, my eyes wide, the chlorinated water of the shower burning in my eyes, but not inhibiting my realization: I'd be more marketable dead than alive. Maybe...maybe it was what I needed to do. Death at Comic-Con...it wouldn't be all bad. I'd at least be having a good time! I'd be surrounded by friends and my brother and sister geeks, and best of all, no clean up if I killed myself in the hotel room! Just a big tip for the maid, and then my roommate back in LA could keep the apartment, get a bunch of sympathy and without the nasty smell of a corpse, too!

I turned off the water, just sitting there a moment, letting the last of the shower drip off of me, watching the steam clouds roll up to the bathroom ceiling. Dear God, what the fuck did I have to live for?

"Liquin, I gotta pee!" Brigham called from the next room.

I forced myself up, toweled off, trying to avoid looking at myself in the steamed mirror. My whole body ached, and I felt my lymph nodes swelling in my neck. I yawned, pulling on my boxers and donning my robe. I kicked my wet towel under the sink, and re-emerged the bedroom. Kate and Roxanne sat on the far bed sipping drinks, as Brigham stood over them, his own cocktail in hand, swishing his weight back and forth, side to side.

"I feel like Hell," I grumbled, hugging myself in my towel, throwing up the terry hood to cover my head. Brigham hurried past me and into the bathroom. A moment later, the door still open venting steam, we all heard the trickle of a steady stream of urine emptying into the commode.

"Were you going to close the door?" Kate chimed with sarcasm.

"I'm good," Brigham yelled back, the sound of his pissing still audible. Just then, the hotel room door swung open again, and Windsor appeared, laptop bag over one shoulder, his arms carrying a large, cardboard box full of vintage action figures. As the door closed behind him, he glanced into the bathroom out of instinct, spying the urinating Brigham.

"Jesus God man!" Straightness howled, juggling the box in his arms. Brigham let out a shriek, accompanied by the sound of clanging porcelain. "Don't miss the bowl!" Straightness added.

"Windsor Kane! Get out of my...get out! Don't look! God Frakking Damnit!" Brigham groused.

"Why doesn't he just close the door!?" Windsor exclaimed, putting down his box and shoulder bag, walking over and greeting Starbuck with a kiss. Her eyes shined as their lips met, and all at once she looked more serene than I'd seen her all weekend. Brigham re-entered the room accompanied by the sound of a toilet flush.

"Did you wash your hands?" Roxanne accused. Brigham frowned and went back to the bathroom.

"Dude," Straightness declared, raising his arms. "St. Sigs of the Weave!" Another Brigham scream emanated from the bathroom, as my Illustrious friend came charging back into the room, hands dripping wet.

"St. Sigs!" Brigham shrieked.

"She's here," Straightness assured us. Brigham screamed, putting a hand to his mouth to stifle the sound. He flapped it away again, revealing his mouth and letting out an even shriller cry, before hinging his hand back in place.

"How do you know?" I asked.

"Twitter," Straightness explained.

"Dear God," I muttered, sitting down between Kate and Roxanne.

"Seriously?" Kate prodded.

"Yes, she's here! I saw it on Twitter!" Windsor said, hellfire in his eyes. "She's walking the floor in a Batman costume!"

"Are you fucking kidding me with this?" I blurted. Kate just stared at her boyfriend, face blank. Roxanne seemed more interested in her vodka. Brigham, however, seemed to vibrate with excitement.

"Which Batman!?" Brigham pleaded. "West? Keaton? Bale? Oh God…" He rested his hand on his imaginary pearls. "What if it's one of the comic costumes? There are so many!"

"This is ridiculous," Kate groaned.

"I'm forced to agree," I added. "I…"

"Hear, hear!" Roxanne cheered, interrupting me. She took another sip from her glass, slipping into zombie mode again.

"I can't imagine Sigourney Weaver has the temerity to dress up like Batman and then tweet about it," I said. "It seems counterproductive."

"She wasn't the one tweeting about it!" Windsor clarified. "It was some 'Secrets of Comic-Con' hashtag that somebody else retweeted."

"All the more credible," Kate injected through a smirk.

"Dude," Windsor urged. "She's here, I know it!"

"I hope she's not that Zur-En-Arr Batman from that awful Grant Morrison run," Brigham mused aloud. "That costume is ugly as fuck. And the writing is bad! Did anyone here read *Batman R.I.P.*?"

"I need a nap," I declared, throwing myself down on the bed and writhing up to the pillows.

"What's with you?" Windsor asked.

"I feel like hell," I groaned, closing my eyes.

"AH! Con crud!" Straightness yelled, making a crucifix with his two index fingers.

"It's the weather," I urged. "I'll be fine. I just need rest."

"You also need better vodka," Brigham chided, swallowing the last of his glass. "Where is St. Sigs anyway?"

"Check my suitcase," I grunted, sliding under the covers. I started to relax into the bed, when another Brigham-shriek jolted me back to attention. I looked up to see him cradling my Lt. Ripley/Power Loader action figure—Sigourney Weaver's character in *Aliens*—like an infant in his arms.

"Just keep it down," I croaked. "I just need a few minutes." I pulled the terry hood up over my head again, and then nestled under the covers, pulling the sheets and blankets up to my neck. I heard Windsor start in about his day and the epic shopping trip he'd had, then...

My eyes fluttered open to behold the pitch-black room. I felt a bit better, rousing myself to try and look around. I reached over and switched on the nightstand light, which revealed that I was indeed alone in the room. I forced myself out of bed, pulling the robe tight around my body in the chilly hotel air. After a quick stop in the bathroom, I dug through my clothes to find my phone, along with a message from the Admiral:

Downstairs in hotel bar. Snackage. Drinkage. Joinage!

I cracked a smile, and went about getting myself ready. I figured I'd had enough time to wallow in my own self-pity and fatigue. Comic-Con came but once a year, and nothing should keep me from attending. I slipped back into my jeans and pulled on a vintage *Thundercats* shirt with the Mumm-Ra logo across the chest. I checked myself in the bathroom mirror, throwing a bit of gel into my hair to refresh the style and a bit of face cream to look a bit more, well, alive. I caught myself shivering again, so I pulled my bathrobe back on before I exited the room, bound for the hotel bar.

The Bayfront hotel bar did not disappoint, decked out in

granite tables and counters, lit with blue and green lights emanating from hand-blown glass fixtures. The bar was packed with industry people still wearing their lanyards and overdressed for the Con, yet despite the douche factor, even true Con devotees like me packed into the booths and up to the bar having a great time.

I found the rest of my crew nestled into a corner, flanked by a glass wall overlooking San Diego Bay. In the clear of night, the Coronado Bridge lit up like a road to heaven itself, silver lights glowing from the support beams, with the colored lights of the marina and sailing ships moving about below. I smiled at the backdrop, sharing a chair with Roxanne. Seating, because of the crowd, was limited, and even at our snug table, the staff had only provided three chairs. Kate sat on Windsor's lap, stacked like spoons, while Roxanne scooted to one side to allow my ass some space. Brigham just sprawled in his seat, martini glass in one hand, the other waving about with furious gestures. He looked like an orchestra conductor on cocaine.

Roxanne leaned over and kissed my cheek as I sat down. Before us on the table sat a half-eaten chicken quesadilla, two beef sliders and a bowl of spinach dip and tortilla chips. Roxanne motioned to the food in front of us.

"Dinner baby?" she offered through a yawn. "You feeling better?"

"Yeah, I'm ok," I said softly, taking a wedge of quesadilla and munching on it.

"Hang in there, chief," Straightness offered. "Nothing is worth missing Con."

"Too true," I agreed, snagging another quesadilla wedge. As I chewed, I glanced at Roxanne as she imbibed a glass of red wine, and Brigham sipped a fizzy, clear drink with a twist of lime— probably a gin and tonic. I held my breath a moment, my eyes narrowing with scrutiny.

"Is it ok to be drinking after the Molly?" I asked. "I mean, does it stay in our systems, or…"

"Oh, Liquin, it's fine," Brigham said, taking a gulp from his cocktail. I scowled at him, turning to Roxanne in hopes of a better explanation. Roxanne glanced over at me with a half-smile.

"You'll be fine," she told me, sipping at her wine. I took the glass from her and downed a swig. The earthy taste of Cabernet Sauvignon burned my tongue and I clenched my teeth at the overpowering bouquet, passing the glass back to the Admiral.

"What've I missed?"

"The usual geekgasms about what's coming up…*Harry Potter, Tron 2, Green Lantern…*" Brigham started.

"*Avengers,*" Kate injected. Straightness leaned in and kissed her shoulder, proud that she would even mention the title.

"*Avengers!*" Brigham repeated with sumptuous relish. "I can't even believe it. That's a bigger miracle than *Watchmen.*"

"Assuming it's good," Straightness added. "Either way, there's a lot riding on it. I'm not sure Whedon can direct."

"Neither am I," I said, mouth half full of quesadilla. "He doesn't have a track record."

"*Buffy* was great!" Roxanne contended.

"Doesn't mean he can direct a movie though," Brigham conceded. "I'd be happier if he was just writing, not directing. Where's Jon Faverau when you need him?"

"Currently rolling around naked in a pile of money," Straightness mused. Kate leaned back against his chest, and I watched him thread an arm around her waist. I smiled to myself, encouraged by their love. If only I had some of my own…

"I fucking hate this thing!" The voice came from an emaciated blond woman, evidently on her third cosmopolitan. She wore a sea green top which more resembled a handkerchief than a shirt in any traditional sense, and a pair of black ass-lifting jeans. She wobbled about next to the bar on a pair of strappy high heels as she slurred and pointed at three other Hollywood douche bags seated nearby—two men in black designer suits, and another woman dressed as if to attend a Steely Dan concert—black leather jacket with sequins and beads, white silk tank top, and leather pants. The copious number of empty glasses in front of the four suggested they'd been at the bar a good while.

My companions reacted to the Hollywood bimbo's remarks just as I did—with sour faces and groans. Brigham and Kate both rolled their eyes, and Straightness muttered something under his breath. Roxanne took a sip from her own glass—red wine, I assumed—and placed it back on the table with a clang.

"Seriously, who the frak do these people think they are?" Kate hissed. "They hold a desk job which eats away at what little soul they have..."

"Assuming they even had one to begin with," I amended.

"Right," Kate went on. "And they come to our convention and then bash those of us that actually love it?"

"In their minds," Brigham explained, "it is *their* convention. They're Hollywood rich people, and if there's one thing that Hollywood rich people feel entitled to, it's..."

"Everything," I blurted, spitting bitterness in my remark.

"Yeah, that," Brigham agreed. "Welcome to Ayn Rand's America." Straightness shivered at the remark. Roxanne scowled.

"I mean have you seen what these dorks are *wearing!*" the bimbo screeched again. "Do these fuckers bathe! No wonder they're all virgins!"

"That's *it!*" I hissed.

"Oh God," Roxanne blurted.

"Liquin..." Brigham started in, his tone trepidacious.

"We're better than this!" I shouted.

"Liquin!?" Kate gasped.

"Jesus God," Straightness grunted.

I stood up, and charged right for the bimbo, landing right next to her at the bar. I lunged over the top of the surface to get the bartender's attention, just as the bimbo teetered again, knocking into me. She spun around, her hair flying about like a peacock tail, looking at me with disgust.

"Sorry," she croaked with condescension, her expression teeming with revulsion. I clenched my teeth, suppressing my rage.

"Barkeep, a shot of Goldschlagger please," I commanded to the nearest server. I could feel the eyes of the crowd—especially the Hollywood d-bags—pouring over me. Yes, I was acting rude, but I had a plan!

"Some people," I heard the bimbo utter. Some people indeed! I just needed to hear one thing…

"At least [STUDIO NAME REDACTED] pays our way down here…" Yahtzee!

I downed my shot of Goldschlagger, and turned back to my friends.

"Hey Brigs, is [REDACTED] still the head of creative for [STUDIO NAME REDACTED]?" In my peripheral vision, I could see the four Hollywood idiots freeze in place. Across the room, Brigham smiled.

"Yep!" Brigham called out to me.

"Good! Thank you!" I called back. I pulled out my phone and dialed. "Hey [REDACTED], it's Liquin Sonos. Hope all is well, sorry to leave you a voicemail this late, but I'm here with some of your deputes and they're behaving like total assholes!" I turned away from the douchebags and walked back to my table, sitting back with Roxanne. "Anyway, didn't get their names, but I'm hoping that you can figure out who and take the appropriate action. Ok-thanks-bye!" I slid my phone back into my pocket and smiled at the group, taking a corn chip, dipping it in spinach dip and munching on the end in tiny, deliberate bites.

"Do you seriously know [REDACTED]?" Kate asked, smug.

"No, but I did just leave him a voicemail! The miracle of net-dialing!" I smirked. Brigham stood up, phone in hand, and snapped a picture of the four panicked Hollywood types, who looked at him in horror, then made their way out of the bar. A group of nearby geeks, still in their Con lanyards who'd been waiting for a drink since I'd arrived at the bar took over the seats of the d-bags, throwing a smile of gratitude in our direction. The Admiral raised her glass back in salute.

"Still the best at what I do," I proclaimed, sitting back.

Roxanne put her arm around me and handed me her glass of wine, from which I took a deep gulp. We sat through another round of drinks while I finished off the sliders and the quesadilla, happy to have flushed the Hollywood roaches from the room and just plain happy to be together in general. My sinuses had granted me reprieve, or at least the liquor convinced me of as much, and I felt relaxed and glad. Maybe God had taken a bit of pity on me after all.

Then it happened. Then *he* arrived.

The five of us closed out our bar tab and swapped a round of hugs with the Admiral, who had to go off to her own dwelling for the night. As we walked her from the bar into the main Bayfront lobby, I noticed the towering, gaunt figure clad all in red at the desk of the Bell Captain, barking orders about how to handle his insane amount of luggage. I didn't say anything, my stomach churning with nervous acid. I thought it might not be *him*, or at least I might escape without having to interact, but my luck failed me again. Or maybe God just *really* hated me that day...

"Minions!" He called out in his unmistakable voice, the sound an odd cross between Hitler and Daffy Duck. Our eyes all lit on him, clad in his fitted red leather trench coat, embossed cow hide tanned deep red, almost purple, with a candy gloss of bright scarlet. Beneath he wore some designer-Banana Republic-Express-Michael Korrs black jeans and a fitted pull over shirt that probably cost all of a dollar to make with child labor, and that he'd probably paid damn near a hundred for. He had a pale, if healthy appearance: good bone structure, ageless face, clear blue eyes and perfect teeth, all accented by his natural ginger hair which, like his coat, seemed varnished with some more-red-than-red gloss, no doubt the result of a special dye rinse to make his perfectly groomed hair just a little too good to be true. He smiled wide, holding out his arms in best "sincere" embrace greeting all my friends, but never taking his eyes off me. Make no mistake about that! Beneath the veneer of style and charm and success burned a cauldron of hate and anger and resentment all directed at me.

His name was Ragnar Wortham.

Brigham first exchanged hugs with Ragnar, then Kate and Straightness. Only Roxanne, not really knowing Ragnar well, stayed at my side, grabbing my arm like an mother out of some protective instinct.

"Kate, my beautiful dear, I'm so looking forward to the shoot Saturday!" Ragnar hissed with silver tongue. "I've been pulling out all my old fencing club moves! Thank you so much for the chance!"

"Here's hoping everyone's well enough to shoot!" Kate said, making polite conversation.

"Oh, beautiful, you know everything will turn out fine, even if I have to duel Windsor! Windsor, bro, how's it hanging? How's the animation?"

"I'm going upstairs," I whispered to the Admiral, kissing her forehead. "Goodnight." I started for the elevator.

"You ok?" Roxanne cooed. I nodded, and continued my bee line toward my escape.

"Liquin, old boy!" My heart sank. "Aren't you going to say hello? We go so far back..." I stopped and pivoted on my heel to face my nemesis.

"Hi Ragnar, how are you?" I seemed to speak the words as a single utterance, sans diction or space.

"I'm fantastic as usual! Things with the production company are grand—four big pictures in the pipeline, you know—and the boss still loves me. Things are looking up!" Ragnar cocked his head back, as if to shake his hair like some Bond girl, relishing her own beauty for the audience. Ragnar always recognized his own attractiveness to others, and loved an audience wherever he could find one.

"Great." I replied, flat in tone.

"How are things going for you?" Ragnar pressed. "Heard you got banned from teaching because of your asinine behavior!"

"Well," I started to rebut. "Not..."

"HEY!" Ragnar screamed, interrupting me. Just beside us, a pair of bellhops pushed a cart with Ragnar's oversized suitcases through the lobby to the elevator bay. "Be careful with those! Those bags are Chanel!" He turned back to the rest of us. "Fucking idiot filth. I guess if they were smart they wouldn't be the help!"

I felt my jaw tense, my back molars grinding together making my mandible ache. I didn't flinch, just staring back at Ragnar with utter disgust bubbling in my core like hot tar. He looked back at me, blue eyes glassy and unyielding, that fucking Mona Lisa smile of self-satisfaction never leaving his face, not blinking once. In fact, Ragnar *never* blinked, at least not that I ever noticed. Something about him just seemed omnipresent. He knew that too.

"Too bad you're not working," Ragnar went on. "And that your script isn't getting you anywhere. Just gotta keep trying, right?"

"Yeah, I'm going to bed, goodnight." I turned and followed the bellhops to the elevator.

"Not too late to start turning tricks!" Ragnar called after me. "You might still get some decent money!"

I looked back to see my friends, my beloved surrogate family, all looking away, their eyes averted from me and Ragnar both, frozen like shamed garden gnomes, looking small, useless and tacky. Only the Admiral, her dark Latina eyes shining in the dim light, displayed any sign of life or sentience. She looked at me, nervous, not understanding what to do. Ragnar's head tilted forward, lit from overhead, his toothy rictus spread across his face, high widows peaks climbing above his forehead. With his perfect, glassy skin, wide eyes and accenting shadows, he glowered like a living skull, ready to accept my fare and ferry me to the afterlife. His hypothetical offer tempted me; maybe he'd just shown me mercy. But I had to see the *Neodämmerung* through to the end, and besides, I'd never give Ragnar the pleasure.

I joined the luggage haulers in the elevator, glancing over the three designer suitcases—two roll away trunks and one hanging garment bag—each with a silver placard with Ragnar's monogram. My head throbbed again, this time with incredible sinus pressure behind my eyes. I rubbed them gently, then looked back at the two deflated bellhops, both staring at the floor like shamed kindergartners.

"Hey," I said, breaking the silence. "Suitcases do get scuffed up. It's just part of the work." Both the men chuckled, and I smiled as I exited the elevator to our floor. When I entered the room, I made no detour on the way to the bathroom where, as if choreographed, I vomited up just about everything I'd consumed all day.

As I sank to the floor, my blood sugar plummeting and head spinning, I clawed up for the handle, flushing away my protein spill and resting my face against the cool porcelain of the commode. I racked my brain, trying to process everything that had happened that day…and I just couldn't. I reached up to the bathroom counter, grabbed my toothbrush, loaded it with paste, and proceeded to scrub my mouth, hoping to eradicate the foul, sour flavor that had flooded my taste buds.

As I finished, pulling myself up to spit the foamy toothpaste from my mouth, I tried to avoid looking at myself in the mirror, but I failed at that too. I looked myself over in the glass, my eyes locking on the pair reflected back at me. They showed no light; I looked fake…old…empty.

Thank God for the *Neodämmerung.*

I reached down to Brigham's pill stash and selected a Xanex, an Ambien and a Viccodin and popped them both in my mouth. Taking them on an empty—*freshly* empty—stomach probably wasn't the best of ideas, but I didn't care if I overdosed and died in my sleep. I just wanted peace! Serenity! Some reprieve from the cruel grind of life!

By the time I lay down in bed, I'd begun to shiver again, and my thoughts started to cloud and dizzy from the medication. I felt as though I might sink all the way into the carpet, plummeting downward to the foundations of the building, and beyond. I wanted someone to poison me. I wanted someone to beat me. I had visions of my ribcage cracking open like a torn piñata, my viscera spilling out as some anonymous surgeon pulled my lungs from my chest like taffy. My body felt like a shell, some hard and sealed container in which my soul floated about, nebulous as the genie in the bottle. Part of me hoped I'd have some other vision of Adam, or that Kate or the Admiral would come upstairs and coddle me, just taking me in their arms and rocking, saying nothing, just quelling my pain through tender contact.

But that didn't happen. I lay in the dark, the blankets drawn up around me, wanting to weep, but finding my tears evaporated, wishing for torture of the body just to distract from my emotional pain. Instead, there was only blackness and silence. Just before the pills guided me into sleep, I did manage to whisper a final plea:

"God, fucking kill me."

FRIDAY

Infinite Crisis

I needed to be alone.

I mean, I'd felt fucking alone all through the night of creepy dreams of wandering an abandoned movie theatre, chased by the CIA, the mob, and my mother, who somehow had sprouted lobster claws and carried a pick axe. Don't ask me—I blame the drugs.

On the upside, other than the night sweats and terrors I'd suffered in bed the night before, I actually slept rather well. By the time I awoke, my three roommates had departed to shenanigans unknown, with only Starbuck leaving a brief text message to call her if I needed her. Well, no doubt I needed something—possibly a straight jacket—but I couldn't see Kate packing one in her luggage.

I rose from bed into the chill of the Bayfront room, jumping in the shower and scrubbing the night from my skin. I still felt like a bulldozer had slammed into my forehead, but even the headache granted me a reprieve as I soaked in the hot water. I downed my usual morning pills—Lexapro, Claratin, Abilify—and dressed myself, pulling on a vintage *Jurassic Park* t-shirt, the stripped and faded material clinging to my chest in a most flattering and comfortable way. I grabbed my Gryffindor hoodie, wadded and sagging at the foot of my bed and pulled it on. Judging by the gloom hanging over the city visible from my window, the Con would suffer another frigid day. I sighed, grabbed my backpack, and headed downstairs.

By the time I reached the lobby, my spirit had deflated even more. Looking at the in-depth Con schedule, I realized there was not a single panel—not *one*—that I much wanted to sit through. I mean, come on! *The Green Hornet* with Seth Rogan? A visionary panel with Joss Whedon, which, no doubt, would make even the ass-smoke-suction of the *Tron* panel look tame? A presentation on the low-rated, impotent *Battlestar Galactica* prequel *Caprica?*

No thank you. But then, I did take some comfort in knowing that my dick wasn't the only flaccid thing at the Con. Oh Hell, no I didn't! Comic-Con used to be exciting and fun! It used to feel like the best theme park ever, like a wild concert of incredible performances or even summer camp, where the attendees bonded, broke down their walls and comfort zones, and evolved as people! Now...this?

Rather than head to the Con, I ventured over to Fifth Avenue and crossed into the Gaslamp District proper, trying to ignore the still-congregated anti-gay protesters and the herd of shivering and wet barkers still trying to pass off their tiny business cards and fliers. I pulled up my hood and tucked my thumbs under the straps of my backpack, my eyes drifting to the muddy and damp ground, not sure what to do about anything. After wandering several blocks, I happened into a Starbucks that, while busy and full of Attendees trying to keep dry and warm, still had room to sit and sulk. I dabbed the rain droplets from my face with my sleeve as I ordered my venti double espresso, and noticed a pair of eyes peeking up from behind an enormous artist's folio. I happened to catch said artist glancing over at me, his blue eyes luminous against the dull Earth-tones of the Starbucks, or the dusty gloom of the outside. I saw a hand fly up behind the sketchpad, which almost seemed to wave, or give a half-assed wave, anyway, as if he'd hesitated at the last second. Instead, his hand landed in the mess of his jet black hair, an artist's pencil entwined between the fingers, stroking his scalp in thought.

I cracked a smile, grabbed my coffee, and made my way over to him.

"Hey Raz-Ar," I said, trying to sound upbeat. Raz-Ar looked up, letting his folio drop to his table top, his eyes lit up and oversized smile emerging from behind the pages.

"Liquin dude! Good to see you!" Raz-Ar made no uncomfortable effort to shake my hand, but did take his own oversized coffee cup from the floor, where it rested against the leg of his chair, imbibing a long sip and adjusting his own faded t-shirt: a pale pink *My Little Pony* tee, fitted for a girl's curves, but somehow flattering to Raz-Ar's lean chest nonetheless. "Raz-Ar got sick of the Con," he explained, sipping his coffee. "Too many people, you know?"

"And not enough to do!" I added in an exasperated gag. "Who fucking watches some of this shit? Why are these people here?"

"Raz-Ar doesn't know, dude," my companion commiserated. "It sucks balls." I snickered at his explicative, looking down at his open folio, then gasped. On one page, he'd drawn an elaborate and menacing Oriental dragon, its body twisted into an "s" curve, smoke flowing from its nostrils and feathers about its neck. On the opposite page, handwritten paragraphs scrawled in pencil flowed over the heavy-linen paper.

"Did you…" I paused, still trying to process the remarkable art before me. "Dude, did you write *and* draw all this?"

"Raz-Ar did, yeah," he admitted with a hint of blush to his cheek. "Raz-Ar wants to write and draw, have his own comic someday."

"That's pretty amazing," I admitted. "You're really good!" Before I could gush on with praise, I noticed the keloid scars on his arms again—dozens, running from wrist to elbow on both limbs. They looked even more pronounced under the jaundice light of the Starbucks. Raz-Ar might have noticed, as he pulled his arms close, folding them against his chest as if to mask the damage to his flesh. He itched the black, spindly hairs of the top of his arm, and though I could tell he'd rehearsed his posture to conceal the scars, I could still see them flicked and plump beneath his arm hair. He'd cut the top of his arms too.

"Sorry," I whispered, turning in embarrassment. I sipped my coffee as we sat there in awkward quiet, both of us too inept to keep the conversation moving. From the corner of my eye, I stole a peek at Raz-Ar. He'd fallen into some kind of daze, one hand scratching at his scarred arm, the other touching fingers to thumbs as he mouthed soft counting in some obsessive tic. I forced myself to sit up in my chair and change the subject.

"So what's the story about?" I could feel my voice crack in my throat like some anxious teenager. I hoped that Raz-Ar didn't notice as he shook from his trance, looking back at me with a smile.

"A dragon," Raz-Ar answered, cheery. "His name is Herb and he lives under a little boy's bed." I smiled at the odd answer, perplexed but charmed.

"Cool," I commented.

"Herb only comes out at night and flies around the neighborhood rescuing cats stuck in trees and finding runaway doggies. He and his keeper, Reggie, are best friends and stay up late playing checkers some nights if Herb doesn't need to do the pet rescue thing."

"Is Herb good at checkers?" I asked as a reflex, the oddness of the question only hitting me after I'd said the words.

"Oh yeah!" Raz-Ar answered in excitement. "He almost always beats Reggie, but Reggie doesn't mind. I mean, they have a good friendship since Reggie puts up with Herb snoring in the daytime and moving around at night. He's pretty loud."

"I would imagine."

"But Reggie has problems too. Herb doesn't care though." Raz-Ar's blue eyes beamed into my face like two spotlights. "They're buds, ya know? They're not afraid to hug or be nice or touch each other. They like to cuddle. Herb would never hurt Reggie."

A strange flutter in my gut made me gasp, but my gaze never left Raz-Ar. He smiled, so proud of his story and illustration, but I could detect an obvious pain buried in his tale. I didn't know how to react to his sincerity over so uncanny a tale, but I knew Herb and Reggie meant a great deal to him. They were *his* friends, which I shouldn't ignore.

"Isn't it so stupid that some people can't show affection?" I observed with soft and deliberate rhythm. "Like, everyone assumes Mr. Rogers was gay because he wasn't afraid to show love and tenderness to other people."

"Yes!" Raz-Ar lit up! "Like that's it exactly! Or some people want to make it all about sexy time, which isn't cool. It's not the same thing."

"Right," I chirped.

"And fucking ass-rape grown-ups try to do it to kids too," Raz-Ar hissed. "It's not cool."

"No," I said, flabbergasted. "It's not." Raz-Ar realized he had, perhaps, said too much of what he really felt—always dangerous in the modern era. He looked down again, biting a nail, head sinking into his shoulders.

"Sorry," Raz-Ar cooed.

"Don't be." He looked up at me again, still biting his nail, and smiled. "I guess it's pretty stupid that we're missing the Con," I said in raised voice, trying to lighten the mood. "Would you want to walk back with me? Maybe hit the floor a bit?"

"Oh yeah!" Raz-Ar perked up. "Raz-Ar wants to see a *Quantum Leap* retrospective panel later!"

"EJO!" I blurted without realizing. I paused a beat, frowning at myself. "*Quantum Leap* was a favorite show growing up! I'd love to see it!"

"Right on!" Raz-Ar said, nodding his head with giddy enthusiasm. "Come with Raz-Ar!" I looked him over a moment, unable to contain a broad smile from crossing my face. I looked away a moment, scanning my thoughts for some reason to decline…

"Yeah, alright, cool," I replied.

"It's not until later this afternoon. Do you want to keep Raz-Ar company until then?"

"Sure," I said without thinking. The weird vibe—ok, the weird *everything* about this guy—should have scared me off. After all, I generally didn't associate with anyone who constantly referred to himself in the third person. Still, something about Raz-Ar seemed alluring, maybe because he was more eccentric than I, which did say something, even if I didn't know what.

"So what shall we do before then?" I posed. "Walk the floor?"

"Raz-Ar isn't a fan of that crowd," my companion replied. He'd already started to close up his portfolio. "Raz-Ar wants to drop off his sketchbook too so it doesn't get ruined. Have you been to the Midway?"

"No," I shook my head. "I assume you don't mean a carnival game thing." Raz-Ar smiled.

"Naw, it's an aircraft carrier. That big ship looking thing out in the bay. It's a museum now." I knew what he meant. I'd seen the Midway at every Con; it was docked walking distance from the Convention Center and the size made it impossible to miss. I'd always written it off as some tourist trap though, and always occupied myself more with the Con rather than take in other San Diego attractions. Besides, it never seemed that geeky.

"Is it expensive?" I went on. "I'm hard up for cash these days."

"Raz-Ar has ya covered," he smiled. "Raz-Ar really wants to see it. My Grandad served on it in the war."

"Cool, I'm down then!" It took a moment for me to realize he'd actually used a first-person conjugation. I didn't quite know what to think...if the whole "Raz-Ar" persona was just an affected one, and he'd slipped in his delivery, or if the mention of his grandfather somehow warranted a different mindset. Then again, as a bipolar nutjob myself, I knew that Raz-Ar's logic might make perfect sense to him, but not to anybody else on the planet. I didn't want to dwell on that thought, however, lest I have reservations about hanging out with him, and he was just too damn unusual to pass up.

The drizzle had stopped when we emerged from Starbucks granting us a reprieve, even if the cool, damp air flowing off the Bay made the walk a bit blustery and the sidewalks damn and slick. Raz-Ar stayed a nearby DoubleTree which took us to the north side of the Gaslamp District, and a bit out of our way to the Midway—one of those walks that would feel healthy on a beautiful day, but seemed just too close to pay for a cab on a disgusting afternoon like ours. His room there looked like a refugee camp—duffle bags everywhere and four pillows spread about the floor, a stack of sleeping bags rolled in the corner, courtesy of his roommates. To my relief, we stayed just long enough for him to grab a sweatshirt and store his portfolio behind a dresser. I dropped my own backpack nearby, liberating my posture of the weight. I preferred to take it with my everywhere, but figured I wouldn't need it at the Midway. It made me nervous to leave the *Neodämmerung* USB behind, but I figured it should be safe for just a few hours.

Back outside, the streets echoed with the tiny splashes of cars and footprints in the all-but-deserted portion of the Gaslamp. Even walking back to the Midway, we saw only a few stray conventioneers, their lanyard badges betraying their destination. Raz-Ar and I kept both of ours on; a pair of Hester Prynnes, wearing our societal ostracization in pride. Well that, and we would need them to get back into that Con, and I had no intention of slogging all the way back to the DoubleTree.

"So you are from LA too?" I asked as we began our trek.

"Yep," Raz-Ar chirped, his head nodding like a feeding woodpecker.

"That's convenient," I grinned. Raz-Ar didn't respond to my flirt. I felt a bit shy and self-conscious, but with him, I had no idea if he'd even picked up on my subtext. We walked in silence a few moments, him distant and me not knowing what to say.

"I grew up in the Valley," Raz-Ar offered after a silent block. "Calabasas. It sucked balls too."

"Ah yes," I said in commiseration. "It's a bit…"

"It's Hell!" Raz-Ar cut me off. "Everybody has to be pretty and hot and rich and normal. Not like Raz-Ar." He grasped the elbow of his left arm with his right hand, hugging himself like a shamed child.

"I'm sure it was rough," I agreed. "I grew up in a small town too." I looked over at my companion, his blue eyes sullen against his angular features. He reached up and ran a hand through the spindles of his spiked hair and sighed.

"Don't ever call Raz-Ar skinny," he commanded at last, clutching his arm again. I flinched and stretched my eyelids, taken aback. Did he have something against the emaciated? After all, I was so thin myself that in the right lighting I swear I could see my kidneys.

"Do you have a problem with thin guys?" I pressed him.

"No, Raz-Ar likes skinny dudes. Raz-Ar just used to get picked on by his Mom for being skinny." He paused a moment, his vocal chords grinding amid the suction of air though sinus cavities drenched with fluid. His lips curled into a bitter scowl as he spit a wad of foamy phlegm from his mouth onto the sidewalk, already grayed with moisture. "Bitch," he added.

"Hot," I muttered, unable to conceal my own frown of disgust.

"Raz-Ar likes you, dude. You're a cute guy." He flicked his hand over a catching it against my stomach, drumming his middle and index finger against my abs. I looked over at him, smirking, enjoying the tap-tap-tap—the closest contact I'd had with a man in ages. He looked away, shy but lit up with mischievous pleasure. I reached up and grabbed his tapping pointer with my own, our two fingers curling together like Tristan and Isolde in an emerald field. He released my grip after a long moment, probably afraid we'd get gay bashed or something while on our walk. I thought the anxiety a silly one, but I didn't say anything. The fear still got to me sometimes, too.

The hulking plateau-wedge of the USS Midway, a behemoth of riveted steel, towered high above the sapphire water of San Diego Bay like some misplaced skyscraper, the needles of its antennae and spinning satellite bars poking up into the churning, ashen clouds above. Though polished and restored with a new coat of gray paint to boot, the aircraft carrier still cast an ominous aura over the quaint neighborhood around it. In a way, with the drizzle and clouds cloaking the decks in shadows and leaving puddles about the gang plank, I found the dour weather fitting. The Midway had served for more than fifty years as a US warship; no telling what skies and waters it had navigated in patrol or battle, or what men had died inside her steel belly as bullet fire cracked the air outside. Now a museum, its status as a tourist trap stoked my sense of irony: an attraction of pride and patriotism—with good reason—reduced to a playground and subliminal reminder of American warrior culture; a soldier painted in grease paint recounting his old war stories eight times a day in vaudeville.

The hanger which once housed a fleet of fighter planes now had a snack bar and video games, and as Raz-Ar and I walked across the noisy indoor tarmac, I shook my head in amazement. Dozens of tourists, even on that rainy day, crowded the deck, looking at TV monitors playing documentaries on the history of the Midway on an endless loop. A few restored, antique planes sat quiet, posing for photographs and open to children to hop in the pilot seat. A handful of retired naval veterans—still classy and proper in their pressed, white polo shirts and pants—slouched in chairs recounting their own experiences out in the waters, and pod-like flight simulators lumbered back and forth on hydraulic legs, inviting long queues of tourists willing to pay an extra twenty bucks to get a taste of air combat. Watching the old timers tell stories made me sigh; they were the real heroes, the real treasures that sanctified the ship and told of the Midway's days at sea more than any placard or documentary could ever do justice. What a pity that we couldn't keep them and their wisdom, their memories restored as we did with the ship.

"Well…" I started, not quite sure what to say or think at the odd display surrounding us. Raz-Ar said nothing, just staring up into the rafters where dangling cranes and other equipment rested under thin but visible layers of dust, also long out of use. "You ok?"

"Sure," Raz-Ar said, cracking a smile. "Let's have a look around!"

Our tickets enabled us to explore the ship at will, and Raz-Ar, to my surprise and delight, made an excellent guide, recounting anecdotes about the Midway's service, or life aboard the carrier. I followed him around, captivated, ducking every time we walked through a doorway or bulkhead. Apparently, the urban legend that people had grown taller in the twentieth century had some validity: I think I had an easy six inches in height above the top of every door. God forbid I ever got drafted to sea!

We entered the former mess hall, where a wall case with plastic letters proclaimed a special showing of *Basic Instinct*, no doubt a leftover from the ship's last tour. I snickered to myself, imagining a boatload of sailors watching a VHS copy of the film on a twenty inch screen television hooting and cheering as Sharon Stone performed her salute to *Leave It to Beaver*. The title couldn't have been more apt...

Raz-Ar took a seat at one of the mess tables and folded his hand against his lips, propping himself up with his elbows. I walked over, sitting down across from him, sensing a mighty weight on his conscience.

"Pretty cool, isn't it?" he asked me as I slid into the metal folding chair. I grinned.

"Reminds me of the *Galactica*," I mused, my geeky sensibility inescapable. "You know, like in the BSG Pilot where the ship is old and decommissioned, and they've made the hangar deck into a gift shop."

"Yeah!" Raz-Ar chimed, coming to life. "I loved that show!" He paused a moment, observing the mess hall. "This would really be like the *Galactica*, wouldn't it? You know, if society fell and the last of the American population ended up on the high seas, running for their lives?"

"I guess it would," I agreed, cocking my head to the right. I narrowed my eyes. "What's on your mind, bud?" I pressed him, my tone deliberate with soothing compassion.

"I'm thinking about Grandad," Raz-Ar confessed with a sad

smile. "I just lost him last year. He served on the ship right after it deployed in the Mediterranean."

"Did he see combat?"

"Naw, the war was over already. Grandad always said he was lucky that way."

"Did he talk about it much?" I wondered as I shifted in my seat, intrigued by Raz-Ar's sudden change in demeanor.

"No," Raz-Ar clipped. "He always wanted to come out and see her again but, um…" He paused a beat. "He never got around to it."

"Sounds like you were close," I inferred. Raz-Ar nodded like a busy woodpecker again.

"My mom and dad are fucked up," Raz-Ar offered. "I mean, they were just like, *mean* to me as a kid. Bad marriage. Crazy religious. Well, and just plain psycho." He snickered. "Grandad knew that though, so he used to take me around. He had a great clock collection. And old cameras! And he loved building model ships, which I used to help him with all the time as a kid. I got him to start building space ships too, which he loved doing even though the models were like way more expensive. He never forgave me for that." He smiled with pride a moment, then lowered his eyes, wringing his hands a bit, as the corners of his mouth twitched, choking back emotion. "I miss him a lot," he said at last, looking me in the eye. His own blue irises looked like precious glass, tear ducts leaking to polish the surface of his corneas.

"I want to ask you something, Raz-Ar," I near-whispered to him, gentle as I could. "Your arms…" Raz-Ar swallowed and nodded again, this time solemn and deferential, as if he'd expected my question all day.

"Yeah, Raz-Ar cut himself," Raz-Ar admitted. "It actually really helps."

"What do you mean?" I blurted, shocked by his answer. Raz-Ar puckered his lips and shrugged.

"When life hurts," Raz-Ar explained with another shrug, "cutting makes the hurt stop. I know it doesn't make sense, but it always worked."

"How long did this go on? Didn't your parents or your Grandad know?"

"I think from like fourteen to sixteen," he recounted. "Something like that. I didn't see Grandad as much when I was a teenager. He started getting old and stuff…couldn't go out much. My folks, they didn't fucking pay attention until one of my dumbass teachers saw me bleed one day. Then they put me in one of those homes for disturbed teens."

"God," I whispered.

"Yeah, then they paid fucking attention!" Raz-Ar laughed.

"So how long were you in the home?"

"Isn't that a great expression?" Raz-Ar snickered with an abrupt change in tone. "Go in a *home*…like I never had one to begin with, or like I couldn't have one unless it was some place for fucked up people like me? A *home* for the *disturbed*…that's another good one! Like, you texted me during sex! I'm *disturbed*! I'm going in a *home!*" He laughed at his own joke, and at his own expense, watching my face from the corner of his eye to see if my expression betrayed any retreat from my query. Maybe it worked for Raz-Ar with other guys, but I was Liquin Sonos, and I was just fucked up as him.

"Like Catwoman said," I offered, "sickos don't scare me. At least they're committed."

"Right?" Raz-Ar agreed. Neither of us said anything as I held his gaze a long moment as he squirmed in his chair, eyes darting about the room, trying to escape. I knew he didn't want to talk about his own mental health battles, but I refused to back down. He bit the nail of his index finger, watching for my reaction.

"So?" I pressed him, leaning forward.

"A year," Raz-Ar told me, matter-of-fact.

"My God Raz-Ar." I realized my own arrogance, not knowing what to say to his confession.

"It sucked pretty bad," he uttered through pinched incisors. "Like I say," he mumbled under his breath. "I mean, I'm ok now," he added quickly. "I see a therapist every week. I'm on meds. I haven't cut myself in years."

"Do you still want to?"

"Um…" He smiled and chortled, uncomfortable. "Kinda. I still feel like…transparent, ya know? Like I'm smoke…there, but not there…people see me but they can't touch me."

I bit my tongue, impressed by his candor but at a loss for words. Out instinct, I dropped my palm to the table, creeping it closer to him, my fingers like spider legs across the Formica. I stopped at his elbow, extending just my pointer finger and resting on his forearm at the crux of his elbow. I moved it back and forth, stroking him with the balled flesh of my fingertip. He wiggled at the sensation, but didn't recoil. He blinked rapidly for just a second, then reached out and took my palm in his own, running his thumb over the raised tendons of the back of my hand.

I think a full minute passed of us hold hands, both quiet, not sure what to say. I didn't feel excited or relieved. I just needed to feel connected.

"I'm bipolar," I spat without warning. Raz-Ar chuckled.

"You *are* bipolar? You are your disorder?" Raz-Ar prodded me.

"No," I rebutted. "I mean, no…"

"Funny how we do that, right? We say 'I'm bipolar' or 'I'm autistic' like we *are* our…issue."

"So, you're…" I gripped his hand tight.

"Yeah, low-level autistic, with comorbid anxiety disorder and dissociative tendencies," Raz-Ar rattled off to me. "Or some shit like that." He paused. "Or I should say, I *have* autism and anxiety. One's enough to give anyone the other." He smiled.

"You know you stopped referring to yourself in the third person, right?" I couldn't let the issue pass.

"Yeah, Raz-Ar does that…*I* do that sometimes. I mean, I say it right." He squeezed my palm. "When I'm comfortable with someone."

"I'll take that as a compliment." I grinned, letting out a sigh. He smiled back at me, eyes still shaking with nervousness.

"Let's check out the rest of the ship?" he said in half question, half suggestion. I cocked my head toward the door, rising from my seat as he did the same. Before our hands parted, I felt a subtle pulse of his muscles, as if savoring the contact before he had to let go. I'm sure in that moment I raised my head in self-satisfaction, just a bit.

"So not to be redundant," I started as we walked through a bulkhead.

"Why not? Tim Burton is all the time!" Raz-Ar joked.

"Hey, I like Burton!" I whined.

"So do I," Raz-Ar admitted. "I love when he's good, but even when he's bad, he can hold my interest because he's *Burton*, ya know? He's interesting even when he's redundant."

"Fair point," I ceded with a smile. "So, do you get insomnia too?"

"Sometimes," Raz-Ar declared. "It's rough."

"Yeah," I sighed. "I've been getting it a lot with my meds. It's like this crackle in my brain...like I'm hooked to a power outlet or something. My body is tired and so is my mind, but my brain is on overdrive."

"Like someone is switching channels right?" Raz-Ar watched for my reaction. "You know, when you go really fast changing the station on the radio or TV and just get noise that you can kind of make out...a word here, a sound there...just a jumble?"

"Kinda, ya," I realized. "I mostly just hear people saying nasty things to me." I rolled my eyes. "Or, I mean, I'm saying mean things to myself." We re-entered the hangar, and walked down to the far end, toward the outdoor runways that extended over the flat deck of the aircraft carrier. The sky had granted reprieve from the nasty summer rain, but the dark clouds still held a threat over the city.

"Do you ever feel like a baby?" Raz-Ar rambled, a pinch in his voice. I stopped in my tracks, eyes locked on him in a perplexed glare.

"Like, in a spank me, diaper me, shove a thermometer in my ass kind of way?" I questioned him, trying to mask my revulsion. Raz-Ar laughed.

"No, not like that..." he backpedaled. "Like, do you just feel like a fussy baby at night, hoping someone with pick you up and rock you? You know, when you have the crackle or say mean things to yourself?" I stepped up next to him, resuming our walk.

"I just want to be held, yeah," I offered, solemn. "Just scooped up and cuddled. I get that."

"Snuggled," Raz-Ar corrected me. "Everybody calls it cuddling. I call it snuggling." A laugh burst from my chest like a baby Xenomorph.

"Snuggled," I countered. "Sure."

We looked out over the agitated waters of the Bay, the gray light of day dulling the beautiful view of the city. Cool air blew in from over the sea, and I hugged myself tight in my hoodie, trying to insulate myself. I glanced at Raz-Ar, who stood with one hand across his waist, the other raised so he could nibble at his left index finger. His eyes looked dilated and distant, as the tone of his skin blended with the outdoor atmosphere, the luster of his skin vanished. A few seconds later, he stopped biting, locking his free arm over his stomach, hugging himself. He panted, his shoulders rising and dropping with rapid, tiny movements. He turned to me, eyes wide.

"Raz-Ar wants..." he blurted, his stop as abrupt as his words. His jaw tensed, as if pulling an anvil out his own throat, wincing at the effort it took to speak. "*I* really want to touch you right now." I didn't respond to him at first, unsure of the veiled question his statement posed. Not knowing what else to do, I held out my hand.

"You can," I replied.

"No," Raz-Ar said, bowing his head. "Like..." His body shook like he wanted to move, but kept hesitating. I took a step toward him, palms up, arms at my side, my posture open.

That's when he grabbed me.

Raz-Ar grabbed my head in his hands, yanking me close to him and planting awkward, electric, uncomfortable, wonderful kiss of my life square on the mouth. I hesitated just as a reflex, then steadied myself, grabbing him at the waist to maintain my balance. In a nanosecond, I closed my eyes and relaxed, savoring the feeling of his tender lips matted by the prickle of his stubble. He smelled of some cologne I'd not detected before, nor could I place, but the aroma suggested youthful rebellion, the joy of good health and boundless energy, defiance of convention and lust for the beauty of life to my senses. I reached up and took both his hands in mine, giving a gentle tug and moving them lower to my ribcage, where he rested them in a firm grip. I wrapped my arms around him, returning the kiss, delighted at his touch and not giving a fuck who saw us. As I had learned at Con years before, we only get a moment once.

When we parted, I took a step back from him, my lips a bit raw from his stubble, but energized none the less.

"Cool," I said, my voice rising in pitch. "And here I thought you were just going to say you had to pee."

"I gotta pee," Raz-Ar sputtered.

"Ok!" I exclaimed with a broad sweep of my arm. "Go pee then!"

"Ok!" But rather than head for the *head*, Raz-Ar grabbed me and we kissed again. We both started to giggle as our tongues intertwined and our lips caressed each other, but we held on anyway, too delighted to stop. Then I felt the vibration against my thigh.

"Sorry, phone!" I croaked.

Raz-Ar released me with a toothy smile, and walked across the tarmac toward the men's room. As I pulled my phone from my pocket, I noticed an elderly man—not a vet, just some tourist in a hat with a giant bass fish on it—staring at him, mouth agape. Raz-Ar noticed him too, and extended his reptilian tongue toward the man in a gesture of flippant, oral defiance.

I slid my phone from my pocket and unlocked the touch screen to find a text message from Starbuck:

WHERE R U? LUNCH W/M&R?

I tapped the side of my phone, staring at the message as I contemplated what to do. I wanted to stay with Raz-Ar, but

I needed quality time with my girls. I didn't get to see them enough at home, and besides, I didn't want them to think I had my head in an oven somewhere.

I messaged them back:

STAND BY GALACTICA ACTUAL.

When Raz-Ar returned from the bathroom, an eager grin on his face, hands dripping wet as if he didn't want to take the time to dry them, I smiled and poked him in the stomach in a playful flirt. He giggled like the Pillsbury Dough Boy, squirming at my advance.

"Hungry?" I asked. "Wanna meet some friends of mine?"

Raz-Ar's expression morphed from ready to anxious as his posture seemed to fold in on itself. I grabbed his hand out of instinct, trying to quell the nervousness bubbling in his stomach.

"Hey," I soothed, "we don't have to, but they're good people. You'll like them." I could see sweat staring to bead on his upper lip and forehead as bit one of his nails again. He looked down, then away from me a moment, then smiled and nodded.

"Sure man. Raz-Ar is down for whatever."

"Alright," I smiled.

"But Raz-Ar still wants to see the *Quantum Leap* panel!"

"Oh, totally!" I chuckled as I texted Kate back. "So let's go get our stuff."

"Wait!" Raz-Ar blurted out. He reached into his own pocket and produced a disposable camera, the kind that used actual film.

"My God, I've not see one of these in years..." I mumbled as Raz-Ar flagged another tourist to take our picture. I wrapped my arm around him and smiled wide as the click-flash spotted my vision and snapped the photo. I rubbed my eyes as Raz-Ar thanked the photographer and put the camera away.

"Is your phone camera not working?" I questioned.

"Raz-Ar doesn't like cell phones," he told me. "Raz-Ar thinks they're expensive and stupid and likes film better than digital. It's more classy, ya know?"

"Sure," I answered, not really knowing what else to say. The truth was I advocated digital filmmaking big time—far cheaper and easier to use than actual film, and not to mention better for the environment. More distressing, I wondered how the man could live without a cell phone. I mean, my phone had already become an extra appendage by which I kept in touch with the world. God forbid I lose touch with the collective—I'd be like a Borg wandering around licking power outlets, which is enough to kill a person.

I wondered if that was a bad thing.

We collected our backpacks from Raz-Ar's room and made our way back through the Gaslamp district to a semi-posh Surf & Turf restaurant to meet my lady friends. Raz-Ar spent most of the walk behind me, picking at my backpack, scrutinizing the glittering pin collection I kept attached to it. That he didn't coddle me or show the kind of open affection he had on the Midway made me uneasy. I mean, maybe Roxanne had a point. Maybe he was impulsive and unstable, and would only hurt me. That's the thing about chemical imbalance—we see each other through the lens of the mind, and sometimes one can't tell the distorted image from the natural one. For that matter, maybe to correct a sick mind, it needed warping into normalcy.

We found Kate & Roxanne sitting in a booth lounging, a half-drunk martini in front of the Admiral. The whole steakhouse had a chic feel, to which the girls seemed adept: floor to ceiling in black and white, every booth and seat trimmed with stainless steel, ultramodern light fixtures hanging over every table. It reminded me of New York in the 1980's, or at least how I imagined it all decked out, *Bonfire of the Vanities* style—pretty, yuppie scum cavorting with more overpaid, oversexed, coked-out trash.

I introduced Raz-Ar to Kate, and I reminded him and Roxanne that they'd met before. As Kate shook hands with him, I noticed a subtle slide of her hand against her waist, wiping it. His palms must have sweated like Niagara.

"I call them Starbuck and the Admiral," I explained to Raz-Ar.

"Roxanne is the Admiral because she is a woman in command."
I didn't think Roxanne would appreciate me introducing her as
the high mistress of dating multiple guys.

"Damn straight," Roxanne added. "Now where's our fucking
waiter? I need another martini!" I grimaced as she downed a
mouthful from the glass in front of her. Kate and I looked at each
other, both of us rolling our eyes.

"What about Starbuck?" Raz-Ar asked. "Why does she get
that name?"

Kate and I looked at each other, both of us waiting for the
other to recount some brilliant answer. We both cracked smiles
and fidgeted in our seats.

"Well," I started, not quite sure how to answer.

"It's the name he gave me a couple years ago at my first
Comic-Con," Kate rattled. "I sort of came out of the closet as a
geek girl. I was a big fan of *Battlestar*, so it seemed natural."

"Yeah, but why'd you pick it?" Raz-Ar pressed, squeezing my
hand. I opened my mouth, hoping some lucid and convincing
explanation might just fall out.

"Why did you pick Raz-Ar?" Kate inquired in an urgent tone.
Her eyes darted from me to Raz-Ar, and I recognized the look as
one of unspoken aid—she knew I needed help, and just gave it
to me without hesitation or question. That's how well she knew
me. That's why I loved her so!

"Raz-Ar is real," Raz-Ar said, wringing his hands, nervousness
flooding over him in an instant. "Full name is Raz-Ar Banning."

"Yeah, but certainly that's not your birth name," Roxanne
retorted, skepticism boiling in her words.

"Don't feel like the ladies are picking on you," I coddled Raz-
Ar. I lay my hand on the black scruff of his neck and gave him
a mini-massage with my fingers. "Raz-Ar is a really cool, unique
name. They're just wondering where it came from." Raz-Ar
looked down in thought, still twisting his fingers together. He
pursed his lips together, shrugged, and lay both arms across the
table, hands folded in front of him.

"It was a nickname," Raz-Ar explained. "Long time ago, in

high school…" He paused swallowing, his eyebrows lifting in some odd realization. "Raz-Ar had some problems, and the other kids used to make fun of him for cutting himself. They called him razor."

I glanced across the table, capturing both Starbuck and the Admiral's reactions of wide-eyed horror and shock. I ran my hand from Raz-Ar's neck down to his back, giving him a nurturing rub, encouraging him to go on with his story.

"Besides, Raz-Ar likes his name better than John, which is what it was," Raz-Ar continued. "When Raz-Ar got better, he decided it was time to start new, so he had his name legally changed. Judge gave him shit, but Raz-Ar doesn't care. I'm not ashamed."

The odd slip made me smile, as did his forthright candor. Raz-Ar had life beat him down to the point where he would have preferred death, had his family toss him into the hell of some psych ward, and clawed his way back out. No wonder he had a few scars, and now he wore them, along with his adjusted name, like trophies: badges of honor for surviving the battles with life and still having the stamina and the desire to stand up and keep going.

"That's really cool," I intoned in a near-whisper. Raz-Ar smiled at me, his blue eyes clear and bright like polished sapphire, and in that moment, he looked perfect, like an Adonis brushed by Michelangelo, if Michelangelo drew comics instead of painting chapel ceilings. That said Raz-Ar would look totally amazing on a cloud in the *Creation of Adam*.

The girls went on to tell us about their adventures in wandering the floor; Roxanne had crossed paths with the Sales Hunk again, who teased the Dooku lightsaber, but without lowering the price. I still toyed with the idea of going back and buying it and letting my estate deal with the lack of funds, but that just didn't seem fair to the people who'd have to clean up the mess after the *Neodämmerung*. Kate finished more prep for the shoot, meeting with Puck and discussing camera setups and lighting for the big duel scene the following night. By the time we recounted our exploration of the Midway, the Admiral had tapped her third martini, and Kate had given me her glassy-eyed "I know you too well" look.

"Another martini for you?" asked our waiter, a stocky if athletic man, probably in his immediate post-college years. His hair had started to recede, though he styled it to cover up the creeping baldness. Stubble covered his face and the extra weight inflated his jowls, but a handsome smile and comfortable air about himself made up for the premature aging.

Roxanne met his question by dropping her head back against the booth, her lips stretching into a grin. She moved like an overcooked noodle—the angles of her body replaced with squiggly lines as she flirted with her answer.

"You're good, Admiral," Kate declared, her annoyance buried in her tone.

"Oh, I don't knooooooow..." Roxanne slurred, stretching out the vowels like a stoned owl. "Maybe one last one, you know? There aren't any panels I want to see today. Though I thought about going and trying on one of those *Star Trek* bathrobes."

"They're selling *Star Trek* bathrobes at the Con now?" the waiter asked in disbelief. "Woa, that's awesome! Are they like the new *Trek* or the old *Trek*, like *Next Gen*?"

"*Next Gen* is considered old now?" Kate groaned. "Dear lord!"

"Twenty some-odd years now," I observed. "I suppose it is."

"And with the reboot last year," Raz-Ar began.

"That doesn't count!" I shrieked! "That noisy, ugly, *illogical* (pardon the phrase) steaming pile of Tribble crap doesn't count!"

"I liked the new one," our waiter offered.

"Say that again and you're not getting a tip!" I bellowed.

"Liquin!" Kate reprimanded.

"No!" I fired back. "That was not *Star Trek*! It was cheap, cliché, DUMB dreck! It's like they just took *Star Wars*, which I do love, and dressed it up in *Star Trek* drag! I mean think about it!" I stretched my arms out across our table between our half eaten plates. "Planet destroying superweapon. Old geezer warrior. Irrational, murderous villain. Cocky farm boy. Weird comic relief alien engineer. Spunky, sexy token woman. It's all the tropes! Not to mention how fucking reductive the whole thing is! Instead of being a deserving, hardworking member of the crew and expert in her field, Uhura fucks her way onto the *Enterprise*. Sulu forgets to take off the 'parking brake,' which I think is supposed to be a joke about Asian drivers, and just what the hell is a parking brake on a spaceship anyway!"

"Liquin," Kate interrupted.

"And the plot holes!" I continued undaunted. Kate rolled her eyes and folded her arms across her waist, slouching. "You mean to tell me snarling Eric Bana comes back in time, destroys a ship, then vanishes for twenty-some-odd years without having to stop for food, fuel or to go to the bathroom, re-emerges and then destroys the entire Starfleet? What the fuck!"

"I'll be back with your check," the waiter promised, backing away in fear. I hardly noticed.

"It's fucking Abrams, that's the problem! J.J. Abrams—which isn't even a real fucking name, it's a moniker adopted by some Hollywood douche to sound cool and hip, not that he has any ideas what those two things would entail."

"What else has he done?" Raz-Ar asked though a grimace. "*Lost* right? *Alias*..."

"Don't get me started on the giant cock tease that is *Lost*," I fumed. "It's appropriate that part of the plot involves idiots arguing about if they should push a button that's function is unknown. It's a big fat middle finger to the audience! There are no answers! And *Alias*? Meh. His other movies? *Cloverfield* was laughable. *Regarding Henry* made me gag with its manipulative idiocy. And *Armageddon* is widely considered to be the most scientifically inaccurate film to come out of Hollywood. It's just dumb. DUMB! And the worst part is, he obviously thinks the audience is just as dumb!"

"His movies and shows do well," Kate pointed out. "Maybe they are. Or maybe people like dumb in their entertainment."

"Yeah, well, your cells like breathing carbon monoxide, but I wouldn't recommend that!" I spat back. "And his Superman script...dear God!" Across the table, Kate grunted. Roxanne just watched me from her half-inebriated stupor, squinting to see me. Raz-Ar grinned, his molars quite visible between his parted lips. "I read the fucking thing! No understanding of the character or the genre! It was loaded with violence against women—the torture and rape of Lara, Ma Kent and Lois! And it was full of gay jokes! And poop jokes!" I raised my hands and balled my fists for dramatic effect. "Poop. Fucking. Jokes! And for some reason Superman did all kinds of kung-fu! It was wretched!"

"Sounds miserable to sit through," Kate hissed. "Kind of like your rants!" I scowled across the table at her, as she burst into laughter, the glow in her eyes and from her skin exuding love and joy for me, and for my fevered pontificating. Raz-Ar did his woodpecker nod again, agreeing with me, or at the very least, relishing my passion.

"He should be tried for crimes against humanity. Send him to the Hague!" I barked, slouching into the booth, a mighty frown contorting my face. I looked at the Admiral, whose confused expression hadn't changed during my entire speech. She sat back in her chair and studied my face through the slits of her eyes.

"So you don't like him?" Roxanne deduced. I smacked my palm to my forehead in frustration. Kate laughed aloud, reaching over and grabbing the Admiral by the arm to steady herself. Raz-Ar squeezed my thighs, and I met his gaze through the space between my fingers, my hands still covering my face.

"Can Raz-Ar kiss you?" he begged, his voice high and pinched. I looked straight into those incredible blue eyes.

"Nothing would make me happier." We kissed long and hard right there in the booth, both of us starting to giggle again. As we did, the waiter returned with our bill.

"Thanks," Kate said through her nasal passages. "Can you two quit with the Pon-Faar long enough to settle up?"

"Sorry," I chimed as I pulled away.

"What's Pon-Faar?" Raz-Ar wondered aloud.

"Vulcan mating ritual," Kate explained. "Something I'll be doing later."

"EW!" I screeched.

"What?" Kate shrugged. "You know about these things!"

"Yeah, but I don't want you and Straightness banging while we're asleep in the room together!" I exclaimed.

"Oh come on, we've all done it," Roxanne grunted.

"We won't do it in the room with everyone asleep!" Kate assured me. "We'll do it in the shower!"

"AHH!" I hollered in revulsion. "What if I have to pee!?"

"Hold it," Kate ordered.

"Hold it," Roxanne agreed.

"Then watch me get a bladder infection! We all have to bathe in there you know!" I frowned as I threw some cash on the table for my lunch. Raz-Ar moved to do the same, and I pushed his money back toward him across the Formica. "I got it."

"Well, it's a shower," Kate defended. "It will be clean because *that's why it's there!*" Starbuck's grin exuded mischief. "Besides, it's not like you've not done the same thing at this very convention..."

I opened my mouth to speak, pointing my right index finger across the table, paused, then shut my mouth again. I plopped my hand down into my lap, looked at Raz-Ar, then looked back to Kate.

"Point taken," I admitted. "Shag on!"

"*Quantum Leap?*" Raz-Ar pressed me.

"Yeah," I answered, giving him a peck on the cheek. "Ladies, interest in a retrospective?" Roxanne and Starbuck looked at each other, shrugged, then gathered their belongings.

"We'll follow you," Kate declared, scooting to the edge of the booth. A doughy Roxanne, however, blocked her exit, sliding about like an amoeba getting out of the booth. It took Kate and I both to prop the Admiral to her feet, and when we had at last, she seemed to gain some extra lucidity.

"Scott Bakula. Chest hair. Warp speed!" Roxanne chanted, pointing with outstretched arm to the door. We followed her meandering pace to the exit. As we stepped onto the street, still damp and grey from the sagging clouds, Kate wrapped an arm around her, signaling me to take the lead. Raz-Ar gripped my hand, and we set off.

I allowed myself a moment of satisfaction as we made our way through the Gaslamp District before the wet chill of the air of the Bay and the reminder of the *Neodämmerung* broke me from my happy pondering. I wondered how Raz-Ar would react when he found out what I'd done. I knew my other friends would feel angry and hurt, but would soon understand why I had to do things the way I would. But Raz-Ar...he'd been there before. I didn't want him to suffer some relapse or think he gave me the idea to boost my career in such an unorthodox way. I just had to hope he would understand too, or at least have the good sense to dump me and sally forth on his own before the final hour came.

"Don't you just hate men," Roxanne sputtered out of nowhere after we'd traversed a few blocks. "I mean, Sister Starbuck, you know what I mean!" I glanced back and traded a fleeting look with Kate as we walked on.

"Windsor is a lot to handle, but I love him," Kate assured the Admiral.

"Yeah, but doesn't he get *annoying*—" Roxanne stretched out the final word in drunken emphasis.

"He does," Kate murmured. "Sure. He snores. He smells bad in the morning. He's a colossal bore sometimes. And he's smoking again, which makes him stink all the time! But that's kind of *all* guys."

"Not all guys smoke," Roxanne pointed out.

"No," Kate admitted. "And he knows I want him to stop."

"But you put up with him not listening to you?" Roxanne cocked her head and moaned. "And all his other bull plop!?" Kate kept the pace with us, quiet a moment. I gazed back again to see her staring off into space, her attention usurped by some unseen mammoth thought.

"I don't know why I do," Kate said at last. "Except I love him."

"This is why I'm single," Roxanne clucked. "Sister, live your life!"

We crossed out of the Gaslamp District at the base of Fifth Avenue where, even in the shitty weather, the crowd clogged the streets and blocked the trolley tracks as it moved like some hive-minded swarm as it poured across the perpendicular Harbor Blvd. to the base of the Convention Center. In the Garden Walk, sheltered by umbrellas and sheets of plastic strung between their protest signs, the anti-gay mob still chanted and screamed through their bullhorns that all of us at Comic-Con were hellbound. I so looked forward to proving them wrong in the immediate future.

Raz-Ar squeezed my hand as we walked by, and I heard Roxanne shout obscenities. The crowd around us smelled of mildew—polluted water soaking into the body heat of ten thousand convention goers, wetting their t-shirts enough to make them adhere to their skin, revealing every unseemly lump & curve, and activating the dormant bacteria on their flesh, the humidity giving off an odor of vermin.

Well, at least it wasn't the overripe parmesan stench of the gink; the geek stink. Though a usual hallmark of Con, it did not in any way add to the hospitality, and I didn't miss the nose-wringing. Still, in an odd way, the lack of gink made the Con feel stranger and more alien, and not in a fun, *X-Files* kind of way. More like my safe haven for years had become something else, something I didn't know or recognize anymore. I'd always lived my life as an outsider, but now I felt shunned from my safe haven. All the more reason for the *Neodämmerung*.

Inside the Convention Center, as we rode the long escalators to the upper level, home of the panel discussion rooms, the great blue and yellow Comic-Con banners strung up around us, I felt a blast of icy air hit me. Damn everything, that fucking arctic, meat locker air condition still pumped cool air into the Center despite the frigid atmosphere outside. I folded my arms, hugging myself, trying to keep warm as I leaned against the escalator banister-belt to steady myself.

"You ok?" Raz-Ar asked me half way up our ascent. I forced a smile and lowered my eyes away from him.

"Yeah fine," I mumbled back to him. Something hit me where I couldn't look at him, nor could I acknowledge Kate and Roxanne behind us on an adjacent step. I looked out the great glass cylinder that comprised the roof of the Convention Center, out to the drab skyline of San Diego replete with its hotel skyscrapers and condos and felt the life draining inside of me. My knees started to give way, and I lurched out and grabbed on to the side of the escalator with both hands. Black spots filled my vision, and all the noise of the Con seemed to melt and muffle, like sound at the bottom of a full swimming pool.

"You sure?" Raz-Ar pressed me, putting a hand on my back. I nodded again as we skipped off the escalator, still without looking at him or the ladies behind us, and set off in the direction of the panel room.

I wanted to scream and cry right there, to make some huge cataclysmic scene in the middle of the Con hall attracting gawkers and powerless Hall Nazis to my side. I wanted to lay in a sprawl on the floor, and to wail, howl, kick and scream like a spoiled child just to prove I still had life inside of me and release all the misery welling in my gut. But of course I couldn't—see, misery isn't like other emotions that burst or erupt forth like geysers, so powerful that we can hardly control or repress them. Misery feels more like a vacuum, sucking inward; a black hole devouring from within, and threatening to consume everyone and everything around me. Had I released it, I knew I'd inflict just as much pain and douse all with around me with despair enough so that none would ever get out of bed again.

I had seen the abyss and could not look away, for the abyss was within me, and I was a colossal narcissist. Not that said fact precluded me from anything; on the contrary, my years working…or trying to work, anyway…in Hollywood had instructed me that outrageous vanity was prerequisite for making it as an artist. All the more reason to proceed with the *Neodämmerung.*

As we entered the tiny meeting room for the *Quantum Leap* retrospective, I glanced back at Kate. I think she caught the morose darkness of my pupils, because as we sat down, she made a point to sit next to me.

"What is it?" she whispered. I sighed.

"Ask me again sometime," I muttered back. The fact was, I knew by the end of the weekend Kate would be angrier with me than she probably would ever be with anyone, but I still trusted her to help me see my plan all the way to fruition. I trusted her, and she'd know the stakes of the *Neodämmerung*. No matter how much she would hate me for what I'd done, I knew my Starbuck well enough to know she would not fail me.

The panel started just a few minutes after we'd found our seats, and the atmosphere reminded me of the golden days of Comic-Cons past. The room hadn't even filled to capacity as the moderator took to the stage, the lights dimmed, and Scott Bakula, the still sexy at 55 star of the show, mingled with a few fans on the edge of the room.

"Dear God," Roxanne purred. "Look at that chest hair!"

Indeed, Bakula, known for his hairy chest, still teased his follicles creeping out from the collar of his t-shirt. The man aged like fine wine; though a few gray hairs now peppered his mahogany waves and curled from out his collar did betray his age, he still looked the same as he had twenty years before as a prime time television hunk. He had no celebrity airs about him, no massive ego or self-righteous entitlement; rather, he just felt like a neighbor or friend of my dad's growing up—warm, friendly, secure and handsome.

The rest of the panel didn't disappoint either. Bakula treated us to some of his favorite clips from the show, in particular the episode where he played three different roles. I'd seen it before, of course, but looking at it again, I had to wonder how the man never won an Emmy. He spoke at length, too, about my favorite episodes where Sam Beckett, Bakula's time-travelling character, encountered another "evil leaper," and how the idea grew out of semi-religious philosophies about balance and the need or opposites, positives and negatives. He also talked about the unceremonious cancellation of the series about which, even after almost twenty years, the star harbored sore feelings. Not that I blamed him—the abrupt end of the show which concluded with a few title cards implying Sam Backett died on a mission felt like biggest cheat I'd ever seen on television.

"Do you think that's true?" Raz-Ar asked. "That for everything good there has to be something bad?"

"People have been asking that question since the dawn of time," Kate observed. "I don't know that we're any closer to answering it now."

"Like matter and anti-matter," I added. "Supposedly there is a whole crapload of anti-mater out in the universe, but scientists can't find any." Kate snickered. I looked over at her.

"Nerd," she chided.

"What, we're at Con!" I contended.

"Raz-Ar doesn't believe that," Raz-Ar said. "The universe is one big mess. Raz-Ar wishes we could fix stuff, travel in time... but we can't."

"Not yet," Kate observed. "Maybe someday someone will invent a *TARDIS*."

"What if it's not even like that?" Raz-Ar speculated. "What if time isn't linear, what if everything just happens at once, and we can't do anything to alter our fates?"

"The end is the beginning is the end," I iterated. Raz-Ar smiled, as Kate laid a hand on my back. A strange choking noise caught our attention, and the three of us shifted our eyes to the Admiral, who sat, her head cocked back against the top of her chair, mouth slack and emitting a modest snore. I shook my head and turned back to Raz-Ar.

"You're right," Raz-Ar declared, a hint of elusive worry in his voice. "And what if that means we can't save ourselves?"

A great chill ran through my blood at that moment, at the sound of his words. I grasped myself, folding my arms across my chest and pinching the sleeves of my hoodie for extra warmth. The nihilism of his question frightened the deepest corners of my soul. What if he was right? What if nothing mattered, and the *Neodämmerung* would fail?

The lights came up in the room, as Scott Bakula waved a final time to the crowd, then exited the stage. Neither I, nor Raz-Ar, nor Kate said a thing, all of us meditating and distracted by the horrific notion that we had no control over our lives.

"I need a nap," Roxanne moaned, rising from her seat. She tipped her head to Kate's shoulder and rested it there with a yawn.

"Doesn't sound bad," I muttered. I looked over at Raz-Ar. "Shall we?" I glanced over at Kate to read her reaction too.

"Naw, time for Raz-Ar to go," he said. I turned back to face him, but Raz-Ar sat with his head bowed.

"Well, ok…" I stammered. "Are you ok?"

"Fine," Raz-Ar answered, standing up. I rose to match him. "Raz-Ar just needs to go." He pushed past me and the girls, out to the main aisle to make for the exit.

"Am I going to see you again?" I pressed him, trying not to sound too desperate. Raz-Ar turned back to me, his blue eyes glimmering, and a timid smile on his face.

"Yeah, you will."

And then he vanished into the crowd. I stood there, shocked, frozen, and speechless. Kate lay an arm on the small of my back, just under my backpack. I didn't even look at her.

"I hope you got his number," Kate chirped.

"Nope," I smacked my lips. "He doesn't have a cell phone."

"Maybe it's for the best," Roxanne yawned. "Can we go now?" I sighed, nodded, and made for the door without looking at either of my friends. Back out in the upstairs halls, attendees flooded in every direction, hassled by Hall Nazis to keep moving and only walk in certain directions down certain hallways. I scanned around looking for Raz-Ar, but he'd already vanished. God knew if I'd ever see him again.

I pressed through the crowd to the great glass enclosures of the stairways, stepping onto an escalator and descending to the ground floor. The sight and sound just melted into noise for me, the death knell of my once hallowed Con. Sitting through the *Quantum Leap* panel with friends—including a sweet-hearted guy—at my side, just relaxing and enjoying the atmosphere of fandom and *love*…it just made me hate the latter-day Con more. Comic-Con had become less a convention than a staging ground, a bountiful crop of joy devoured by a horde of Hollywood locusts and parasites. Outside the Convention Center the chanting anti-gay protesters, undeterred by the sloppy weather, continued their cruel and ugly assault like the plagues their thumping Bibles derided. Dear *God*, was it ever enough?

Wasn't it enough that Hollywood had their own trade shows and media to peacock around and blow smoke up their own asses? Did they have to then blow smoke in the eyes of their audience? Must they treat us with such condescending disdain? And as for the inexplicable protesters…wasn't it enough they'd stolen away our right to marry with that heinous Proposition 8?

Couldn't life just be *good?* Did it always have to be mean?

I stormed back into our room at the Bayfront, trailed by Starbuck and the Admiral. Kate walked with her arm around Roxanne, I assumed, to keep her from wandering off or doing anything else crazy. I tossed my backpack in a corner and flopped down on top of my bed, burying my face in the pillows a moment, holding my breath. I imagined what it might feel like to suffocate right there, what a mercy death could offer me from this torment. Comic-Con had once been the closest thing to heaven I could imagine encountering in this life. Now I just wanted life to end.

I reached up under my shirt and felt the USB drive with my fingers. Maybe I would have to precipitate the *Neodämmerung* sooner than I'd planned.

I looked over as Kate helped Roxanne settle onto the other bed, mothering her by getting her comfortable and folding the comforter in half over her body like a half-sandwich. She pushed Roxanne's long caramel tresses back over her ear, and I saw the Admiral relax, her body going limp as she slid into sleep. Kate then walked over and sat down on the other side of the bed, closer to me. She looked down at me, folded her arms, and frowned.

"Darling, if I die, can you be a dear and make sure people read my work?" I moaned to Kate. I could hear her sigh in disgust.

"And what makes you think you're going to die?" Kate murmured in sarcastic annoyance.

"Everything does," I said, burying my face in the pillows again.

"What is with you this Con?" Kate croaked. She took a pillow from her bed and tossed it across to my head.

"Yes, please, smother me." I turned over and faced her, pulling my body about as if my limbs had become dead weight. I frowned. "Ragnar Wortham?"

"Oh Lord," Kate whispered before I'd even said the entirety of his awful name. "Yes, Ragnar."

"You know he's like, Satan right?" I pushed. "I mean, like Brett Ratner-J.J. Abrams level reprehensible." I held a beat. "Well, almost."

"Like I told you earlier, it solves a lot of problems..."

"Like?"

"Like getting this short film seen, and getting me and Puck and a lot of other talented people work! You can't begrudge me that."

"Even if he treats one of your friends with open loathing and contempt," I croaked, sitting up and matching her arm-crossed posture.

"I don't know what happened between the two of you..."

"No, you don't."

"But I'm staying out of it," Kate declared.

Just then the hotel room door swung open and the rotund, glowing countenance of Brigham strode into the room carrying two large plastic shopping bags.

"This weather!" Brigham declared, putting the bags down next to my backpack. "And this crowd!" He bent down rummaging through one of the bags and pulled out a large water filtration pitcher, still in its original packaging. Brigham stopped and looked at us through the coke-bottle lenses of his eyeglasses. "What am I interrupting?" he asked with caution.

"Ragnar!" I spat, my eyes firing daggers at my illustrious friend. Brigham gave a duck-faced frown and plopped down on the bed next to Kate, the water filter in one hand, the other clasping at his collarbone at his imaginary pearls.

"Liquin," Brigham started. "I have no special love for Ragnar Wortham."

"Evil!" I cried. Roxanne shifted in the bed with a muffled whine. She distracted me from my anger for only a moment.

"Necessary evil," Brigham corrected me. "You know how this business works. *Orrrrrr*," he stressed the consonant out in dramatic fashion. "Or maybe you don't. Maybe that's why you are where you are."

"What's that supposed to mean?" Kate asked, revulsion in her voice.

"Same thing I told you Kate, dear," Brigham continued. "It's a game. One big tabletop RPG with shifting alliances, chance rolls of the dice, changing lines of power, and little plastic figurines to signify pawns that provide function according to the player strategies. But the game always has the same players." Brigham sighed, his face turning grave. "If you want to join, you need their approval."

"Is this why everyone in Hollywood is two-faced?" Kate asked with a giggle.

"No dear," Brigham mumbled. "Everyone in Hollywood has multiple faces, with only some attached through surgery. They call it 'versatility.' But really, it's just how we all need to survive."

"Maybe I just need surgery then." I stood up and went to the window, looking out over the Bay. Gray haze floated in off the marine layer, churning clouds overhead to match the angry waves below. "You know, if I hurled myself out this window right now, and splattered on the ground like a crushed egg, everyone in the world would want to read *Leopard Messiah*. The studios would have a bidding war to see who got the movie rights."

"And you'd be dead," Kate observed.

"Why's that bad?" I shot back. "My work gets made, my friends get famous, my family gets the money, and I'd have accomplished something in my life. Not to mention, I wouldn't have to put up with Ragnar or his stupidity or any of this other torture we call life."

"Did you stop taking your meds?" Kate cooed. I spun around on my heel and glared at her.

"No, Starbuck," I explained. "This is me in a good mood, as good as it gets these days." I walked back to the bed and sat down across from Kate & Brigham, rubbing my eyes in nervous frustration. "And remind me, I need to give you something later."

"You've gotta let it go, Liquin," Brigham said, rising to his feet and shaking his head. He walked over to the desk and started to unwrap the water purifier next to the First Aid Kit.

"Soon enough," I muttered under my breath. I watched as Brigham took the pitcher from the packaging, assembled the water filtration system, and took the cap off the shampoo bottle of vodka. "What are you doing?"

"Making better liquor," Brigham grunted, pouring the whole contents of the shampoo bottle into the purification unit. The vodka dripped down through the filter in starry droplets, settling into the container below. "I'm getting old, Liquin. I can't stand to drink this lighter fluid-bottom shelf swill."

"Funny, I thought you liked the bottom shelf," I chided in monotone. Brigham glared at me over the top of his frames, his blue eyes piercing. Kate snickered.

"See, that's what you need!" Kate insisted. "The snark! Your spirit!"

"Oh God, Kate," I blurted. "Can you just give me one good reason why I shouldn't hurl myself out the window?! One good, easy, legit, fucking reason why I need to live?!"

"You're braver than that," Kate declared, her voice like a bell. "Brigham?" She raised an outstretched hand, beckoning to Brigham for a drink.

"Give it a minute to distill," Brigham said, adjusting his glasses. "And Liquin, you still have to meet with Monty Doyle. Don't kill yourself off until after your meeting! That'd be counterproductive." Brigham looked at me with a Loki smirk, and something in his eyes put me on edge. I knew my Illustrious friend well enough to know when he had something sneaky in mind.

"Brigs," I prodded, drawing out the vowel sound. "What did you do?"

"What, me do something wicked? The very idea!" Brigham teased. "What time is it?"

"Almost five," Kate observed.

"Oh good," Brigham chirped back. "Monty will be here soon."

"What?" I grunted, my voice dropping two octaves, stretching out my arms as if to part the Red Sea.

"Yeah, I invited him up before he and I go to dinner." Brigham bounced in place, pleased with himself. From the corner of his eye, I could see him scan for my reaction, and when he saw what must have been total shock and flabbergast on my face, he bent over and taped the water filtration unit, forcing the droplets to fall through the purifier a bit faster. "Another reason why we need good vodka."

I looked at Kate, whose own shocked reaction must have matched my own. I opened my mouth to say something, but couldn't find a witty comeback. I shook my head at a loss, and Kate just shrugged, not knowing what to do either.

"Fuck," I whispered, overwhelmed. "Fuck!" I looked at Brigham, who replied with a big Cheshire grin and bounce of satisfaction. I could hear my heart pounding behind my ears, my cheeks flushing, my lungs stretching my ribcage for more air as the adrenaline flowed into my veins. "Fuck!" I shrieked again.

"ROXANNE!" I screamed, diving across the room, past a mortified Kate, landing on the bed next to the Admiral. She shifted under the comforter, emitting a low murmur as my hand connected with the round sinew of her Latina ass. "GET UP!"

I pushed at Roxanne's backside with all my weight, throwing

her from the mattress into the narrow crack between the wall and the bed. She came to full consciousness somewhere midway between thin air and the crash of her body into the carpet, yelping and thrashing her head around, whipping her ebony tresses like a cat-o-nine tails.

"Jesus!" Roxanne shrieked as she thudded against the wall, limbs flailing.

"Monty Doyle is on his way up!" I barked. "Get it together!" Roxanne sat up from the floor, her hair mopped and messed like Cousin Itt in a hurricane. I started re-making the bedding, smoothing out the wrinkles in the comforter as the Admiral parted the hair obstructing her eyes. I tore off my shirt and went to the dresser, searching around for the perfect ensemble. Monty Doyle was my last best chance to get anyone to look at my script before the *Neodämmerung*.

Kate snickered as she accepted a vodka-Red Bull from Brigham. Both watched as I riffled through my drawer, whimpering to myself in anxiety. Roxanne ducked into the bathroom where I heard her grunt and whine at the sight of her appearance.

"I hate all my clothes," I snarled.

"Drink?" Brigham offered.

"In a second!" I seethed back.

"Kate I'm borrowing your make up and brush!" Roxanne declared from the bathroom.

"Fine!" Kate called to her.

"Will your skin tones even match?" Brigham asked, reaching for his pearls.

"I'm good!" Roxanne called out with relish.

"Ok, ok, ok…" I panted. "Dress shirt or pop culture?"

"Did you bring a dress shirt?" Brigham questioned.

"No!" I realized. "Fuck! Ok…um…" I pulled out two shirts and held them up to my collarbone. "Vintage Disney or Corey Haim?"

"Corey," Brigham decided without hesitating.

"Corey makes a statement," Kate observed. Roxanne peeked

her head out of the bathroom, her complexion transformed from puffy and sleepy to silky by way of some under-eye powder. In one hand she held a tube of lip gloss, and in the other, a brush which rested in the waves of her hair about halfway down her back.

"Aww, Corey!" Roxanne frowned, before disappearing back into the bathroom.

I pulled the Corey Haim shirt, a sort of vintage-hipster memorial, down over my body. I'd found it at a boutique in Los Feliz that specialized in celebrity wear—shirts saying "Free Winona" or "Never Forget" with a picture of Winona Ryder or Michael Jackson underneath. I never knew how they got away with it all without getting sued, but since they generally used mugshots, maybe they had public domain. In the case of my Corey Haim shirt, it combined images from his heartthrob days with a memoriam for his untimely death. I never had been particularly attracted to Corey Haim as an actor or as a grade school crush, but his premature death and rocky career stuck a chord with me, as he took his place in the pantheon of tragic Hollywood tabloid stories of victims of the business' excesses, or their own.

I grabbed my robe from the closet and slipped it on over my shirt, leaning into the bathroom to check myself in the mirror. Roxanne looked over, curling her sparkling lips into a smile.

"Good, relaxed, powerful, semi-mysterious?" I questioned the Admiral.

"It's a bathrobe, Liquin," Roxanne grumbled.

"Well?" I pressed, ignoring her bemusement. Roxanne paused brushing her hair and smiled. She leaned over and gave me a light kiss on the cheek, careful not to mess her painted lips or leave smudge on my cheek.

"Adorable," Roxanne said, resuming her brushing.

"Good, thank you," I replied, making a bee line back into the bedroom to Brigham and Kate. "Still the best at what I do. Drink!" I ordered. Brigham handed me a vodka-Red Bull, which he had ready and waiting. "Good, thank you," I repeated.

"It'll calm you down, girl!" Brigham trumpeted. Kate snickered, taking a seat on her bed, mindful not to leave any wrinkles.

"Damn straight," I declared after a long swig from my glass. I swallowed another mouthful, just in time to hear a rattling outside the door. My posture stiffened, as I rushed to the door and swung it wide open, thrusting my body into a grandiose pose in the doorframe.

"You ok, chief?" Straightness asked, as I met with the sight of his disheveled, Con-worn form standing in the hallway. In his right hand he dragged an oversized, yellow bag which contained, from the look of things, anyway, some massive box that stood almost three feet high when tipped on end.

"Dear God! Get in here!" I hissed, yanking him by the shirt into the room. He yanked the bag and its contents behind him, which thunked about as it grazed the door.

"Dude, what the fuck?" Straightness protested. "That's a rare G.I. Joe aircraft carrier in there! Be careful!"

"How much did you spend?" Kate said rising to meet him. I stormed past her in a nervous frenzy walking back to the window and slurping my cocktail. Roxanne emerged from the bathroom, beautified and restored, and accepted a cocktail from Brigham.

"Good to see you too, Booboo," Straightness wheezed. They exchanged a perfunctory kiss as Windsor took note of the cocktail distribution. "Ooh, can I get one Brigham?" Brigham obliged, mixing a cocktail for Straightness. "Check it out!" Straightness proclaimed, holding out his phone.

We all crowded together to peer down at the screen, beholding a grinning Straightness standing alongside a svelte Batman, dressed in the 1960s TV show costume. Kate, Brigham and I all exchanged confused looks.

"It's Batman," Kate observed.

"It's St. Sigs of the Weave!" Windsor chided. "It's her! I totally got a picture with her in the Exhibit Hall."

"Good fucking God, Windsor," I groused. "You did not get a

picture of Sigourney Weaver in a Batman costume!"

"I did so!" Straightness contended. "Brigs! Boo-boo! Back me up here!"

"Insufficient data," Brigham equivocated, handing a cocktail to Straightness.

"No idea," Kate said, flopping back down on the bed. Straightness cocked his head sideways, observing my angst.

"What's with you, chief?"

"Monty Doyle is stopping by and I have to look professional!" I groused, tidying the room a bit, my drink in hand.

"So you're wearing a bathrobe and a Corey Haim shirt?" Straightness observed, his left eye flinching in a nervous tic.

"Oh God," I said, my nerves a flutter.

"Sit down, Licks," Brigham ordered me.

"Licks?" I repeated, perplexed.

"Well you get to call me Brigs, Illustrious and the rest of us God knows what fucking else!" Brigham retorted. "I'll call you Licks if I want!"

I plopped down on the edge of my bed. Roxanne and Kate both moved over beside me, flanking me on either side. Straightness and Brigham sat across from us on the opposite bed.

"Found my G.I. Joe aircraft carrier!" Straightness reminded us with pride. "Had to haggle the guy down hardcore, but it was worth it! And I've got my eye on a couple bootleg DVDs!"

"Windsor," Kate muttered to herself, putting a hand to her mouth, concealing a smile.

"Which DVDs?" Brigham inquired, sipping from his glass.

"Special *Magical World of Disney* triple feature!" Straightness declared. "You guys remember that, right? The Sunday night Disney movie? We all nodded. "Ok, so the guy has *Mr. Boogedy* and *Bride of Boogedy* as one package..."

"Oh my God, I remember that!" Roxanne squealed.

"Ah, yes," Brigham chimed, "another one of those 80s TV movies...well, two actually...where New England in late fall looks more like southern California in the spring..."

"As was the style of the time," I offered.

"The other," Windsor continued, "is this obscure backdoor pilot about a bunch of kids in space..."

"*EarthSTARVoyager?!*" Kate gasped, her eyes widening.

"That's right BooBoo," Straightness chucked with delight. "Can't wait to see how it holds up!"

"Give you one guess," Brigham scoffed. "It didn't even make it to series!" Brigham paused, swigging the last of his drink, then marching back to the First Aid kit for a refill. "William McNamara, on the other hand, the hunk who played the lead..."

"You actually remember that?" Straightness piped.

"Oh sure," Brigham said, pouring a generous glass of vodka from the filtration pitcher. "He's right up there with young Chris O'Donnell, young George Takei, Jamie Bamber and Hayden Christiansen as my genre hunks!"

"Hayden Christiansen?" Straightness bellowed. "Are you kidding?"

"He was hot in *Revenge of the Sith*," Roxanne said.

"He was not!" Straightness protested.

"I dunno," Kate uttered, cocking her head to the side in consideration.

"He kinda was," I added. "He gained like thirty pounds for that part..."

"Oh he did not!" Straightness whined.

"They say he did," I maintained. "He worked out like crazy."

"Mmmm...with his cock," Brigham purred with a naughty smile, eyes distant as he no doubt fixated on the image of naked Anakin Skywalker.

"No way," Straightness spat in his timpani basso. "What did he eat?"

"Cock," Brigham muttered.

"I think like fish and chicken six times a day," I said.

"Hayden Christiansen is built like me!" Straightness charged. "Where did he gain the muscle?"

"In his cock," Brigham relished.

"Will you stop with that!" Straightness exploded.

The girls and I looked at Brigham, who rolled his eyes, pursed his lips and shrugged before returning to his train of thought, a sensuous Tim Curry-smile crossing his face. He sighed, twitching his ass and letting out a grunt.

"Jesus God!" Windsor sighed, collapsing backwards onto the bed. The girls both burst into laughter, as I dove forward and grabbed Windsor by the shirt.

"Don't mess up the bed!" I howled. Kate and Roxanne laughed even harder, grabbing each other's hands in hysterics.

"Dear God, chief!" Windsor shrieked. "It's my bed!"

"Yeah, but Monty Doyle is on his way up, and I want everything to look…" I paused, catch a whiff of the rancid, smoky odor emanating from Windsor's body. My eyes widened in horror.

"What?" Straightness asked.

"You have *gink!*" I screamed. "You have geek stink!"

"I do not!" Windsor claimed.

"Yes you do!" I growled back. Kate climbed over next to us, sniffing about her boyfriend.

"Oh Windsor," Kate winced. "You stink bad like Comic-Con and cigarettes!"

"You and my smoking," Straightness dismissed. "I do not have geek stink!"

"Whatever it is," I began, marching into the bathroom. I found Kate's make up bag and started rummaging for a certain spray bottle. "I will not let you smell that way in front of Monty Doyle!" I plodded back into the bedroom, bottle of Febreze in hand, and pointed it square at Windsor. Kate had just enough time to dive out of the way before I let out a fog of deodorizer spray onto Straightness. The drizzle formed droplets on his glasses as he coughed and wheezed in protest.

"Douche!" Straightness ejaculated. He squirmed and stood up, backing away from me. I followed him, pumping the spray nozzle with each step.

"Hold still!" I commanded, spraying.

"Douche!" Straightness repeated.

"Go back on the patch!" I yelled, spritzing him again, chasing him into the bathroom.

"You're a douche!" Straightness whined, wiping the fluid from his glasses onto his shirt.

That's when we heard the knock at the door.

"Fuuuuck!" I mumbled in low voice. I tossed the Febreze down on the counter and ran back out into the room, sitting down next to the Admiral and tried to look casual. Windsor followed me, scowling and adjusting his moist clothes. Kate rose to answer the door.

"Cock!" Brigham muttered again. Kate paused as we all looked over at him. Brigham snapped from his daydream and strutted past Kate, throwing open the door.

"EJO! Monty!" Brigham screamed. He embraced our guest in the hallway, then lead him into the room. I crossed my legs and tried to look casual, avoiding the shooting looks of Starbuck, the Admiral, and Straightness as they all tried to contain their laughter and excitement. I raised my glass up a bit and smirked.

Monty Doyle stood all of five feet tall with graying, curly hair, a sagging gut hung from his modest frame and the fashion sense of a nebbish. Had I not known who he was and seen him on the street, I would have thought him a Peter Falk doppelganger. Fortunate for me, I *did* know better and realized this nondescript man was one of the longest-working, shrewdest, most-respected agents in the business. That Brigham could introduce me to him might prove one of the most important moments of my life.

"Monty, I want you to meet everyone!" Brigham giggled. "This is Roxanne, she's in music. That's Kate, she's in film school. This is Windsor, he's an animator." Monty exchanged quick hellos and handshakes with the rest of the group. "And this..."

"I'm Liquin Sonos," I said, rising to my feet, hand extended. I gripped Monty's hand and met a firm, confident handshake and a smile of bleach-white teeth.

"You've heard about him!" Brigham oozed in a faux whisper.

"Ah, Liquin!" Monty greeted me in his rough, nasal voice. "So happy to finally meet you! I'm so excited to discuss your work!"

I could feel the eyes of my compatriots fix on me with veiled excitement. I continued my forced smirk, trying to keep cool.

"Thank you Monty," I said, trying to conceal the nervous pinch of my vocal chords. "I look forward to it."

"I just wanted you to see the new Bayfront rooms," Brigham went on, presenting the room to our guest. "It's totes fab!"

"I'm diggin' it Brigham!" Monty chuckled. "Fine digs. Though wherever you are there's always a party!"

"Ain't that the truth," Straightness muttered. I swallowed down the rest of my cocktail in a single gulp, my eye never leaving Monty. My gaze locked on the vodka pitcher, waiting next to the First Aid kit.

"Monty, would you like a drink?" I offered, moving to the pitcher. Monty grinned and scanned the room again, surveying his company more that the decorum. For a split second, I sensed his hesitation.

"Love one, Liquin!" Monty answered with a flash of his phosphorescent teeth.

"Vodka ok?" I asked.

"Top shelf!" Roxanne injected with a tip of her glass. Across the room, Kate snickered.

"Vodka's great!" Monty acknowledged. "So what do you guys think of the Con?" The room let out a collective moan of annoyance.

"The crowd!" Roxanne spat.

"The weather!" Kate whined.

"I'm with BooBoo," Straightness added. Monty gave him a blank look. "Oh sorry," Straightness realized. "I mean Kate. She's my *lady*." Monty chuckled.

"And I agree on all counts!" I declared, raising my index finger for emphasis. "Brigs, glass?"

"Oh!" Brigham grunted. He started to slide open the drawers, rummaging about through our stores of towels and other maid-cart contraband until he found a clean goblet.

"Thank you," I nodded to Brigham as he passed me the glass. I filled it with vodka and a splash of Red Bull, mostly for color.

"That's some serious linen you got going on in there, Brigham!" Monty observed. "Planning a bath house?" Brigham shrieked with offense, clutching for his imaginary pearls.

"Oh Monty!" Brigham gasped. "You know what it's like down here these days, people always coming and going!"

"Like a bath house," Straightness snickered.

"Windsor!" Brigham snapped. "I'm a respectable man and a respectable agent! I'm prepared for all possible contingencies like any good agent should!"

"Or any executive geek," I amended, passing the drink to Monty. "Tell me if it's too strong."

"Like any respectable agent, it's never too strong!" Monty teased, taking a sip. He coughed at the taste, eyeing the liquid. "What'd ya mix with this, some kinda Red Bull or something?"

"Yeah, just a bit for flavor," I explained, almost apologizing.

"That's fine, that's fine," Monty grizzled, motioning to me to relax. "My heart can't take all that caffeine. Better just a splash for the color!"

"Terrific," I said, pouring myself a generous cocktail and sliding down on the bed next to Roxanne.

"This is quite a set up you got here," Monty complimented us. "I love this box of travel mini bar thing. Reminds me of my late grandfather."

"Why your grandfather?" Kate inquired.

"Oh, he never went anywhere without a flask. I still have his glassware. He used to label everything with an etching tool. So now I have all these old frosty glass bottles with his handwriting. For the ages!"

"That's lovely," Kate smiled, genuine as usual.

"What's with the robe? You some kinda Eskimo or something? It's July!" Monty groused at me.

"I like to sing 'Blue Velvet'," I quipped, pulling one side of the terry over the front of my body. "Besides it's fucking cold."

"What's *Blue Velvet*?" I heard Roxanne whisper to Kate across the room. So much for acting discreet...

"It's a movie," Kate replied. "We'll have girls night and watch it. Drink a box of wine!" They clanked glasses.

"No shit, ain't it awful cold though!" Monty exclaimed. "Fuckin' worst July ever! I hear it's something to do with that volcano in New Zealand, but who the fuck knows. Red sunsets or something." Morty took a long drink of his cocktail and swallowed it down, clenching his teeth. "It's a good fuckin' drink, Liquin."

"Still the best at what I do," I spouted, looking down with bashful humility.

"We'll see," Monty said, downing the last of the vodka. "Hell of a drink. Liquin, Brigham and I are headed to dinner in Little Italy. Why don't you come along?"

"Well…I…that…" I stammered. I wanted to play the whole *woe-is-me*, I'm a starving writer card since I knew I couldn't afford the kind of dinner Monty had in mind. Before I could protest, however, Monty read my mind.

"I'll expense it. But don't wear the robe!" Monty tossed his glass aside on the dresser.

"Um…"I started.

"Yes, Liquin," Kate said, striding over to me. "Leave the robe!" Kate's blue eyes shined with excitement as she tugged the robe from off my back, gently nudging me to join Monty and Brigham.

"Why not!" I decided, my voice higher pitched. I raised my glass and drank, as Brigham and Monty did the same. Both Brigham and I watch Monty down the entirety of his beverage in one long swallow. My eyes met Brigham's, both of us impressed at the seasoned agent's imbibing skills, if indeed drinking large quantities of alcohol qualifies as a skill.

The vodka hit me halfway down the elevator shaft. I watched the digital floor numbers above the doors go blurry as I teetered backward, steadying myself against the wall covered in the *True Blood* poster. Brigham looked at me and smacked his lips, detecting my inebriation. I just smirked.

"Comic-Con!" I grunted as the doors swung open.

"I think it's fabulous," Brigham declared as he exited the elevator. Monty chuckled, as he and I followed behind. The lobby of the Bayfront hummed with activity, as guests, random convention attendees and Hollywood schmoozers milled about, coffee or cocktail in hand. I smiled to myself, staring up at the banners of silver beads dangling from the ceiling. They accented the white marble of the floors so well, and considering the modest accommodations I usually boarded in during the Con, I had the satisfaction of feeling like I'd somehow moved up in the world.

"Ya know, we could walk," Monty said as we exited out to the curb. "But this fucking weather-rain-shit is too much. Let's cab it, shall we?"

Brigham and I didn't protest, as the night wind blew off the Bay, shivering both of us to our respective cores. Besides, in the company of success, one must act successful, especially if he desperately needs the help of the successful. We loaded into a minivan cab and pulled out into the traffic surrounding the Con.

"Might have been fucking faster to walk," Monty muttered as we sat in the glut of cars that filled Harbor Blvd. The street ran parallel to the trolley tracks and the Convention Center, and thus flooded with pedestrian traffic in addition to the cars. Moreover, the constant run of the trolley stalled the crowd from exiting the Con into the Gaslamp District. Thus, we'd sunk into one giant clusterfuck.

"So, Monty, you ever been to Con before?" I slurred, trying to manage the buzz of the alcohol with my conversation skills.

"Oh sure," Monty croaked. "Every now and again. Clients, ya know. Like Brigham here."

"Dear lord," Brigham exasperated for dramatic effect. "Today was un-fucking-believable! The crowd! I had clients on two panels and it sucked up my whole day from ten in the morning until three in the afternoon! Didn't get a chance to eat lunch."

"Your poor guy! We gotta get you some good Eye-talian!" Monty leaned forward to the driver, asking about alternate routes. I snickered to Brigham at his pronunciation of "Italian," but didn't correct him. I knew better.

Forty five minutes later, only about ten of them in motion,

the cab dropped us in Little Italy, one of San Diego's most charming neighborhoods. With tea lights strung back and forth over the streets and painted awnings and sidewalk cafés, I fell smitten, even with the bad weather. Monty led us into a smaller eatery—it must have only sat about fifty people with every table full. An elaborate mural covered the walls, a sort of pictogram telling the story of San Diego from the days of the Spanish Missions to the present. As a hostess escorted Monty and Brigham to our table, I stopped off and studied the brush strokes close up. I could see the faint outline of penciling beneath the paint. I smiled…someone had painted it by hand.

I rejoined Brigham and Monty at our table, watching the two agents peck away at their smartphones without looking up to acknowledge me. As I sat down, my glance ping-ponged between both their faces, stern with concentration.

"Everything ok?" I asked.

"Email," Brigham muttered. Monty didn't say anything. He only groaned. After a moment, Brigham snapped back to the present, sliding his phone away into his pocket. He looked up at me and smirked.

"Sorry," he said, glancing over at Monty. Monty ignored us another minute or two, then put his phone down on the table next to his silverware.

"We got another one comin'!" Monty declared. "Colleague. Smart guy. You'll like him. He's into all that comic shit stuff too." He looked around for the waitress. "Darlin', can we get some drinks here?"

Three straight-up martinis half imbibed later, the three of us cackled at maximum volume. Brigham had turned as red as a singing crab, and Monty had lit up with flushed patches of rosacea about his face. No doubt he'd done this before, many, many times over the years with clients. As for me, I kept catching myself slouching forward on the table, braced with my left elbow, pointing my index finger and whipping my wrist about as if flogging the conversation. I'm sure I looked oh-so professional, but in that moment, I didn't give a flying frak.

"Melanie Griffith, Tippi Hedren, and a pride of untrained lions..." Monty pontificated. "You gotta see if some fuckin' bootlegger down here has it. It's some kinda scary fuckin' movie."

"Wait, what was I called?" I slurred.

"*Roar,*" Monty growled. Across the table, Brigham let out an orgasmic yelp, covering his mouth with his hand in embarrassment. I raised an eyebrow.

"*Roar,*" I repeated.

"*Roar,*" Monty said again. Brigham chirped again, this time in an even higher pitch. I couldn't help but snicker.

"Did you, um, hurt yourself there, Brigham?" I teased. His blue eyes burned with annoyance from behind his Kissinger glasses, his hand still planted across his mouth.

"I'm fine," Brigham uttered in a near-squeak. "Sounds like a fascinating film."

"Yeah, all the fuckin' lion attacks were real," Monty recounted. "Thought it would help some kind of wild lion fuckin' preserve thing or something. Instead, everyone got mauled."

"Oh my," Brigham said, eyes wide.

"*Roar?*" I asked again.

"*Roar!*" Monty confirmed. Brigham squealed again, just as Monty's phone lit up with a message. "Hang on a damn minute...second...damn it..." He began pecking at the screen, closing one eye as he looked down at it. Apparently, his depth perception had blurred.

"Did you just get hard?" I whispered to Brigham. At last he moved his hand away from his mouth and promptly slapped me on the arm.

"I like Monty's voice," Brigham admitted, turning his nose up at me.

"So that's a yes?" I pressed him. Brigham's eyes widened with fury.

"Our guest is here!" Monty announced. Brigham and I looked up, scanning the restaurant. We both froze when we saw who approached.

"Ragnar, man!" Monty welcomed, as Ragnar Wortham approached the table. As a reflex, I began to rise from my seat, a serrated knife in hand. Brigham grabbed my hand, calming me down.

"Monty! Brigham!" Ragnar greeted. His eyes shot across the table to me. "Gonna give me a hug Liquin, old friend?"

"Aw, how 'bout that, you boys know each other!" Monty exclaimed.

"Something like that," I mumbled.

"Oh yeah, Liquin and I go way back!" Ragnar went on, taking a seat at our table. "I brought Liquin to his first Con."

"You did?!" Monty stammered. "Well how about that!"

"A client of mine paid for a room at the Westgate," Ragnar recounted. "That place is like a palace. Liquin and I were much closer back then." He smiled wide, displaying all his perfect teeth, eyes wide like some grinning piranha, his ruby hair burning in the dim light of the eatery. "But things change. People burn out, if they're lucky. Otherwise they just fade away." His dilated pupils never moved from their fixation on my face.

"Real interesting theory," I shot back, taking his bait. I knew Ragnar tried to engage me with his little dramatic monologue. I didn't give a flying frak that it was bait, and that he probably employed it only to humiliate me. He'd done that enough simply by getting me to sit idle.

"Care to qualify that assessment, Liquin?" Ragnar said without a hint of anger in his voice.

"I don't think our companions really want to see us engage in this kind of debate here," I countered. "I think they just want to eat."

"Now that's a good fuckin' idea," Monty roused. "Where's that girl-waitress-girl anyway?"

"Still writing, Liquin?" Ragnar further goaded. "Is that how you got Brigham here to introduce you to Monty?"

"We're just having a Con dinner," Brigham contended. "Like we all used to do, back in the old days."

"Oh stop it Brigham! You're better than that pithy excuse for diffusion, you know that!" Ragnar grinned as an oblivious Monty waved for the waitress, and then ordered another round of martinis to go with our extra large pepperoni, mushroom, olive, onion and sausage pizza.

"That good with everyone here?" Monty inquired as the waitress walked away to give our order to the kitchen.

"Just fine," Ragnar said, his gaze never leaving me. I could almost taste the rage dripping from every one of his pores.

"Still bitter," I spat at Ragnar through a crooked smile.

"Bitter, me?!" Ragar erupted, his voice pinched with tension, volume intensifying. "Why should I be bitter, Liquin? I have a great life! I'm doing what I want, meeting beautiful, talented people, making great money and generally enjoying the life of an executive at a up-and-coming production company with four great pictures in production or pushing toward release. I hang out with ridiculously talented, beautiful people all the time and have sex to the point of absolute boredom."

"Yeah, with what stray animal?" I quipped. Ragnar smirked and drummed his fingers against the tabletop. Brigham didn't move in his chair, staring off into space, probably too scared to look at either of us. Monty seemed only half interested, waiting for the waitress to return with his drink.

"Here's a pitch for you, Monty," Ragar articulated with smooth, cool elocution. "Two young film school grads come to Hollywood and arrive on the same day. In fact, they live in the same apartment building. They meet and have everything in common. They hang out together, go to the movies, of course, go for happy hour, to parties, everything. People are sure they're a couple, but that's not true. Neither dates much, they just prefer to be together dreaming about making it big in Hollywood, and how they'll help all their talented friends achieve their dreams too."

"Where's the drama?" Monty asked as the waitress returned. He took a long drink from his full martini glass, then rested his chin on his fist. I looked down at my own refill as the waitress set it in front of me. I didn't bother to even sip it.

"Oh, wait for it!" Ragnar chided. "One day the two best friends get an offer from a major Hollywood player...someone with immense power in the business. He wants to film the two of them having sex with each other, and with himself, and with his friend that he already got a job at a big movie studio through his influence."

"*Showgirls* meets *Indecent Proposal*," Monty laughed.

"It's better than that," Ragnar continued. "One of the guys is flat broke. Can't pay his rent. The other gets a job as a substitute teacher, making barely anything. Naturally, since the starving guy will have to resort to selling drugs or prostitution anyway, he wants to do it. But the teacher guy...he has some high-minded moral objection and refuses. So what happens? The poor guy does have to turn tricks, and he does have to degrade himself to get by. The executive doesn't want to fuck him alone."

"I'm not sure where this is going," Monty interrupted.

"Oh it's a fun revenge story," Ragnar mused. "Eventually the poor boy does become successful, and the substitute, morally self-righteous one doesn't. Think of it like an erotic version of *The Player*."

"Altman, huh?" Monty grunted. "Well, his movies never made a dime, and the whole premise is a bit outlandish..."

"Too much?" Ragnar asked. "The kind of thing that would have to be a true story, otherwise nobody would ever believe it?"

By that time, I'd gone from having butterflies in my stomach to pterodactyls pecking away at my innards. I thought I might projectile vomit—actually, I kind of wished that I could. I would have aimed straight for that son-of-a-bitch Ragnar in full Linda Blair fashion. But I couldn't. I looked down at my hands, which I realized I'd balled into fists. My palms were covered with tiny crescent-shaped lashes, courtesy of my fingernails digging into the soft flesh. I curled my toes in my shoes, and felt the tendons in my neck and shoulders spasm with tension. My breathing had swallowed to a mere pant, penetrating just my upper thorax. And my eyes burned with bitter tears, trying to force their way down my cheeks, burning the skin in their paths.

"I need to go," I said quietly, rising from my seat.

"Oh, now?" Monty slurred. "We got dinner comin'! You don't want to stay for dinner?"

"Liquin," Brigham uttered, low and as deadly serious as I'd ever heard him say anything.

"I need to go," I repeated to Brigham.

"I really think you should stay," Brigham encouraged me.

"I need to go," I said again. "Thank you for everything." With that, I turned and sped out of the restaurant. As I fled, I heard Ragnar call after me.

"Feel better, Liquin! Don't just eat shame for dinner!" Ragnar yelled.

In that moment, I wished I'd had a gun, not to shoot Ragnar, but to shoot myself. What better way to solve *all my problems at once* than to walk back into the fine Little Italy hotspot, whip out a revolver, smile wide and yell out to the stunned dining patrons "Virgin eyes, cover them up! This might be graphic!" And then I'd blow my brains out right there.

It'd be so easy.

Ragnar would feel guilty and be scarred for life. The sensationalism of it all would catapult Brigham and Monty into the spotlight, they'd get better clients, sell their life rights, and get a Oscar-bait movie based on their lives. And even though I'd be dead, every news network, every newspaper, everyone in Hollywood would want to know about suicidal lunatic who died at Comic-Con. They'd fight to get their hands on my script... the one artifact I'd left behind, the one possible answer to the heinous question of *why*. Kate, Windsor and Roxanne would all get hired on to consult or work on the film version of *Leopard Messiah*, and at long last, I'd have done something with my life! Something to earn my place in history and benefit the people I care about!

If only I'd had a gun. The thought wouldn't leave me as I wandered my way from Little Italy back into the Gaslamp District in the damp, frigid night air. My teeth chattered and I folded my arms across myself, hanging my head in shame. As I reached the intersection of First Avenue and Broadway, the tears finally arrived. I thought they'd make me feel better, but of course they didn't. *Nothing* ever made me feel better.

The hot, salty tears ran down my face, stinging the skin in their path. I hugged myself tighter, feeling my insides trembling, unable to find any comfort in anything. I only cried harder, feeling so worthless, so alone that even in the Heaven of Comic-Con, I felt empty. I passed an alley behind a grocery store on my left, and detoured inside. The street still packed with Con attendees, and I didn't want any of them to see me blubbering, or recognize me later. If there's one thing people hate more than their own pain in Hollywood, it's acknowledging someone else's.

The alley smelled of rank and sour trash, and the ground felt slick from motor oil and used diner grease dumped over the pavement. It seemed so appropriate that everything around me wreaked of death and decay. I figured my hollow insides probably smelled the same. I rested myself against a brick wall, the masonry covered in dirt and slime. Nearby, from a stack of rotting boxes and a dumpster, I sensed movement. Dismissing it as a rat or some other pest, I chose to ignore it.

"Gimmie your fucking wallet, Marv."

The sudden words, along with a silver flash amid the shadows jarred me from my brooding. A vagabond, clothes soaked in filth and sweat, his face smeared with black grime and his hair wild and frizzy edged toward me, an open pocket knife in hand. Swollen, festering sores covered his bare arms, and his cracked face and decaying teeth betrayed a crystal methamphetamine habit.

"Your wallet! Gimmie your wallet, Marv!"

I just looked at him. I didn't move, I didn't respond. I just stared.

"I'll fucking kill you Marv!"

"Go right ahead," I demanded. I took a step toward him, my hands raised up by my head. "Please, go right ahead."

"Your wallet!"

"Kill me and take it," I demanded. "I don't fucking care." I took another step toward him.

"You're fucked up, Marv." The tramp took off running down the alley in the opposite direction. I watched him vanish into the darkness, my arms still raised, still waiting for him to stab open my chest and release my soul from the burden of mortal coil. But the meth-head didn't come back. I just stood there, alone and disappointed again. How I craved death!

I collapsed down to the ground, balling myself up, resting my face in my hands. I shook my head, thinking, trying to find some alternative, but I knew...I knew I had to die at this Comic-Con. I would proceed with the *Neodämmerung;* I would give Kate the flash drive, still dangling about my neck. That would insure she had the master file to *Leopard Messiah*, along with my final wishes and a thank you note to my friends. Death was my only solution.

"It's the only way," I whispered to myself.

"You don't know that." I looked up to see my friend Adam, glowing somehow in the moonlight, dressed in his Jedi robes and towering over me with some metaphysical authority. "You're drunk, Liquin. If you kill yourself, there's no assurance that your plan will succeed."

"So what, I'm supposed to take advice from some cosplaying, drunken vision?"

"Ragnar hates you for your inner strength. That's why he wants you to suffer." The spectral Adam walked over to me and squatted down, looking me in the face. "You're on the brink of doing something he never thought possible in his own cynicism. He blames you for all his failures and hates you for your perseverance."

"The script is finished, and that's all that matters! All that matters is getting it to Monty and helping my friends! Paying them back for loving me all this time when they had no reason to. When I wasn't worthy of their love."

"You can't control what happens after your own death. Nobody can. You must have patience."

"But I can't do this anymore!" I screamed, my eyes wide with fury and burning with tears. "I don't want to do this anymore! Con is corrupted by the very place it once offered me refuge from, and I'm just a burden to the people that I love!"

"Liquin, don't give in to despair! Only you can do whatever it is that you do!"

I rose and turned away from my vision, walking back toward First Avenue.

"This is my last chance, Adam. I have to do you justice. All of you."

"It's not just about the love you feel, Liquin. It's not all about you."

I spun around, and my hallucination had vanished. I paused a moment, wondering if the spectre of my friend might appear again, but he didn't. As I walked back toward the Bayfront, looking at no one as I did, I pulled out my phone. I had a text message waiting from Brigham:

SRRY.

I ignored it, instead messaging Adam, wondering if talking to the real thing instead of some drunk or drug induced vision might produce better results. When I arrived back at the empty hotel room, he still hadn't messaged me back.

I took a hot shower, then went straight to Brigham's pharmaceutical bag. I opened it, finding half a dozen prescription painkillers and sleep aids, and took them all into the bedroom. I switched on a lamp, and pulled the silver serving tray from the First Aid Kit. Sitting naked on the floor, I opened each medicine bottle and poured the contents onto the tray, then just sat there, looking down at the multi-colored shapes. I took a deep breath and looked up at the liquor bottles still stored in the First Aid case. No doubt, I had the means to finally end my life. The hour approached.

One thing remained…

SATURDAY

Masters of the Universe

D on't ask me what time Kate, Windsor or Brigham got home. Don't ask me what time I finally fell asleep. And don't ask me what I dreamed about that night. I have no frakking idea. Bouts of escaping or lapsed memory had become an increasing vexation on my life since my diagnosis. As if the crazy mood swings weren't enough to wipe my memory— and they were—the Lexapro and Abilify screwed with my brain chemistry in order to keep me sane, and caused memory loss as a side effect in addition to flaccid wiener. I'd become an impotent, lethargic amnesiac, which somehow still managed to classify as healthier, at least by medical standards.

Not that it would matter much longer.

I woke up the next morning in the dark. The room felt like a meat locker, and the only light to break up the blackness of the room came from the LED alarm clock on the nightstand. Through the blur of mucus and dust in my eyes, I could make out the 6am-hour on the readout, and the curvaceous silhouette of my dear Starbuck crouched beside me alongside the bed. Next to me, Brigham emitted glottal sighs, not quite a snore, but still a disturbing choke from his rotund, warm body next to me.

My mind darted to the pills. I'd hidden them after two long swigs of whiskey underneath the bed, still arranged on the serving tray. I assumed, with confidence, that my roommates would not discover them missing—not even Brigham, who had a nasty habit of forgetting how many he'd taken or handed out at parties. Finding the bottles empty wouldn't faze him much; rather, it would just make him find the nearest pharmacy for a refill. The serving tray was rarely used for anything but show. I couldn't imagine my friends noticing it missing before I did what I had to, and even if they did, they wouldn't think too much about it.

"Hey," Kate whispered, running a gentle hand across my back. I squinted and grunted, rubbing my face with my left hand.

"Hey," I winced back. A moment of alarm jolted me to full consciousness as I reached down under the sheets, confirming that yes, I had remembered to put boxers on before bed. Lord knew what my compatriots would say if they woke up to my exposed lightsaber.

"Come with me. We gotta go get in line," Kate instructed me.

"Mmm," I whined. "For what?"

"Warners. Just come on."

I closed my eyes again, burrowing under the covers. Kate patted me through the comforter, her nurturing instincts matched by her patience.

"I want to die," I mumbled. Kate swatted at my back.

"Go brush your teeth. Come on."

A few minutes later, and with fresh and sparkly teeth, I followed Kate down the hall of the Bayfront, backpack over my shoulder, a black and red *Thundercats* cap concealing my messed hair, clad in jeans, a vintage *Superman* t-shirt, and my hoodie. I didn't shave or bathe before leaving the room, so I had to wonder just how much I would add to the aroma of the gink by day's end. Well, Kate had insisted that we hurry. She knew full well the perils of Con, so I trusted that she had good reason for making me delay my personal hygiene.

"Where are we going? What about Straightness & Brigham?" I asked as we boarded the elevator.

"Warner Brothers panel," Kate explained.

"That's not until like eleven!" I screeched, my head throbbing. "Why are we getting in line so early and in this shit weather? And why aren't the other two with us?"

"The lines this year are out of control," Kate said, watching the descending floor numbers above the door. "Brigham needs his beauty sleep, and he has clients he needs to see later this morning. Windsor just needs…"

"What?" Kate shook her head.

"I don't know what Windsor needs," Kate admitted. "But you and I need quality time. Like in the old days."

"Sounds nice," I uttered, cracking a smile.

"With the shoot tonight I'll have to prep most of the afternoon," Kate mused. "This might be our last opportunity."

I looked at her, admiring her ethereal beauty. Even in the early morning with little sleep and minimal make-up, Kate still had a natural radiance to her, in her perfect complexion and crystal blue eyes. I had to wonder if she had any idea of the prophecy of her statement. In less than 24 hours, I'd be dead, and she'd have custody of my script. I sighed. Kate glanced over at me with a warm smile as she exited the elevator. I followed.

The lobby of the Bayfront already rumbled with activity, even at that ungodly hour. Other conventioneers, their Con badges strung about their necks with lanyards, milled about, light morning snacks or paper cups of coffee in hand. Kate and I shuffled across the polished marble floor, half dazed with sleep. I ran a hand across my face to try and jolt myself into full consciousness, but ended up picking the sleepy crumbs from the corner of my eyes. Kate must have noticed, because she let out an empathetic snicker. That made me smile.

Armed with overpriced coffee, we made our way out to the shanty town/line for Hall H. I plopped down in the moist grass, feeling the morning dew seep up into the ass of my jeans. I grumbled and frowned as Kate did the same, only with the foresight to drop a dirty t-shirt down to the ground to soak up the moisture.

"So," I said, pulling my hoodie up over my head to muffle the chilly morning air. "What's up Starbuck?"

Kate half smiled and took a sip from her coffee. She looked down and shrugged with a sigh, then met my gaze with her own shimmering eyes.

"I dunno, Liquin," Kate confessed. "Everything. Nothing. Stuff." She paused a beat, taking another sip from her cup. "Windsor."

"He's pissing you off," I charged.

"No, not exactly," Kate replied. "Well, the smoking pisses me off," Kate admitted with a steely look. "But it's just one of those things…I have to wonder if it's worth it to stay together."

"Do you not…don't you love him anymore?"

"Of course," Kate said before I'd even finished. "I love him like crazy."

"You know he loves you…"

"And I know that," Kate assured me. "But all this crazy stuff with the short film, and him trying to get in with that animation academy…I have to wonder if it's worth it." I nodded in understanding.

"You could always do the long distance thing," I suggested in a half-hearted attempt to comfort her. Kate scowled and rolled her eyes, seeing the emptiness of my platitude.

"It's one of those things," Kate observed. "We have to prioritize. Is it better to stay together or split, and if we did stay together, who would sacrifice what in the name of the relationship? I mean, if either of us is on the brink, or even just the path to making our lifelong dreams come true…is any relationship worth that?"

"I see what you mean," I confessed. "I guess this is why the divorce rate in Hollywood is so high." I paused a moment. "And I guess that's why I can't blame anyone for it. It's the nature of the business." I took a swig from my coffee cup. "Not to mention the innate hypocrisy in a single guy like myself telling others how to run their relationships."

"Oh stop," Kate chided me. "You'll meet some guy. You just have to…"

"I won't, Kate," I cut her off. "I'll die alone." Kate let out an uneasy chuckle, studying my face for some hint of sarcasm. Her expression of amusement faded in rapid course. I reached up under my shirt and hoodie to feel the flash drive strung about my neck. The time had come to give it to Kate, but how?

"Well," Kate sighed, breaking the awkward silence, "no dying before the shoot tonight. I might need you."

"That makes me feel so much better, Starbuck," I grumbled with sarcasm. Kate smiled.

"Don't want you to forget," Kate nudged.

"Just as well," I muttered, "considering I can't remember a damn thing from the drugs."

"The med-drugs or the drug-drugs?" Kate pressed.

"Well both," I admitted. "Though the drug-drugs can't help what's already an uphill battle. Like what did I do the other day after the Admiral gave me the Fuckitall?"

"Do you remember any of it?"

"Screaming," I said, my thoughts distant and laborious. "Lizard queen…something about 'stick it in.'" I sighed. "God knows what that could mean."

"Ok, enough with the somber," Kate urged. "Can we talk about something fun?"

"*Green Lantern*?" I suggested.

"Right!" Kate chirped. "So you think DC movies will hit their stride the way the Marvel movies did?"

"Who knows," I shrugged, taking another swig of coffee. "It seems like they want to do their own cinematic universe, but that's hard since the Christopher Nolan Bat-films are still in production. Do they really expect the audience to accept multiple Bat-men in different film franchises that are still made by the same people?"

"Good point," Kate observed. "But doesn't the bloated cast of *Green Lantern* suggest they're trying to do that?"

"Angela Bassett, you mean," I offered. Kate nodded.

"Amanda Waller," Kate said. "Even though Angela Bassett is totally wrong for the part. I'm guessing they want her to be the

Sam Jackson/Nick Fury of the movies."

"You're probably right," I nodded.

"And I love Angela Bassett!" Kate added. "She should have played Storm in *X-Men*."

"Agreed."

"But Amanda Waller is supposed to be short and kind of stocky, a female form we don't often get in the movies. I mean, was Latifah busy? Mo'Nique?"

"Damn, either of them would have been great," I uttered in a pensive monotone. "Some days it just seems like there's no justice in the universe." I looked up to find Kate staring at me with powerful fixation. Something about her countenance sent a spasmodic chill through my core.

"What?" I asked, disturbed by her gaze. Kate shook her head.

"Nothing. You're right," Kate cooed, averting eye contact with me. "No justice," she murmured.

We sat there, quiet a long time, then engaging in idle chatter for the next few hours, discussing our favorite topics—graphic novels, *Battlestar Galactica*, and our favorite memories of Con. It only served to make me sadder. From what I observed, Kate felt the same way, her face unusually sullen, no doubt from the lingering concerns about Windsor and the realization that Comic-Con had become almost unrecognizable in just the course of two years since she'd started attending. I wanted to comfort her, but I felt the same kind of despair. By 10am the doors to Hall H opened, and the line began to move inside. Kate and I made it in, despite the droves of attendees camped out in the shanty town. Finding good seats proved tricky, but we managed to secure a couple off to the left of the stage about half way back in the hall.

Then we just sat there again, both of us too distracted to find triumph in making it into the panel.

"Do you think they should move the Con?" Kate asked after a protracted silence.

"Oooh," I rumbled. "Careful how loud you say that."

"Why?"

"The geeks get passionate about that subject," I explained. "But…it is a question worth addressing."

"I saw some of the coverage in the trades earlier this year," Kate mentioned. "Comic-Con renegotiating with San Diego. Other venues lobbying for the Con…Anaheim, Los Angeles, and Las Vegas, I think."

"That sounds right," I uttered, my gaze fixed straight ahead, eyes lost in oblivion as I considered the possibility. "Of the three, Vegas makes the most sense in my mind. Plenty of hotels and space. Those would both be issues in LA or Anaheim. The LA Convention Center is surrounded by downtown, and Anaheim would have to compete with Disneyland."

"But it's so hot in Vegas!" Kate squealed in a half-laugh. "Think of the gink!" I chuckled.

"True," I admitted. "Nowhere is ideal, but I fear the Con has outgrown San Diego. I read that the Con signed a five year extension on their lease for this Convention Center. The city of San Diego has promised to build more hotels and expand the venue." I turned to Kate with a wry smile. "Think about that… the Convention Center is surrounded by the bay on one side and Petco Stadium on the other. Where will they build?"

"And how long will it take?" Kate added. "And how would it affect the Cons in between?" She sighed and shook her head. "Is this the end of Comic-Con?" Kate asked, channeling the melodrama of the announcer on the *Batman* 60's TV show.

"Everything dies," I chimed low, to Kate.

"The end is the beginning is the end," Kate murmured, a quiver of optimism in her voice. "The circle opens, the circle closes again."

"Does it make you happy I'm so strange?" I asked aloud, but not to Kate. I asked myself. For years I had relished my eccentricities, reveled in my weirdness, but in that moment…I had to wonder if I'd been wrong the whole time. I scanned the room, lost in the amoeba-like site of the fluxing crowd, climbing over themselves to get the best seats in the hall as the Hall Nazis barked trying to control the influx.

This is what Comic-Con had become—my home, my place to belong, the celebration of love and joy and friendship, reduced to some biblical plague infesting a city, devouring the space even as the city devoured *us*—exploiting and oppressing and condescending to the whole fucking lot of us. Just another buck to make, another market to tap. And more people to just hate.

I reached up under my shirt and grasped the USB drive a final time before I slipped the lanyard over my neck and held it out to Kate.

"Sweetheart," I said, my voice dead and devoid of feeling. "I need you to keep this, Starbuck." Kate took the data stick and turned it over in her palm before looking at me with utter confusion.

"What is it?" Kate inquired, anxiety buried in her words.

"The best of me," I whispered. "You need to keep it secret. Keep it safe. You'll know what to do when the time comes."

"Liquin," Kate pressed, urgency bubbling forth. "What..."

Kate paused, interrupted by the dimming lights as the moderator took to the stage to introduce the Warner Bros. presentation. The cast of *Green Lantern*—Ryan Reynolds, Blake Lively, Peter Sarsgaard, Mark Strong and the director Martin Campbell filed onto the stage amid the strobe of flashbulbs and squeals of the crowd, the loudest of which came from the studio plants given preferential seating at the front of the hall.

I forced a smile to my face as the panel began with the usual smoke-in-the-ass banter glorifying the movie, the cast, the direction, and generally anything else conceivable. They showed some footage, which looked colorful and promising, and then Reynolds, cast in the titular role, recited the Lantern Corps. Oath, the iconic poem that served as a premise for the character. He also gave away a movie prop power ring to a young kid that asked a question. As the poor lad walked away from the mic with his new toy, a cabal of middle aged, slovenly men descended on him, no doubt, memorabilia dealers ready to cut the kid a deal. If he did sell it, I hope the kid got enough to pay for college, or at least his weekend at the Con.

Watching the Lantern presentation, I couldn't get excited. Granted, Green Lantern wasn't my favorite hero, though I did have nostalgic memories of wearing a visor with the Lantern emblem to a rave once in college. Though the bright and vibrant footage looked promising, something seemed off, like everything felt forced somehow. Nothing about the movie seemed alive.

There again, given the antidepressants and resolve to the *Neodämmerung*, maybe my frailty of emotion had at last began to fade. Maybe to lose the pain, I had to lose the joy too.

"What do you think?" Kate asked as the cast exited the stage.

"I think it lacks character," I muttered. "But we'll see."

Next in the panel, young Tom Felton, Draco Malfoy from the *Harry Potter* film series introduced what turned out to be little more than an extended trailer. Though the seventh *Potter* film featured heavily in announcements for the Warner Bros. presentation, apparently the studio just didn't give enough of a damn to cobble together anything interesting. Maybe they didn't have the time or finances to put something together. Or maybe, like me, they sensed the death of the Con at hand and didn't see much of a need for effort anymore.

My ambivalence waned as Zach Snyder, Executive Geek and director of *Watchmen* returned to the stage after a two year absence. Snyder had come to debut footage of his first auteur project, a female-driven action picture called *Sucker Punch*. He first introduced his tag-along cast: Emily Browning, Vanessa Hudgens, Jenna Malone, Jamie Chung and Abbie Cornish. None of the girls had seen any finished footage, and because of the heavy green screen special effects, none of them really had any idea what the movie would look or sound like. As it happened, the footage, set to Lords of Acid's *Crablouse*, a techno track about crabs infecting an unsuspecting snatch, packed a hell of a wallop. It looked like a cracked-out videogame directed by Russ Meyer on speed.

"Holy crap," Kate uttered. The cast, for their part, went nuts. Hudgens sat in complete shock, while Malone and Browning looked as though they might cry. Snyder grinned from ear to ear, obviously proud of what he'd shown.

"Looks pretty cool," I said. "Lots of explosions and plunging necklines. Looks like a hit!"

"Does seeing an Executive Geek like Snyder make you feel better about everything?" I shrugged.

"Maybe," I offered. "Just a little."

"Liquin, what is going on?" Kate confronted me. I started to roll my eyes when she grabbed my shoulder and gave me a violent shake. I looked down at her shining blue eyes, as she held the flash drive up in one hand, almost threatening me with it. The panel hadn't finished yet, but I stood up and walked toward the exit. Kate followed without my prompting.

Outside the Convention Center, in the gray light of day and damp breeze, I stood like a pillar of salt, looking back at the self-destructing mess that had become Comic-Con one last time. Kate marched up to me, her face only inches from my own, the USB drive clutched in her fist. For a moment, I thought she might actually slug me.

"I'm going to die, Kate," I declared, not a hint of emotion in my voice. "That data stick has the master file to *Leopard Messiah* and a letter containing details for my cremation and division of my property." I winced. "My very modest property. You get to inherit my backpack..."

"Stop it!" Kate ordered me, waving her fist even close. "This is absolutely crazy, you know that?"

"So am I," I observed. "Apparently. Totally batshit nuts." My voice softened. "And I don't want to be alive anymore."

Kate looked at me with desperate shock, eyes aglow, mouth agape. She shook her head in the negative, little twitches, as if unable to believe what I'd said, or what she felt. She kept the USB drive locked in her right hand, as she raised her left, palm outstretched. She took a step back, looking down a moment, then back up at me, her face hardening.

"You're out of your mind," she chimed.

"Isn't that what I just said?" I shrugged in indifference. Kate clenched her jaw.

"Walk!" Kate ordered, grabbing me by the collar of my shirt and dragging me to the Fifth Avenue crosswalk. I obeyed; for one thing I didn't feel like fighting anymore. For another, she had the USB stick with the master file of *Leopard Messiah*. If anything happened to it—if she got fed up and chucked it in the ocean—that'd be the end of my one chance at making an impression.

"Gore Vidal said it," I observed as we sat down at a table tucked in a shadowy corner of TGIFridays. Kate had led me there —the first place we ate at her first Con years before—without a word. She sat across the table from me, her arms folded, elbows propping her up against the tabletop. I paused, waiting for her to finish my sentence for me, but apparently she didn't know the punch line. "Death is a great career move."

"If you're dead you don't get to enjoy your success," Kate said, her voice quiet and monotone.

"Well, if I'm dead, I won't care," I rebutted.

"How do you know you'd be better off? What if you end up in Hell or Purgatory or…"

"Oh come on," I interrupted her. "You know I don't believe in that crap, and neither do you!"

"I do," Kate assured me with affirming cool.

"No, you don't," I pressed. "Deep down, no you don't. I don't want this to morph into some dissection of the afterlife," I declared, my palms open in front of me. "I'm not in the mood for theological debate, and if the best you can do is offer Hell as some kind of cosmic blackmail, there's no point in even continuing this conversation."

"Fine," she conceded. "It doesn't change the fact that you'd be abandoning your own moment of triumph."

"No darling, I'd be fulfilling it," I said, matching her even temper. "I need to die in a sensational way to get the world's attention. Why can't you see that? It's what I need to do to get an interest in my work! And why can't you understand that this is best for everyone?! For me, you, Straightness, Brigham…they'll pay attention to you too! They'll want to know what I was like in my last moments, what you had to do to keep me sane! They'll look at your work, and suddenly you won't need people like Ragnar..."

"Lord, this again," Kate grumbled.

"You won't need him. And I'll win! You'll win! I won't have to put up with any of this sham of life anymore, and people will pay attention!"

"That's all this is to you," Kate erupted, her voice. "A cry for frakking attention! It's so desperate, Liquin! You're better than that!"

"Well," I sighed. "I have your attention now, don't I?"

An unremarkable waiter came to the table, tossing cocktail napkins in front of Kate and I.

"Greetings, hobbits!" the waiter chirped with faux glee. "Are you guys Gryffindors or Hufflepuffs?" Kate and I broke from our furious stare down of one another, and in unison, turned our bemused looks to the waiter. "Ravenclaws?" the waiter squirmed, sensing our ire. "Aren't you guys here for Comic-Con?"

"I'll have a club sandwich and a Coke," Kate requested before turning to me. "What do you want?"

"I'm not hungry," I sighed.

"You've barely eaten all day," Kate urged.

"I'm not hungry," I repeated.

"Get something," Kate pushed.

"Not hungry."

"You need to eat." Kate turned to the waiter. "Bring him baked potato soup and a Coke too, please."

"I'm not hungry!" I insisted. The waiter began to look scared.

"You're eating the soup!" Kate declared.

"I don't want the soup! What for? Where I'm going it's not like I'll need it..."

"Get the soup," Kate growled, shooting daggers through her eyes.

"I'm not eating the soup!"

"Get the soup or I will bite your frakking nuts off," Kate threatened with icy calm. From the corner of my eye, I could see the waiter shudder. A beat of silence passed.

"I'll have the soup," I conceded, smiling ear to ear at our waiter. He nodded and walked over to a touchscreen kiosk to enter our order. I turned back to Kate, my smile vanishing. "I hate it when they try to cater to the Con attendees, or think they are by attempting lame ass product-tie ins, or just clumsy ones, like confusing *Lord of the Rings* with *Harry Potter*."

"It's enough to make you lose your appetite," Kate mused. I opened my mouth to spout a witty comeback, only to have her cut me off. "You're eating the soup."

Kate leaned forward and buried her face in her hands, letting out a deep sigh. She spread her fingers, peeking out at me through the gaps between them, and sighed again.

"You know something?" she muttered. She ran her hands back through her hair, locking them behind her neck. "You. Exasperate. Me." She punctuated each word with perfect diction.

"I'm sorry." I slouched forward to face her. "Are you new at this party?"

The waiter returned with our Cokes, and we just sat quiet a few minutes, no doubt, both of us exhausted by one another. It's hard arguing with someone I knew so well, and more important, who knew me well. And I hated arguing with someone I loved so much. We both needed it though; no doubt the hysteria that had become Comic-Con put us in bad moods.

"I do believe in an afterlife, you know," Kate affirmed after a long silence. "I believe in God, and I think you do too."

"A benevolent being that tortures us our entire lives and then condemns us for not wanting to go through it?" I grumbled. "And don't get me started on religious dogma…"

"All doctrine aside," Kate said with a wave of her hand. "I do. I mean, I don't pretend to know why everything happens the way it does, but yeah, I believe. For all I know this could be some dream. Maybe death is where we wake up."

"Time for a wake-up call," I joked. I smiled at Kate, who rolled her eyes. "In which case, life begins at death."

"The end is the beginning is the end," Kate offered. I grimaced and shook my head. She leaned forward and folded her hands, her manicured nails shining under the lamplight. I groaned.

"I used to come to this Con and feel such love," I mused. "Such joy. Now I come here, and it's just anger and frustration and *hate*. Disdain. Just like every other day of my fucking life. And when refuge...when home...becomes a place of torture, what's left?"

The waiter came back with our lunch, and we ate in silence, both of us heavy and tired. Halfway through my soup, I tossed the spoon into the bowl and crossed my arms. I didn't want to eat anymore, in part because I wasn't hungry, and in part because I was a stubborn bastard who still needed to make the point to Kate that no, I didn't need food if I didn't want it.

"I think I need to go be alone for a while," I uttered at last, looking through the floor and into blank space.

"I don't think that's a good idea," Kate insisted.

"Kate, please..."

"Here," Kate growled, tossing the USB drive across the table. It almost landed in my soup, but instead fell to the table top with a *clack*, spinning around from the force of her throw. The lanyard dragged behind the spinning ends, spooling around in its wake. "Do your own dirty work. I want no part of it."

"Kate, please," I repeated. "I just want to be done. I don't want to do this anymore. I don't want to weigh down my friends with my depressive glum. I don't want you to worry."

"Too late," she spat.

"It's for the best. Now all you have to do is open the drive. There are two documents...you'll know what to do when you see them."

"Frak you," Kate declared, digging through her own backpack and tossing cash out onto the table. "Whatever happens, Liquin, just remember: I need you for the shoot tonight."

"You do not," I whined. "You have Windsor."

"I'm telling you now, I need you!" Kate pressed. "Be there or else!"

"Or else what?"

"Or else..." Kate rose to her full height, her eyes darting around as if looking for some Holy Grail of spite. "Or else, I don't care what happens to you, I'll throw that damn USB drive in the bay and be done with it!" I knew from the stony resolve in her face that she didn't kid. I edged a hand up to the table and grabbed the data drive, slinging the lanyard over my neck again and tucking it into my shirt. I tossed my own share for the lunch I didn't want to eat onto the table and followed Kate to the exit.

"May the Force be with you!" our waiter called at us. I glanced back to see him wave as he counted the money left behind on our table. Ahead of me, Kate scoffed.

"You're right about the imitation geeks," Kate grunted outside the restaurant. "They're everywhere." I nodded in silence.

"So what now?" Kate sighed.

"Don't you have to prep for tonight?" I asked.

"Yeah, but I don't want you to be alone," Kate told me. "Besides, Con comes but once a year. I would like to enjoy a bit of it."

"That makes two of us," I grumbled. I looked up into the gray clouds still churning above us. My eyes lit on one pocket, a lighter shade of gray than the vapor around it. It seemed to flicker as the clouds moved overhead, like the flame of a candle.

"Sun's trying to come out," Kate observed. I grinned.

"Maybe there's hope for some good weather yet." Kate and I looked at each other and smiled. She moved over to my side and grasped my lanky arm with both hands, nuzzling her face against my shoulder, pulling me back in the direction of the Convention Center. I felt her exhale, her breath warm and damp through my sleeve. I glanced down at her again, still buried against me as she peeked up, then looked ahead, her noggin still resting against me.

"You hear more from that guy?" Kate asked. "That Raz-Ar

guy?"

"No," I confessed. "Maybe that's a good thing." Kate murmured her disapproval.

"Boys can be so stupid," she said, her tone distant. "Speaking of," she muttered under her breath. She took out her phone and started punching at the keys.

"Not that I ever prove that statement," I chided. Kate smiled, stepping back from me and raising her head high. She ran her tongue over her back molars, the bulge protruding in her cheek and she hit me with a sideways glance.

"You're the best at what you do," Kate declared. She looked down at the phone, still in her hand, as it began to vibrate. She ran a finger across the screen, reading some message.

"I used to be," I whined.

"Stop," Kate ordered. "Come on."

She led us back down Fifth Avenue to the railroad crossing, just beside the still-chanting crowd of anti-gay protesters. We fought our way past the barkers and the crowd, back up to the Convention Center, where Kate marched half the length of the building toward Hall E, not even stopping to notice the group of Imperial Stormtroopers dressed in hip-hop colors and accessories, dancing to LMFAO's *Sexy and I Know It.* I had to stop for a moment, watching their vivid pink and orange armor adorned with oversized gold chains and rings. A grimace snuck across my face—at least they showed some creativity. I mean, despite my own occasional donning of *Battlestar Galactica* combat fatigues, I never really dressed up. It always seemed expensive and uncomfortable for a weekend I knew I'd spend on my feet walking almost the entire time, and through crowds and in the heat. Not that we had any heat *that* day, but it seemed an exception to the rule.

On the other hand, with all the crazy warping of Comic-Con into some abominable douchebag freak show of publicity and smoke-ass blowing, maybe dark clouds portended the future.

I hurried along and caught up to Kate just as she cut through the Hall E lobby and walked out onto the Convention Floor. The crowd had swelled to near paralysis—the marching of the aisles looked like sick conga lines, marching in rhythm from one end of the Convention Center to the next. As I took my place next to Kate facing the massive crowd of the Exhibit Hall, I could hear her murmur in annoyance.

"Of course he'd want to meet in on the Floor," Kate groused.

"Where is he? What's he doing?" I inquired.

"I don't know, you know how Windsor is," Kate rattled. "And now I can't even get any signal in here." She tapped the screen of her phone in frustration.

"That's weird," I said. I pulled my own phone from my pocket. "You've never had trouble getting signal in here before. And neither have…" I stopped short as I looked at the readout on my own cell phone screen. It too showed the graphic for no service.

"Something's up," I declared, fiddling with my phone. "WiFi?"

"Already tried it," Kate confessed.

"Dear God," I realized. "The whole cellular network is overloaded! And the WiFi!? That's insane! These were just working a few blocks away…"

"And we have different service providers," Kate reminded me. "Think about *that* one. It must have something to do with these new smartphones and all the bandwidth or something."

"Probably," I agreed, my eyes widening. "Dear God, what's going to become of us?"

"Well, Windsor is going to get his butt kicked unless we can find him in this mess," Kate spat, shaking her head. "He was looking at animation stuff."

"This way," I ordered, leading Kate into the masses toward Hall A at the far end of the Exhibit Hall.

"How do you know!?" Kate exclaimed. I could feel her grab on to my backpack, coupling herself to me so as not to get lost in the crowd.

"Most of the vendors rent the same space every year," I explained. "You never noticed that?"

"No," Kate confessed. "And I don't know how you did either!

The way you tell it, every Comic-Con is just a blur of sex, drugs and superheroes for you!"

"Very true," I conceded. "But consistencies add up after damn near ten years of doing this craziness!"

As we approached the edge of Hall A, I could spot our target: an animation vendor, who specialized in discarded animation cells, mostly from Saturday morning or syndicated cartoons of the 80s and 90s. I scanned the booth, which actually took up the space of two booths with snaking tables and boxes forming a maze of acetate, paper and paint. Sure enough, I cited a pair of familiar hands locked to the edge of the table, a head of greasy, black hair bobbing up and down at its edge.

"Hello, Straightness," I chimed as Kate and I entered the booth. Windsor popped up from beside the table to his full height, a naughty smile on his face.

"Hellooooo, chief!" Straightness greeted me with his low, timpani voice. "Hello BooBoo!" He leaned down and gave Starbuck a kiss on her cheek. She responded with an empty grin.

"What are you buying and how much are you spending?" Kate grumbled, folding her arms across her abdomen.

"Check it out!" Windsor exclaimed. He ducked back under the table and returned with an oversized manila folder—the kind used in old-school animation to turn in or store a series of drawings. "Ta-da!" Straightness flipped open the file cover, revealing a slightly crumpled animation cell of bright blues, pinks and purples.

"Is that…" I began to ask.

"The Peculiar Purple Pieman of Porcupine Peak!" Straightness bellowed in triumph. Kate just looked at both of us, blank confusion in her eyes.

"Dear Lord," Kate moaned, planting her face in her left palm, unable to stifle her giggles.

"From *Strawberry Shortcake*?" I grunted in incredulity. "That!?"

"Peculiar Purple Pieman of Porcupine Peak!" Straightness repeated. "I've been looking for one of these for years!"

"I don't know what's more astonishing: that you spent years looking, or that you actually found one!" I grumbled in monotone.

"Why are you looking for the Pieman?" Kate questioned in vexation. "That's not your usual…" She searched for the right word. "Taste."

"Seriously," I strained. "That's like even gayer than I am! Even gayer than Brigham!" Both my companions began to laugh. "Well, it's true!" I insisted.

"The Purple Pieman was an awesome character!" Windsor insisted. "My Mom and big sister used to call me that when I was three. I used to walk around the house doing his dance!" Windsor smiled wide, his left eye twitching in his nervous tic. Kate and I twisted our heads with slow perplexity, exchanging a look of confusion before turning back to Straightness.

"Do you remember the dance?" Kate asked, soothing.

"Oh sure! It's…"

"Please don't!" I begged, raising my arms in a blocking gesture. "I'm not sure I can today." Windsor shrugged. Kate rolled her eyes.

"So are you buying it?" I questioned, returning to the matter at hand.

"It's seventy bucks," Windsor replied. "Of course!"

"Lord, Windsor," Kate moaned. "Where will you put it?"

"My bedroom," Windsor said.

"Your action figure collection is in your bedroom," Kate observed. "And your Iron Man bust and *Thief and the Cobbler* cells are in the bathroom. The living room is full of vintage movie posters and framed comic books."

"The kitchen!" Straightness exclaimed. "Perfect for a Pieman!"

"Why do I bother?" Kate grumbled. Windsor flagged down a booth attendant and started the haggling process to buy his Pieman cell. I watched Kate, her eyes turned upward, staring into some invisible vortex of inner reflection. I lay a hand on her shoulder.

"You alright?" I asked.

"Peachy," she uttered. "Why does he buy this stuff?"

"Starbuck, you understand the geek principles. You know this is how he operates, just like the rest of us."

"That's true," Kate replied, still looking upward.

"You knew what you were getting into a long time ago," I nudged, trying to get her to relax. Her eyes drifted over to Windsor as he handed a roll of cash to the booth attendant and slipped the folder with the cell into his messenger bag. I watched her chest expand with a deep inhalation, then relax again.

"Also true," she confessed. "But..." She paused a moment. "That doesn't make it easier."

"No, but then you also can't be angry when he does things like this," I reminded.

"That's fair," Kate said with a nod. Her blue eyes fixed on me. "But that doesn't mean I can't get frustrated."

"So!" Windsor blurted with self-satisfaction. "We doing the *Avengers* panel? It's the first time ever the cast has been assembled in one place!"

"There's no way we'd get in to that mess of a hall," I protested. "And I don't much want to wait in this weather."

"And I have to start prepping for later," Kate added.

"Aw, come on!" Windsor pleaded. "Liquin, please?" I sighed and threw back my head in exhausted protest.

"Ok fine," I acquiesced. "But I need a drink first!"

The three of us traversed the crowded insanity out of the Convention Center, down the block, past the shanty town and into the Bayfront hotel bar. I protested getting drinks at the bar when we had perfectly good, ultra-purified liquor in our room, but Windsor offered to buy my cocktail. Under no circumstances—stress, euthanasia or otherwise—should I ever turn down a free drink.

We tucked ourselves in a corner alcove in the bar, a small nook big enough for only two loveseats and a small table, but surrounded by glass like a bubble on the side of the building.

Sitting there, I allowed myself a smile, looking out over the stormy waters of the bay up and down the coastline. Windsor sat down with his arm around Kate, who seemed to share in my satisfaction. He leaned down, and snatched up the bar menu from off the tiny table. His eyes widened behind his glasses, his mouth turning downward in a scowl.

"What?" Kate asked. Windsor leaned over to her and showed her something on the menu. Kate rolled her eyes and planted her face in her right hand, leaning against the back of her chair. "You've got to be kidding."

My eyes darted back and forth between them as I waited for some explanation. I shrugged, opening my arms as if to embrace the problem, my face the picture of perplexity. Straightness leaned across the table and handed me the menu. It didn't take long for me to see what had them so upset.

"A Spock martini?!" I blurted. "X-Men mojito?! Superman cosmo?!"

"They're just regular cocktails with arbitrary geek names attached," Windsor observed. "And a two dollar uptick in price."

"No doubt," I agreed, still agog at the menu. "A fourth stage guild navigator bloody mary?"

"What?" Kate clucked, confounded.

"That's an obscure one," Straightness commented.

"No kidding," I grumbled, just as the waitress, a busty brunette dressed in all black arrived at our table in a huff.

"Did you guys want to order something?" the waitress greeted without looking at us. Her gaze was fixed across the room at some Hollywood-biz lothario with a bad tan and not enough Botox.

"We're right here," Kate needled. The waitress wrested her gaze back to notice the three of us, snug in our nook.

"Yeah, did you want something?" the waitress asked again. "If you're not ordering you can't sit here. We're too busy with the nerd convention."

"I'm going up to the room," Kate announced in a huff. She rose to her feet, fired a faux smirk at the waitress and then charged past her, heading for the lobby.

"Love you honey!" Windsor called after her.

"I'll have a martini," I told the waitress. "A real martini, with gin. Not vodka."

"Oh so you don't want it with vodka?" the waitress asked in confoundment.

"Gin," I repeated, annoyed.

"And you?" the waitress asked Windsor, her eyes darting back to the lothario across the room.

"Scotch on the rocks," Straightness requested. Without another word, the waitress stomped off back to the bar.

"What's with her?" Straightness wondered aloud once the bitchy brunette was out of earshot.

"Crowd must be getting to her too," I waxed. "I understand that." Straightness nodded.

"What's with Kate?" he asked me. I cocked my head sideways, raising an eyebrow.

"She's your lady friend," I reminded him. "Are you not perceptive enough to know? Can't you ask her?"

"I'm not psychic chief," he said. "And yeah, Kate's a peach, and I love her, but peaches have the pits."

"Dear God," I muttered. "How should I know?" I evaded. "Go ask her?"

"Naw-naw-naw," Windsor stuttered. "I don't want to make it worse."

"Who said you'll make it worse?" I squawked. "Maybe she wants you to ask!"

"Don't want to risk it, chief."

The waitress returned with our drinks, but not a word to us. Straightness and I exchanged an obligatory clash of the glasses, then imbibed long swigs from our drinks. The gin stung my mouth with its proof, the alcohol coursing to my brain numbing me into chemical blur. I propped my head up on my arm, resting my elbow on the back of my loveseat, and let out a sigh. My eyes fell on Windsor, who looked out into the gray of the bay, the waves churning with an angry undercurrent. Between the gin and the hypnotic bob of the water, I slipped into a sort of trance. Maybe I could just go throw myself in the bay; at least if I did, there'd be no clean-up of my corpse, and it'd be a green burial!

"I heard from my animation academy friend," Windsor uttered without prompting. "He made an offer."

His words jarred me from my brooding. I felt my jaw loosen and my wrists tighten as I searched for what to say.

"That's...awesome..." I managed to get the words out, but couldn't think of a follow up. Windsor was my friend, my geek brother, someone I trusted...

"I haven't answered him yet. I haven't told Kate."

"When do you plan to?" I asked. Windsor's eye pulsed with nervousness. He took a sip from his glass and shook his head.

"Guess I should figure that out," Windsor confessed.

"She loves you," I stuttered, still at a loss.

"I love her, chief. I really do." Straightness reached up under his glasses and rubbed his eyes with his free hand, shifting in the love seat. "But I don't know. She seems so repulsed sometimes. It's hard. I just want to be close to her. I hold her at night and bury my face in her neck, just smelling her. Feeling her. Hearing her breathe. She tells me sometimes that I hold her too tight, that I'm smothering her. She laughs about it, and I guess I do to but...it always kind of hurts. I know I drive her crazy. I drive *me* crazy. It scares me that I care about her so much. I'm always scared she'll leave."

"You're the one talking about leaving," I observed. "Have you thought about asking her to go with you? Maybe you should be talking about getting married or something."

"God, no," Windsor grunted. "We can't get married. We both are too fucking...we want...ambition, Liquin!" He stared toward me, as if fighting the urge to look away. I could tell he wasn't looking directly at me, but fixing somewhere above my line of sight, afraid to look me in the eye, as usual. "Kate and I both want to create, and you fucking now what that's like! I can't ask her to give up her dreams, she'd hate me! I would hate me! Her ambition is part of why I love her. She's..." He paused a long time, his head shaking a bit, his mouth muscles tightening as he swallowed back and suppressed some flood of emotion. "She's Kate," he uttered. His voice dropped into a whisper, barely audible and breathy. "She's Kate."

"Then don't give up," I murmured, my own emotions beginning to drown me.

"Oh come on, Liquin, how long are you going to do this? Why do any of us need to be here?"

"At Comic-Con?" I asked.

"Comic-Con. Hollywood. California. Any of it! I came out here thinking I'd be some hotshot animator, some great movie guy but we all know that's not happening! I can't anymore!"

"You can't give up!" I pleaded. "You don't know what could happen! Tomorrow..."

"You made me believe that a long time, chief, but not anymore. I hate this godforsaken place." His face hardened with resolve. "And now I think it's time."

It nauseated me to admit, but I felt the same way he did. That realization frightened me to the core. I looked out over the waves again, trying to distance myself from all the awful that surrounded me, but I felt even more trapped, as if layers of glass coated my skin, suffocating me, freezing me in place like a waxwork dummy, an imitation of life.

I downed my martini in a single gulp, the gin stinging my head almost immediately. I ran my hands back through my hair, pulling on it, trying to numb the inside throbbing with more pain. I sighed, took a deep breath, and sighed again, not knowing what to do, or where to go, or even what to think anymore. My whole life seemed to fray and disintegrate right there. I looked at Windsor, who watched me, captivated. I gazed at him through the separation of my fingers, my palms still concealing my face. He said nothing, just sipping at his drink. I felt a quiet understanding pass between us. We both had to do what we had to do.

"*Avengers*?" I asked in a near whisper.

"Yeah," Windsor sighed back. He stood up and stretched his

arms and back, and I did the same. I slung my back pack over my shoulders, climbed out of our nook, and marched towards the lobby. Across the room, our bitch waitress didn't even notice.

"We have to pay!" Straightness called after me.

"They can suck my ass!" I hollered without turning around. I heard the rapid footsteps of Windsor charging up behind me as he rushed to catch up.

"That was cold, chief," Windsor observed.

"They can suck my ass," I reiterated.

Outside as we approached the shanty town formed outside Hall H, we both recognized something afoot. Just before the crosswalk between the Bayfront and the island of pavement that houses the Convention Center, I stopped short, and Windsor did the same. I slackened my jaw and ran the tip of my tongue over my incisors, scanning ahead over the migrated crowd flocked and clumped around the edge of the Convention Center.

"Dude, what the Hell?" Straightness wondered aloud. He'd obviously noticed the same thing I had—about a half dozen police officers and several Hall Nazis holding a strict perimeter around the outside of the building, and glowing red and blue emergency lights flickering from the front of the structure. Something had happened. Something *bad*.

"I think we'd better find out," I replied, my pulse quickening.

We rushed across the street, dodging other gawkers like Frogger dodging the water. That game, incidentally, always drove me crazy. Frogs are amphibious, so why do you die if you hit the water? I mean, crossing a busy highway with cars and semi trucks I understand, but fucking water? I'll even concede dodging the alligators, but even then, you can ride on their backs without getting eaten! Seriously, what the Hell kind of water is in that pond, and if it's that toxic, why the Hell would I want to get to it anyway?!

Frogger, however, was just about the furthest thing from my mind as we saw a group of three EMTs pushing a gurney out to the waiting ambulance. Windsor and I stopped at the edge of the crowd between the building entrance and the shanty town, both of us standing on our tip toes and craning our necks to see what had happened.

"What the fuck?" Straightness grumbled.

"Licks!"

I turned in the direction of the familiar voice, but before I could even spot the source, I felt the athletic arms of Roxanne wrap around me in a vice grip, making me grunt as her embrace knocked the wind from out of my gut. The Admiral planted a wet kiss square on my forehead.

"AHH!" I howled in reaction, not expecting the kiss. "Admiral, Roxanne, darling…" I strained, wresting myself from her grip. She laughed, pulling her flowing hair back from her face, mugging with lips puckered in a come-hither bombshell pose. Behind her, Brigham shuffled up, one hand resting on his collar bone, the other fixed in the air, palm open, as if to block out all the chaos in front of us.

"Dear God," Brigham moaned, moving his hand from his invisible pearls to straighten his thick glasses on his head.

"How are you darling?" Roxanne asked me before immediately rushing to give Windsor a hug too.

"What the Hell happened here?" I demanded, my eyes darting between Brigham and Roxanne.

"We're waiting to find out," Brigham explained. "Word is something *happened*."

"That's a rather astute observation," Windsor muttered in his smooth timpani voice.

"There was a fight," Roxanne clarified. "At least that's the rumor in the shanty town."

"What's going on in Hall H right now?" Windsor queried.

"*Avengers*," Brigham observed. "They were supposedly about to start. We were going to try and go—I was going to work my agent mojo—but all of this happened."

"Told ya we wouldn't have gotten in," I hissed to Straightness. He shrugged.

Just then, three police officers lead a small attendee—short with dark features in nondescript Con clothes—out of Hall H in handcuffs to one of the nearby patrol cars. Brigham pulled his smartphone from out of his pocket and punched his finger at the screen.

"EJO!" Brigham screamed. The other three of us crowded toward him, trying to get a glimpse of his phone readout.

"There was a stabbing!" Brigham gasped. "My client inside the Hall says some guy got up to go to the bathroom right before the *Avengers* panel started, someone else took his seat and wouldn't give it back, and so the guy stabbed him with a pen!"

"Jesus God!" Windsor exclaimed.

"In the eye!" Brigham added. "It was chaos in there! My client was afraid of mass panic that the room monitors or just a handful of cops couldn't handle!" Brigham slipped his phone back into his pocket. "Luckily nobody else wants to lose his seat, either."

"Shit," Roxanne said, trying to wrap her head around what had happened.

I felt a bit dazed as I tried to process it all too. Crowds and Hollywood douchebags were one thing, but violence? Attendees stabbing each other over a seat? I watch as the patrol cars and ambulance pulled away from the curb, leaving a crowd of onlookers, their camera phones erected in the air to catch some tweetable shot of the ruckus. My heart sank. If the love of Comic-Con had dwindled to the point where violence replaced it, there was no hope for the Con. Nor was there any hope for our species!

Nor was there any hope for me. I wanted off, I wanted out.

"Comic-Con is dead," I shouted, the venom of my bitterness almost burning my lips. My compatriots all snapped their heads to attention, staring at me with disbelieving horror. Brigham's hand shot up to his mouth, clutching it with disgust and hurt. Roxanne took a step back from me, confused. Windsor lit up a cigarette right there, saying nothing.

"You ok, baby?" Roxanne cooed.

"I'm fucking done," I said, stomping back towards the Bayfront.

"Liquin!" Brigham called after me.

"DONE!" I shouted back.

By the time I reached our hotel room, I wanted to die. I thought about finishing it all right there, especially when Kate was nowhere to be found in the room. I stood there, backpack still slung across my shoulders, drumming my fingers against the desk, my eyes distant, contemplating my own demise.

I poured myself a vodka-Red Bull and went to the window, looking out into the muted, washed-out light of evening. I couldn't stop with the finger-drumming, tapping my fingers against the window pane, then, after passing my drink to my busy hand, against my cocktail glass. I couldn't stop the inevitable. I had to die, and I had to get the USB drive to Kate, and I needed her assurance that she wouldn't fuck me over in anger.

The door flew open and Brigham and Roxanne entered, both looking like stern babysitters, not quite sure of themselves, but self-aware enough to know they needed to look authoritative. Roxanne watched my Illustrious friend take the lead, walking over and snatching the cocktail from my hands.

"Dude!" I exclaimed.

"You don't need any right now," Brigham said. He downed half the cocktail himself and held the glass out to the Admiral, who took the glass and downed the rest herself.

"Does everyone need to bust my balls today?" I complained. I turned my back to them, bowing my head against the window glass. Brigham reached out, grabbed my shoulder, and spun me around to face him. I'd never seen him look so grave.

"Liquin, you need to stop. Right now." The usual effervescent energy that made Brigham so fun, so loveable, indeed, so ironically charismatic, had vanished, replaced by pools of sadness behind his eyes.

"I want to stop, Brigham. I really do." I croaked out the words, feeling tired and sore. Brigham gripped my shoulder tighter for just a split second, his eyes widening with intensity.

"Stop. Now." Brigham repeated.

"I must agree," Roxanne chimed from across the room. My

eyes lit on her, as Brigham took a step back and sat down on the edge of the bed. Roxanne plopped down on the other bed and folded her arms, both of them looking stern. I reached up under my shirt and grabbed the flash drive, starting to pull the lanyard out my collar and off my neck.

"Don't," Brigham commanded. "Don't even."

"Somebody just got stabbed!" I bellowed. "At Comic-Con! In the eye!" My knees gave out, and I collapsed to the floor in a heap, pulling the backpack straps from off my shoulders and tossing my bag into a corner. "This stupid shit isn't supposed to happen here. This is Con! It's all about the love! And I'm sorry, I'm not fucking OJ Simpson. Don't tell me stabbing someone is a sign of love and affection!"

"You're right," Brigham intoned after a long pause. "This isn't what it's supposed to be. It sucks now, and it's a personal affront to those of us that have been coming here for years, and feel a sense of community and love." He shook his head. "I wish I could comfort you about that, but I feel just as bad about it as you do. Nothing I say would ring true, and more importantly, you probably wouldn't believe anything I said, even if it was true."

"You think you feel as bad as I do?" I seethed. My steel gaze lit on Roxanne. "Do you?!"

"I…" Roxanne began.

"We do feel bad," Brigham cut her off. "And I do know how you feel."

"Bullshit!" I cried. "You don't know how I feel! Ragnar Wortham-?!"

"Ragnar is a jerk, and we all loathe him, but he's good at what he does!" Brigham insisted.

"If I asked you to drop him because he's an ass and a jerk to me, *me* your friend, would you? No!"

"No, of course not," Brigham admitted. "This is how the game is played, Liquin. I'd never drop you if he asked either, because you're my friend, and I love you! But these are the rules. And if you want to win the game, and I do, and I've worked my *whole life* to get what I have, you do what you have to!"

"We do love you, Liquin," Roxanne croaked, crawling across the other bed, next to Brigham. She stretched out on her stomach, shaking her dark hair back over her shoulders, letting out a deep sigh. "You need to believe that."

"Do I?" I hissed in defiance. I pulled my knees into my chest, resting my forehead against my patellas. "I just want this to be over."

"It will be soon enough." Brigham rested a hand on Roxanne's back, rubbing it with vigor, the way he might pet a sheep dog. Roxanne gave him a sideways look, then exchanged a skeptical glance with me. She cracked a smile. I didn't.

"Tonight, after the shoot, you and I can go to Rich's," Brigham offered. "I'll buy you a drink there. We can meet cute boys to make out with or something."

"I'd go too, but I'm meeting a guy for a drink myself," Roxanne admitted with glee. "He's cute. Works at Fox."

"Careful, he's probably psychotic then," I rattled, trying not to sound too bitter.

"He's right," Brigham added.

"Probably," Roxanne sighed. She rolled onto her back, stretching her arms over her head. Her perfect locks poured over the edge of the bed like syrup, shining even in the muted light. "But a girl needs a snack every now and again."

"So do guys," Brigham nodded. "Rich's. Tonight."

"If I live that long," I stipulated. Roxanne snapped her attention toward Brigham with a look of alarm. Brigham just stared at me from behind his Kissinger glasses, his steely pale blue eyes unwavering. I gazed back at him, indifferent. I wasn't about to engage him in another debate about the pointlessness of my own life with Brigham and Roxanne too. What little energy I had left needed to get me through the shoot that night before I imbibed all the pills. Or threw myself into the bay. Or out of a window. Or picked a fight with someone in the shanty town in hopes he'd stab me to death, because, evidently, that had become vogue.

I stood up and stripped down to my boxers as Brigham and Roxanne watched, not really giving a damn anymore about anything. Without a word, I slid into bed, with Brigham and Roxanne still sitting on top of the bedclothes. I twisted and writhed, trying to get comfortable, wanting to argue, but without the energy to do so.

"To die would be an awfully big adventure," I sighed.

Just then, the door to our room opened again, as Kate burst into the bedroom looking forlorn and exasperated. Windsor trailed her, the tic under his eye spasaming like mad.

"I thought you said you wanted Liquin to do it!" Windsor rumbled. He itched at the fine, black hairs on his arm, picking and twisting at the skin, making it plump with redness as he stripped away the tissue, layer by layer.

"I do, but I want you on hand!" Kate pushed back. "I have a lot to worry about right now, and I don't think it's too much to expect a bit of frakking support! You're my boyfriend!"

"Yes, and I have my own shit to worry about right now!" Windsor hollered.

I wiggled up by my shoulder blades to a more erect posture, my attention rapt. I noticed Roxanne scoot closer to Brigham like a frightened child, clawing for assurance from a parent. Both of them didn't wince, shocked at the rage between Windsor and Kate. Kate raised her hands, as if Windsor had pointed a shotgun in her face.

"Can you please just stop, Windsor!?" Kate shouted.

"No, I can't, Kate!" Straightness bellowed back at her.

Kate pressed her fingertips together across the t-zone of her face, covering her nose and mouth. Her eyes dipped low to the carpet looking for composure, deliverance...something. But it wasn't there. She dropped her arms to her sides, her azure eyes flicking up to meet Windsor's gaze. Out of instinct, Windsor took a step back, retreating from her penetrating stare.

"Ok then," Kate whispered. "Go on." Windsor shifted his weight backwards onto his heel, his nails digging into his arm even deeper.

"So later?" he queried.

"I guess," Kate dismissed without passion.

Windsor sighed in a half chuckle, shaking his head. He spun around without another word to Kate, or to even acknowledge the rest of us in the room, threw open the door, and slammed it behind him.

None of us said anything. Brigham, Roxanne and I just watched Kate, motionless for a long moment, then wringing her hands in anxiety. She paced the length of the room, back and forth once, then sat on the edge of the empty bed, clasping her hands about her face again.

"Kate?" Roxanne murmured, leaning towards her.

"I can't," Kate whispered back. "I don't have time." She took a deep breath, and turned to me. "Liquin, please meet us down at the edge of the bay, just outside the cabana bar at nine. We'll have a costume waiting for you. Hopefully shooting won't take more than an hour."

I opened and closed my mouth in futility, trying to find some answer. I wanted to ask if she was ok, but I knew she wasn't. I wanted to offer comfort, but I realized I couldn't do that either. I'd never seen Kate upset like this before, and it frightened me to the core in a way few things did. Suddenly, my problems seemed minuscule. I wanted to reach over and hand her the USB drive again, and just be done with *everything*, but somehow I couldn't. It felt like all the joy and life had drained from the room... drained from all of us.

"Ok," I said at last, leaning back against the pillow, staring up at the popcorn ceiling. Another moment of silence passed between the four of us.

"I'd better go," Roxanne chimed at last. She stood up and walked to the door, nonchalant. As her hand rested on the latch mechanism, she paused a second. She walked back to Kate, leaned down, and planted a tender kiss on her head. The Admiral ran a gentle hand over Kate's cranium, smoothing her hair, then left without another word. Brigham downed the backwash left in his cocktail glass, then turned to me.

"I'll text you about Rich's," Brigham affirmed. Then, he too got up and left.

I'm sure neither Windsor nor Brigham had any particular destination in mind. They just had to get out of there as fast as they could. Roxanne had her date, but I figured she had time to spare, and just wanted to get away too. And just when I thought my life couldn't blow any harder, an even greater weight pummeled me—my friends, my group, my clique, my surrogate family, had just dispersed, too afraid to confront a problem, too scared to offer comfort. It felt like the whole world had pulled itself apart, like gravity had reversed: instead of a natural attraction toward one another, love turned to hate, each atom repulsing all the others in some Diaspora of geekdom.

"I really love him," Kate declared, voice cool and devoid of passion. "I always have. You've known that longer than I have." I sat up in bed, pulling the bedclothes up to my neck like some scene from a bad soap opera. I pulled my knees up close to my chest, tucking the edge of the blankets between my kneecaps and my collar bone, pinning them in place. I folded my arms over my shins, resting my chin on my patellas. I nodded in quiet agreement.

"Sometimes love isn't enough, though, is it?" Kate queried. "Sometimes the universe is just indifferent. Ambivalent."

"Yeah, it is," I uttered, not knowing what else to say. I reflected a moment, then: "He loves you too."

Kate raised both eyebrows in realization, and gave a slight nod of her head. She didn't look at me though, just staring off into the void. She shifted her posture against the sag of the mattress and let out a sigh.

"Yeah," she agreed. "And what does it matter?"

Kate rose to her feet and gathered her own backpack, slinging it over one shoulder. She tucked her hair back behind both her ears, bit her lower lip, and sighed again.

"I'll see you at nine," she ordered, just as she marched out of the room.

I listened as the room door closed, and the world faded into silence. I lay back, rolled onto my side, and pressed my face into the pillow, just enough so that my right eye could still see over the white edge of the cushion. And I lay there. And I lay there. And nothing changed. I prayed that it would, but God, fate, the universe, whatever—it was just ambivalent, just like Kate had said.

I wanted to cry, but my tears had run out long ago. I wanted to scream and yell, to trash the room in a fevered rage, but the fires of my fury had extinguished. And I wanted to chase after Kate and Windsor...Brigham...Roxanne...all of them, and promise them it would get better. I wanted to *swear on my life*, on my love, on Comic-Con itself, on everything I held dear that I would make sure it would get better, that everything would be ok. I wanted to remind them I loved them, and that somehow, some way, we'd all survive.

But I couldn't promise that, not really. Nobody could. We want to believe we have control over our lives, that through it all, some mystical Force did bind us together—the Force of friendship and love. But all the love in the universe couldn't save us. Kate was right; sometimes love wasn't enough.

The last rays of daylight vanished beneath the horizon, along with all my hope for, at the very least, a happy Con. I knew I should get up and get ready for the shoot, that I should go eat and beautify myself and try and have a bit of good sportsmanship about it all, even if Straightness & Starbuck fighting would be a giant elephant trampling our shoot, and even if my own animosity toward Ragnar would stir every negative emotion in my being. But I just lay there in the dark, counting down the seconds, the minutes, until the end of the Con. Suddenly dying wouldn't even be enough to satisfy my pain. I wanted to *unmake* myself—to erase myself from existence in some twisted Doc Brown-George Bailey alternate timeline kind of way, to liberate myself from reality, and free my friends from the weight of my ever-negative being.

I had to help Kate; no amount of selfish death-wishing could change my moral obligation to her as a best friend. I had to help her get through the shoot. But after, I would die. One way or another, I would end it all. I didn't want to be a part of such a cruel, indifferent universe anymore. And if my friends, my family, or even God would somehow hold that against me, well, then fuck them all. Their objection would make them sadists. And I still had enough pride not to allow myself to be blackmailed into weathering the torture of life just to satisfy them. Why did I matter anyway?

I slipped back into my clothes and hoodie, USB drive still hung around my neck, and inched my way downstairs. The lobby of the Bayfront still bustled with activity...mostly Hollywood douchebags—men in tailored suits, women in low-cut dresses stumbling about in high heels trying to look cool, to look important. I ignored all of them, making my way to the ground level of the hotel, and out the back door.

The rear of the Bayfront gave way to a waterside walkway, twisting around the coastal curves of San Diego Bay. An artificial peninsula jutted out into the water, offering clear view of the Coronado bridge on one side, and the open water leading into the Pacific on the other. Upon the concrete of the peninsula sat a cabana bar—a fancy watering hole for daylight beach parties for high-paying guests. White canvas couches and chairs surrounded heat torches and a fire pit, along with wicker tables and a glass perimeter, separating it from the rest of the walkway. Though vacant that night, the heat torches were lit and the fireplace blazed, providing some much needed heat from the frigid wind coming in off the water. No doubt Kate and Puck had arranged—or begged—for the hotel staff to turn the heating elements on for a few hours while they shot their duel scene.

I walked into the abandoned bar, listening to the waves crash against the shoreline and the wind howl against the tower of the Bayfront. I stood next to the fire pit, gazing into the flames. A gas line fueled the fire, of course, one of those ultra-modern designs with crystal stone covering the pilot jets. It shimmered like something out of a sci-fi movie, or some wizard's magical furnace, prepped and ready to cast some vicious curse over all the world.

"Cigarette?"

I didn't have to look to know the voice, but none the less spun around to behold the source. Ragnar Wortham strolled toward me, lit cigarette clasped in his left hand, his right extending an open pack toward me. He wore black cargo pants, polished leather riding boots, and a karate gee tied with a black cloth belt, all encased in a red leather trench coat. He smiled, running his left thumb over his receding hairline, unafraid of the cigarette ember burning his vampire-crimson hair. He smiled his creepy, lupine grin, relishing every moment.

"I don't smoke anymore," I told him, turning back to the flames. He walked up next to me, taking a long drag off his cigarette, the open pack still offered to me.

"Maybe now you do again," Ragnar mused, his cold, glassy eyes locked on my face. I looked at him a long time before I accepted a cigarette from the pack and placing it between my lips, holding out an empty hand to await a lighter.

"Here," Ragnar said, plucking the cigarette from my mouth. He placed it in his own, and touched the burning end of his own cigarette to the unlit end of mine, puckering his lips and working his cheeks like a bellows. The tip of my cigarette ignited, and he handed it back to me, taking another drag from his own. I inhaled a deep breath of smoke, choking and coughing a bit from the stinging carbon dioxide. I looked back at the flames of the fire pit, pensive.

"Same brand I used to smoke," I muttered, trying to make awkward conversation.

"I know that," Ragnar reminded me. He took another long drag from his, spitting a thick plume of smoke as we both let silence fall between us.

"You learn a lot about a person by hating them," Ragnar mused. "Of course, I didn't hate you when you got me started smoking these. If I die of cancer, I'll have you to blame."

"Somehow I think you'd blame me either way," I observed, a musical tone in my words.

"Probably," Ragnar confessed. "But that's part of the fun of it." He flashed his phosphorescent, perfect smile, the flicker of the firelight reflecting off his glassy skin. The light and shadow made his features look more skull-like than ever. I scoffed, taking a hit off my cigarette.

"You really don't fucking stop, do you?" I seethed, refusing to look at him. I didn't need to see his face to know his shit-eating wolf-smile mocked me.

"No, I don't, Liquin." I hated the sound of my name in his voice. Somebody once said everyone's favorite sound is that of their own name. I never quite understood that—when someone said my name, which I admit is an unusual one—it always stung, like the pierce of a thorn through a child's finger. The sound of my name meant I was in trouble, that someone was angry, that someone was mocking me. Coming from Ragnar, it felt like a dagger in my side, twisting and jerking to inflict as much pain and butchery as possible.

"I'll never stop," Ragnar proceeded. "I absolutely *hate* you, and I derive pleasure and satisfaction from causing you pain and humiliation." I stared up into the clear blue of his eyes, and found no hesitation in them. He meant what he said.

"Why? For how long!?" I fired back. "Because of what happened, we're going to do this for the rest of our lives? Do either of us deserve that?"

"You do, in my judgment," Ragnar grinned, dispassionate. "And what I think is all that matters."

"You're a petty fucking asshole…"

"Oh bullshit!" Ragnar growled back. He edged his face close to mine, snarling like a ravenous animal, ready to decapitate me. "You think I'm the asshole here? Are you that fucking stupid?" He took one last puff from his cigarette, and tossed it into the fire. "Look at where you are, Liquin! Look at where I am! Look at this Convention! You say you hate all of it—the executives, the Hollywood types, the price gougers, the protesters—but you don't. You *resent* them. You resent them because they are getting and doing what they want. They are succeeding while you fail. The only thing you really hate is *yourself*, Liquin. That's why you flounder as you do."

"You don't think I hate you?" I pressed him, trying my best to hide my shame.

"You wish you did!" Ragnar continued. "You're too afraid. You're not strong enough to hate me! See, if you did, if you had the fucking balls to hate me as much as the world hates you, you might have a chance at happiness. It's not enough to be angry. It's not enough to resent me or the fucking executives who treat you like a serf and loathe your very existence while they make money off you and exploit the things and people you love! You have to *hate* them! You have to hope and strive to hurt them at every possible opportunity until they break! Life is a competition. It's not enough to succeed in a goal. Anybody can do that; success doesn't command respect!"

"Oh, then what does? Petty grudges? Petulant bickering?"

"Winning," Ragnar snarled. "And you know what it means to win?   Of course not, you've never won a day in your whole worthless life! Winning means someone else has to fail. Someone else has to lose. That's the pleasure and power of winning that commands and demands respect from everyone else in the world. I'm here to win, no matter what, and that's always been the difference between you and I. You have some high-minded morality that you think will save you, but it just damns you to failure. You can't do what's necessary to win! But I can, and I have, and I will! I will see you broken for crossing me. I'll see you shamed and disgraced and destroyed and will take utter satisfaction and joy in hurting you. And nobody, none of your prized friends—not Brigham or Windsor or Kate—will come to your aid, because they're smart enough that they want to win too. And they know how to do it. Everyone you know and love will turn their backs on you in order to survive to fight another day, and you will be alone and even more worthless than you are now!" He reached up and rested both his hands atop both my shoulders, moving in so close that I could smell the stain of tobacco on his breath, rancid and expired, like cremated ashes. "After all, what's the point of success if you can't hurt the people who doubted you?"

"And that's not petty, Ragnar?" I did my best to sand firm and not let me fear show in my posture. I don't think it worked. "After all the pain it takes to succeed, and you'd still hurt other people just as deeply?"

"Pain is a force of nature," Ragnar shrugged. "It's like money, given and earned. Or electricity…it can't be created or destroyed, only transferred." He looked me up and down. "Or stockpiled. Pain transcends life. And on the last day of your life, Liquin, when you're alone and dying and miserable, you will realize how empty and wasted your life was. And you will beg for my forgiveness. And I shall whisper *no*. Because on that day, my beloved friend, I will have won." He smiled again, broad and proud, his widowed peaked-hairline curling with the edges of his lips. His whole face looked as though some artisan had carved it in glass. "And you'll die alone and forgotten. Another rotting body on the ash heap of this polluted driftwood we call a planet. That's the power of hate, Liquin. It's just like love, except it's rational and honest."

I stared into the shimmering light of his eyes, the flames reflected in the gloss of his corneas. For a second he waivered, and I thought I could see hurt and sadness drowned in the rage… maybe even regret. But, whatever his suppressed emotion, it vanished again beneath the relish of his hate. He would destroy me and everything I cared about; I had no question about that. I'd seen that look in his eyes once, years before, standing out on a balcony overlooking San Diego, Comic-Con in full vigor below, moon shining on us from above, and the chance of a lifetime presented at our feet…

"Hey Liquin!"

Ragnar and I parted to see Puck, armed with a clipboard and wearing an oversized headset connected to a walkie-talkie clipped at his belt. Even in the dark of the evening and the cold of the air, I could still see the stains of sweat under each arm.

"Hey Ragnar dude!" Puck greeted. "We're almost ready guys!

We gotta get you into costume though, Liquin. Kate's almost ready with the camera!"

"Ok," I said, trying my best to sound confident. I tossed my cigarette butt into the fire and gave Ragnar one last icy glare. He just smiled again, my Satan incarnate, feeding on my anger. He lit another cigarette as Puck and I walked out of the cabana bar. "What am I wearing?"

"Well, you gotta wear Frank's costume, which kinda sucks," Puck explained.

"Will it even fit? He's like a totally different body shape!"

"Oh yeah, totally. Didn't even fit him right," Puck rambled.

Puck escorted me down to the set, where Kate stared through the viewfinder of a heavy-duty digital camera atop a tripod, her own spiral notebook tucked under her arm, its pages dog eared and scribbled with ink. Kate & Puck had selected a plain area of concrete walkway against the edge of the pay for their shoot, and a trio of high-powered lamps marked the edge of the shooting area, each pointed at different angles and all three powered off. Beside her, a key light aimed forward into the viewing area, lit to test the power of the lamp. Kate reached up and adjusted it with gentle precision, not noticing Puck lead me down beside her. The equipment containers used to transport the camera and lights were stacked in front of the camera, adding banal set dressing to the shot. Behind Kate & the camera, a plain wheelchair, stenciled with the words "First United Methodist Church" spray painted on the back of the seat, looked out of place parked alongside the rest of the equipment.

Puck threw open a large plastic container, filled with random audio equipment and cuts of raw fabric. He dug about a moment, before presenting me with a black kimono and microfiber trench coat.

"Puck, can I get a lighting temperature on the key light?" Kate asked, still not acknowledging me with even a look.

"Just put 'em on man, and I'll get you wired," Puck assured me. I pulled off my shirt and tied the flowing kimono around my waist, its hem poised just below my groin. The USB drive still hung from my neck, which I tucked into the folds of the kimono. The chill of the night barreled right through the thin polyester making my nipples harden and teeth chatter. I donned the trench coat right away for comfort, and found it actually fit pretty well. I watched as Puck navigated over the snaking chords of the lights and camera, taped to the ground with black electrical tape, each plugged into one of two surge protectors, which in turn joined with two orange extension cords tracing the walkway to some unseen outlets closer to the hotel. In front of the camera, Kate and Puck fiddled with a light meter, with Kate making notes on her pad and Puck tinkering again with the key light.

Ragnar joined us on set, tossing away the remnant of the cigarette, taunting grin still plastered across his face. He exhaled a lung full of smoke, tapping his foot against the cement, cracking his knuckles.

"We about ready, minions?" Ragnar asked.

"Yeah," Kate said without looking up as she made notes on her pad. "Let's get 'em wired," she ordered to Puck. Puck dove into the storage bin again, pulling out two tiny vinyl cases and handed one to Kate. She came over to me and affixed a tiny body mic to the collar of my kimono, tucking a long wire down against my bare skin, and plugging it into a battery pack which she strapped to my waist. Puck did the same for Ragnar.

"Now, we're probably going to have to rerecord you in post anyway," Kate explained. "But even so, try not to jostle too much." She pulled a roll of black electrical tape from her back pocket and tore off several pieces, reaching up under my coat and kimono to tape the chord to my skin.

"And what am I doing?" I inquired, adjusting my kimono a bit, retying the belt for maximum stabilization.

"Standard duel," Kate directed. Her eyes flashed up across my face a split second before she went back to the storage container. "You remember your stage combat?"

"Um, no," I confessed. "Remember, I'm a last minute replacement!"

"Amateur," Ragnar stabbed as Puck ducked under the back of his trench coat, fastening his battery pack to his waist.

"It's just basic," Kate called back. She produced two full-sized replica lightsabers from the container, screwing the white, Plexiglass blades into the hilts. She handed me one and the other to Ragnar. I gripped the cool aluminum tight between my fingers, getting a feel for the weight of the weapon.

"When you swing," Kate explained, coming back over to me, embracing me from behind and sliding her hands over my own. "Keep the sword parallel to your body, the point of the blade between ten and two." She puppeted my hands back and forth as if the blade were a clock hand, the tip bouncing back and forth between the ten and two positions. "That's for safety. Don't make any true lunges or stabs. Just swing it like a bat. We can speed up the footage a bit in post to make it look more intense."

"Ok," I sighed, a wave of sudden nerves tingling in my gut.

"I'll give you some direction from off camera," Kate assured us. She went back to the tripod and started adjusting the stabilization knobs, tugging at the camera.

"Here," Puck grunted, running over to assist Kate. The two of them lifted the camera from off the tripod, which Puck tossed aside with a loud rattle. Kate balanced the camera over her right shoulder, eye through the viewfinder, as Puck pulled the wheelchair up behind her and helped her to sit down.

"What the..." I stammered.

"Nice," Ragar uttered, swinging his lightsaber about, loosening his muscles. "Instant steadycam!"

"It's how Friedkin shot *The French Connection*," Puck mused. He seemed to bob about like a ball on the surface of a swimming pool, barely able to contain his excitement.

"The edge of our shooting range is spiked with the blue tape on the ground," Kate said. "But I don't expect you to cross it. Sound effects and the lightsaber beams we're going to add in post, along with a digital matte for the background. Just imagine you're on Bespin!"

"Dressed like Neo and Morpheus?" I squawked.

"It's a mash up!" Puck quipped with pride.

"Ok," I mumbled. "What's the dialogue?"

"Make it up, you're a writer!" Kate ordered. I glanced at Ragnar, and he & I actually shared a moment of camaraderie at our mutual perplexity.

"We're ad-libbing?" Ragnar asked, incredulous.

"No, Liquin's ad-libbing," Kate clarified. "Your line, Ragnar, is 'From Hell's heart, I stab at thee!' Just make it cold."

"No problem there," Ragnar assured her. I didn't have to look at him to know he'd shot a playful glare in my direction.

"Ok, we ready for a take?" Puck asked, switching on the lights and pulling Ragnar and I into position alongside the equipment cases. I squinted at the overpowering, white glare from the lamps. All at once, the chill in my bones subsided; the heat from the arcs overpowered the cold of the night.

"Lights!" Puck proclaimed. He jogged over the wheelchair and plugged his headset into an audio jack on the camera. "Can I get a sound level?"

"Check," Ragnar spat.

"I hope I'm getting hazard pay," I grumbled.

"Ok, blades up! Face each other!" Kate directed us. Puck grasped at the wheelchair handles at the top of the seat, wiggling the contraption just a bit. "Easy, dolly."

"Copy that dude," Puck muttered with anxious intensity.

"Ok, ready?" Kate squinted through the viewfinder.

I turned to face Ragnar, his devil smile never looking more evil. I took a deep breath, ready for action, just wanting to get the whole thing over with as fast as possible. Just think: my big screen debut at hand, and I was hoping to check out before they'd even ran dailies.

"Camera rolling!" Kate declared. My heart fluttered as I leaned forward, staring into the crystal skull of Ragnar's face. I could hear my pulse banging in my ears and throbbing behind my eyes. I clenched my teeth together, all the anxiety and frustration and anger and *pain* that had tormented me over the whole weekend of the Con about to explode from inside me.

"Go!" Kate yelled out.

Ragnar and I both chopped the air with our lightsabers, the plastic blades connecting with *crack* that echoed against the walls of the Bayfront and out over the water. Both of us leaned our heads over the locked blades, teeth bared, foreheads leading like two frenzied rams on an ultraviolent edition of *National Geographic*, or some godawful Fox show like *When Animals Attack.* I stared past the blue of his eyes trying to see his soul. I could feel him try to pierce me the same way.

"From Hell's heart, I stab at thee!" Ragnar growled through his clenched jaw.

"Get away from *her*..." I seethed. I pulled back my sword, and swung it back with all the force I could muster. "YOU BITCH!" I screamed. The words exploded from my throat with volcanic ferocity, as I felt my vocal chords grind in my larynx. I thrust all my weight against Ragnar, who met my charge with stubborn resolve. His feet skidded across the pavement as I pushed my blade hard against his own, as he knocked into one of the storage containers, tipping it over.

Somehow though, he maintained balance, and came at me with hellish fury. I blocked his attack, but felt myself lose ground against his velocity. He came at me again, and again, and again, as I retreated from his advance, Puck spinning Kate around in the wheelchair with our every move. I brought my sword down against his, panting for breath. Ragnar held his ground pressing back against me, his own breathing labored at wet, his smoking habit apparent.

"By God I swear..." I hissed. "I'll never stop!"

"You're a fucking disappointment!" Ragnar screamed, jumping backward. I seized my moment and batted my saber towards him, just in time to feel the USB drive fly out from under my kimono. It spun on its lanyard, tethered about my neck as Ragnar parried my advance and caught the tip of his lightsaber on the nylon of the lanyard chord. It pulled taught like a guitar string, just before the plastic hook that bonded the drive stick to the necklace snapped and the momentum of Ragnar's lightsaber knocked it flying out into the dark where it landed in San Diego Bay with a modest splash.

The sword slipped from my hands as I felt icy cold run up through my wrists and into my forearms, my blood turning to formaldehyde. I could only hear my heart thunder under my eardrums as I wheezed for air, running to the edge of the bay and bracing myself against the guard rail. My knees went slack and I collapsed to the ground in a heap, the world around me lost in a haze of panic and desperation.

It was gone. My would-be masterpiece, my magnum opus for which I had endured years of agony and struggle, the fucking script that would insure my memory for all time, was lost. *Leopard Messiah*, along with all my instructions for the *Neodämmerung,* had sunk into oblivion, and with it, any hope I had for some meaning in my life.

Somewhere in my daze, I knew Kate and Puck had cut filming, and rushed up behind me, calling out my name. I didn't hear it, but I just *knew* it, like I'd read the factoid in a magazine or something. I have no memory of experiencing their cries. I do, however, remember looking up into Ragnar's face as I tried to comprehend the magnitude of my failure. Lit by the halogen lights behind him, he cocked his head sideways looking down at me, fingers of light cast over his glaring, glossy skin, his eyes and expression lost in the dark. He wasn't a man, but a faceless demon sent to destroy me and everything I cared about, a fountain of pain and loathing.

And he'd won.

"I'm cold," I remember whispering in the dark of our hotel room. I've no idea how much time passed between the duel and Kate's getting me upstairs, nor do I remember the walk up through the Bayfront. I came to as Kate threw a second comforter over my back, my body already wrapped in a bathrobe and the bedclothes of my mattress. I became aware of the shaking—the uncontrollable oscillation of my limbs when Kate placed both her hands on my wrists, trying to steady me. I could hear her talking to me in some muted distortion, like sound from under water.

"Hey!" Her howl registered with me at last, and I found myself staring into the pale blue of her eyes, shining and moist as she tried to maintain her own composure. "Drink this," Kate ordered me, handing me a paper cup of hot water.

"It's so cold," I said again as Kate slipped the cup between my fingers.

"I know, sweetheart, I know..." Kate rubbed my arms through the blankets, trying to warm me with her maternal instinct. "Don't spill!"

I clutched the cup tighter in my hand before shifting to grasp it with both hands just above my abdomen. The warm soothed my frigid digits, and though by body still quaked, my teeth had stopped chattering. My vision came back into better focus as I looked down into Kate's majestic crystal blue eyes, her resolve masking her overwhelming fear. She steadied my hands, lifting the cup to my lips, urging me to sip. I took a modest drink, cringing at the aluminum taste of the hot tap water, forcing it down my throat, recoiling my head from drinking more.

"I can't, Starbuck," I whimpered. "I can't." I shook my head as Kate kept stroking my arms with tender affection.

"I already messaged Brigham and Windsor and Roxanne," Kate told me. "Brigs should be back here soon. I can't find the other two." Her words teemed with bitter frustration at Roxanne for being so flighty, and no doubt at Windsor for a myriad of reasons.

"I can't," I whispered again, teetering back on the edge of catatonia.

"Hey, hey, hey," Kate urged. "Stay with me now. I have to go help Puck the equipment..."

"It's gone, Kate. My script is gone."

"I know."

"I want to die," I croaked, my body tremors intensifying.

"Liquin..." Kate searched her heart for words of comfort, but both of us knew she'd find none.

"I want to die," I sputtered. My body shook and my fingers

went limp, the cup slipping to the floor. Kate hopped backward to avoid the spilling water, which poured out over the carpet, setting in a wet splotch. I didn't care. I slumped backward, flat to the mattress, my hands clawing at each other over my stomach as I tried to find some existential way to steady myself. I writhed, inching my way up the bed toward the headboard, the pillows stacked and fluffed awaiting a sleepy head.

"I WANT TO DIE!" I screamed, burrowing my head under the pillows, scratching my bare arms. I could feel the tiny peels of skin gathering between my fingertips and my nails. I pulled one of the pillows against my face with all my strength, hoping to suffocate myself and the world around me, to stifle the pain and agony and awfulness into serenity. I screamed into the pillow, the hardest, loudest scream from the depths of my soul that ever escaped my lips. My whole body vibrated as I howled.

I started punching my right hand into the pillow toward my face, the fluff of the stuffing cushioning my blows. I wailed and yelled. I wanted to kill the world too; it deserved it as much as I did. I wanted to murder those who had hurt and crossed me for what they'd done, and more than that, I wanted to kill all the people that loved me too. After all, they'd led me on, they'd made me have faith in myself, they'd encouraged me to keep going. They needed to be punished for what they'd done—for the mistake of believing in me, or worse, the lie they told me to keep going.

Life was a lie. Love was a lie.

I cried and cried, rolling into a fetal ball, the pillow smushed between my face and knees. Why couldn't I just have peace? Why couldn't I just have serenity?

Why couldn't I just be happy?

I felt the bed sag and the springs of the mattress contract under the weight of another body as Kate lay down next to me, resting her arm over my own, cupping my body against hers. I shuddered and sobbed in her warm embrace, neither of us saying anything. I just lay there in hysterics like the maniac I was. Kate just held me like the tender soul I didn't deserve.

I'm not sure how long we lay there, but after a while, I heard the *snikt* of the key-lock on the door, followed by the creak of the pneumatic arm. I felt Kate sit up, and heard her murmur something to our caller. He whispered something back. I didn't have to look to know it was Brigham, come back to check on me.

I sensed their exchange as Kate rose from beside me, and exited the room, saying nothing else to me. I didn't hold it against her for not saying goodbye; she didn't owe me anything more.

After a few more minutes, I raised my head from the pillow to find the blurry form of Brigham sitting on the bed across from mine, slurping at a drink. He just watched me but didn't say anything. When I finally had choked back my cries to mere sniffles, I sat up and wiped the tears from my cheeks.

"Hi," I managed, a whimper escaping with my words.

"Girl, you're a mess." Brigham sipped his drink again, the light of a nearby table lamp reflecting in the Coke bottle lenses of his glasses. "And for the record," Brigham added, "don't even think about the pills." I froze, staring back at him, hiding part of my face behind the pillow again. He didn't waver.

"You think I'm stupid?" Brigham asked, sounding more apathetic than angry. "Do you think Kate or Windsor or Roxanne are stupid? Well, I suppose we all can be sometimes..." He trailed off, gulping down the rest of his drink, then rising to pour himself more. "But do you really think we'd be stupid like *that*?"

"Would you like one?" he asked me, pouring a splash of vodka from the water filtration unit into his glass.

"No," I coughed, resting my chin on my knees.

"The pills are all gone, Liquin," he declared. "You're not going to die tonight, at least not with my drugs, or on my watch. And really, I think deep down you know, you couldn't kill yourself anyway."

"No?" I pressed him. He shook his head and scowled.

"You're a survivor by nature," he said, taking his seat on the bed again. "You wish you weren't, because that'd be easier. But you never did anything because it was easy."

I sat quiet a long minute, letting his words marinate in my brain. I relaxed a bit, my shudders at last subsiding. I took a deep breath, exhaled, and took another.

"I really hate it when you're right about shit like this, ya know that?" I grumbled. "Or at least you sound right."

"Girl, when am I ever wrong?" Brigham chided me. He raised his glass in my direction, took another sip, and put it aside on the nightstand. "You know it's getting late. We should get going if you want to get to Rich's."

"I'm not going to Rich's!" I moaned. "I want to go home!"

"EJO, aren't you finished yet?" Brigham howled. "Pull it together Mr. still-the-best-at-what-I-do! Yes, the script is gone, but what can you do about it?! Now let's go meet boys! Sitting here isn't going to make you feel better!"

I sighed. I knew he had a point, even if it drove me nuts. I tossed the pillow aside and sat another long moment before I glanced up at Brigham again. He looked at me over the crest of his eyeglass frames and I replied with a nod. I got up and went to the bathroom, switched on the light and tried not to look at my puffy face.

"God, now I look like the one in *The Shining*," I grumbled. "I look like Hell, Brigham! I can't go out like this!"

"Concealer!" Brigham barked. I poked my head back out of the room and frowned at Brigham, who took another swig from his glass and proceeded to lead me back to the bathroom. He sat me down on the toilet and started pecking about in his toiletry bag.

"I'm not wearing a pound of make-up," I stipulated, "and even if I were willing I don't have the same skin tone! You're paler than I am."

"Yes, darling," Brigham purred. "I'm a Tilda Swinton. You're a Nicole Kidman."

"There's a scale?" I asked.

"Yup. Casper the friendly ghost is a zero. Tilda's a one. Nicole's a two." Brigham took a tube of liquid foundation, dabbed bit on my finger and started blotting it around me under eye.

"How high does the scale go?"

"For Euro mutts like you and me? Ten. Which is like George Hamilton-John Boehner."

"Eew!" I shuddered. "Remind me to get a spray tan next time." I snickered to myself.

"See! Making progress already!" Brigham observed. I chortled again. He leaned down and kissed the top of my head. I sighed.

"Why is it all so hard, Brigs?" I whispered in reverential tone. "Why Ragnar?" His name escaped my throat like a serpentine hiss.

"That's the business part of show business," Brigham observed. "Ragnar is a means to an end. But if we had to choose one of you, or if we had to ask who the better friend is, do you think that any of us would pick him over you?"

"I'm not sure I'd feel better if you did," I admitted.

In the end, I don't think Brigham painted me with much make-up. For one thing, he knew I hated it and my fragile masculine self-image would crack under too much. He also probably realized that if he wanted to get me out of the room and back into public life where my mood could stabilize, he needed to do it fast.

A few drops of Visine to quell the redness of my eyes and a slather of moisturizer later, Brigham shuttled me out of the bathroom and started digging through the dresser to find my going-out clothes. I hadn't brought much—my frugality and self-loathing somehow convinced me that I wouldn't hit Hillcrest for fear of embarrassing myself. I really should have known better given that I roomed with Brigham. Somehow or another, he always managed to get me into trouble. That's part of why I loved him. Sometimes in life we need a friend to push us out of our comfort zones and into some mischief.

"Maybe you should just wear a bathrobe and nothing else," Brigham suggested.

"Pssh!" I scoffed. "I'd need to wear pants! I need someplace to put my wallet and keys! Besides, it's so fucking cold out there I'm afraid my junk would fall off before we even got a cab."

"A cab," Brigham reflected. "It's going to be heinous getting one out there tonight."

"Yeah," I nodded. "We should cut up into the Gaslamp District and try to get one there. That way we can bypass the traffic from the Con."

"See?" Brigham chimed. "That's the Comic-Con paladin I know! Go ahead and say it…" Brigham stared at me, head bowed, fingertips drumming against each other, his hands folded together in a semi-prayer stance.

"I'm still the best at what I do," I uttered in dispassion.

"Not really convincing," Brigham critiqued, "but getting better."

"I know!" I said. "Why don't I just wear the kimono from the shoot? Kate forgot it up here…" I looked down at my body to see the black satin wrinkled around me and adjusted it, retying the belt chord around my waist. "What do you think?" I posed with my hands on my hips to Brigham.

Brigham eyed me up and down, walked to the nightstand and took a large gulp of vodka from his discarded glass. He winced as he swallowed, then looked me up and down again.

"You look like a 70s porn star crackhead pimp or something," Brigham declared.

"That's a lot," I observed.

"I think it's fabulous!" Brigham cheered, grabbing me by the hand and leading me from the room. Down the hall as we waited for the elevator, my Illustrious friend turned to me again and grinned a wicked grin. "Besides, it's coming off five minutes after we walk in!"

We descended the elevator, evaded the perplexed looks coming from the Hollywood douche bags as I strutted through the lobby in my kimono, cut down another escalator, and then crossed over Harbor Blvd. on a giant walkway populated by other Convention attendees. The wind blew harder above the main thoroughfare of Harbor and the train tracks and I shivered against the wind. Brigham rested a hand on my back, I suspect, to keep me from running off. His hand was warm, so I didn't mind.

The pedestrian walkway dropped us on the far side of Petco Stadium, so we had to walk around the massive circumference of the ball park to get back to the main streets and a cab. I remembered that Sixth Avenue ran north one way, so we cut over a couple blocks and met with a peculiar sight.

"Are you seeing this?" I asked Brigham as I beheld the massive line for Flynn's Arcade.

"Yep," Brigham smacked. "Looks like Disney is going all out on *Tron: Legacy*."

Flynn's was a major set piece in the original *TRON*, the home and business of Jeff Bridges' character. Disney had gone to the trouble of recreating the entire arcade right there on Sixth Avenue, complete with the red brick storefront and glowing neon *Flynn's* sign, and as we walked up the block, Brigham and I could hear the rumble of deep bass signaling a live DJ, and the beep of old style cabinet arcade games.

"Maybe there's hope after all," I uttered. "Now if we could just get a..." I spotted the headlights of an approaching cab and jumped out into the street, my left arm outstretched. "TAXI!" I shouted as the cab screeched to a halt.

"Still the best at what I do," I declared to Brigham.

"Excellent," Brigham sneered, doing his best Mr. Burns impression.

"Nice shirt," the cab driver complimented me as Brigham and climbed into the back seat. "Who are you supposed to be?"

"Myself," I purred, taking one last look at Flynn's before the car sped off.

For all the chaos and decoration for Con in the Gaslamp district, Hillcrest, the historic part of San Diego that housed a preponderance of gays, never seemed to change no matter how many times I visited—an island frozen out of time and place. Now, I'm sure it did change. Businesses, no doubt, opened and closed and buildings underwent refurbishment. But compared to the chaos of Comic-Con, or worse, the everything-lasts-fifteen-seconds turnover of Los Angeles, Hillcrest seemed almost draconian. It surprised me how good it felt to get away from the Con and back to some kind of reality.

The cab dropped us right in front of Rich's, its façade repainted a shade of deep blue. A sizable crowd had packed in the enclosed patio out front, a haze of tobacco smoke hovering over it. A giant banner over the door sported the Comic-Con logo, welcoming the geeks. I didn't object to Rich's advertising the Con; the gays had known about the geek counterculture for years and, for the most part, embraced it. I'd always felt an odd kinship between my gay friends and geeky brethren: they'd all known what it was like to feel like a freak, to play the outsider. That gay culture, more or less, and geek culture had hit the mainstream pop-American culture around the same time only intrigued me more.

Brigham and I entered the sea of hot geek soup in the front bar of Rich's, the bass dwarfing that of Flynn's Arcade, the patrons crowded in, drinks in hand, the bartenders naked but for well-placed speedos and body paint. Brigham and I made a bee line for the bar, and he ordered us two vodka-Red Bulls and two shots of Goldschlagger. I stared down into the tiny shot glasses, the bits of gold leaf floating, suspended in the thick cinnamon schnapps. The colored lights above shifted and danced over the clear liquid, as Brigham raised his glass in a toast.

"To old friends!" Brigham declared, his eyes concealed by the reflection of the light gels in his Kissinger glasses.

"The sun also rises," I said, downing my shot. Brigham did the same, fanning his face with the burn of the liquor in his throat, then resting it atop his collarbone at his imaginary pearls. I washed my shot down with a swig of the vodka-Red Bull, choking a bit on the cinnamon aftertaste.

"Christ, Brigs," I coughed. "Why do we do this nasty shit?" Brigham straightened his glasses, resting atop his nose.

"Think how *boooooring* we'd be otherwise!" Brigham purred over the roar of the music.

"Or just plain bored!" I added. I took another sip from my drink and scanned the room for familiar faces. "Ok, we're gonna go work the room. Who are we gonna flirt with?"

"Oh my!" Brigham exclaimed. "First things first..." He grasped my arm with his free hand. "Body paint!"

Brigham lead me to a corner of the room where some wooden bleachers covered in carpet scaled one of the walls. We found our favorite Bostonian make-up artist—the one we'd seen at every Con for years—perched with a airbrush gun and different canisters of body paint, finishing the Batman logo on the an inebriated, dark skinned muscle dude, no doubt on leave from the nearby naval base on Coronado Island. As he stumbled down from the bleachers, the make-up artist turned around, wiping down a brush in a paper towel. He cocked his head side to side like a confused chicken, trying to place our faces.

"Ahhh, yah finelly shaaawed!" He squawked though his east coast brogue. "I been wayteen foh yah!"

Brigham pushed me up into the bleachers, sitting me down in front of the make-up man who snatched up a nearby miner's helmet and fixed it on his head. Brigham and I exchanged a look of confusion as the make-up dude switched on the head light—the literal head light that is—and shined it into my face. I squinted and cowered away from the blinding light, and the artist turned it off.

"Dear God!" I muttered.

"Saw what ahhh we dooooin this yeeeah?" The make-up dude asked. "Awff with yahh sherrrt!" I set my drink down next to me as Brigham started pulling at the kimono draw string. I smacked his hands away and undid the tie myself, taking off the shirt and tucking it into the belt line of my jeans.

"Oh, I dunno," I whined. "Brigs?"

"How about the Phoenix logo," Brigham suggested. "It fits with the weekend." I nodded.

"Why not?" I smirked. *"It's better to rise than fade away!"* The words stuck in my head like an arrow, in one ear and out the other. Suddenly, the Hole song "Reasons to be Beautiful" made all the sense in the world: there's always more than a choice between life and death. Sometimes, we just have to find the option.

I mused on the lyrics, humming the song to myself as the make-up artist went on a bout his work, painting the giant golden emblem of the Phoenix on my chest. For a split second, I thought again of the godawful movie *X-Men: The Last Stand*, and how it managed to botch the comic arc of *The Phoenix Saga*, bastardizing it into unrecognizable noise. Fucking Brett Ratner.

I looked up to find Brigham, but the make-up dude's headlight kept me squinting blind. I decided to wait as he seemed almost finished, the emblem drawn, as he painted over it with gold glitter. The phoenix looked amazing shining there on my pasty white chest...so pasty in fact, that I wondered how the make-up dude could see to even paint! I worried his retinas might detach!

"Ah, yah dunn theyhhh!" The artist switched off his headlamp as black, twitching spots consumed my sight. You know, those weird, moving specks after looking into a camera flash? Yeah, those, though in my post-shot, darkened environment with spinning colored lights above, I had a hard time distinguishing the club effects from the blind spots. For a split second I even thought I saw Raz-Ar standing in front of me, a goofy smile on his face. I tipped the make-up artist, thanked him, and took a long swig of my drink.

"Raz-Ar's been looking for you!"

My eyes darted back to the dancefloor, where Raz-Ar, stood grinning. He decked himself out in a pair of jeans with vertical tears up each leg held together by safety pins and an oversized gray thermal shirt with *The X-Files* logo embroidered in green thread across his left pectoral. He raised up his right palm and gave a modest wave, the way a five year old might at a fire engine passing by in a parade.

"Raz-Ar?!" I uttered in confused shock. He just waved again, emitting a goofy chuckle.

"Hi!" he said with his rapid nod. Without even thinking I opened my arms and outstretched them for a hug. He jumped into my arms and held me tight, whispering "hi" again.

"Wait!" I panicked, pulling the two of us apart. "The paint!" Sure enough, I looked down at Raz-Ar to see the phoenix emblem and its surrounding glitter had imprinted on his thermal, leaving a perfect reflection in the middle of his chest.

"Aw man!" Raz-Ar groaned. "This is vintage!"

"GOD DAMNIT!" Raz-Ar and I spun around to see the make-up artist shaking his head at us. "Don't messs up mah werk!" He grabbed a brush from his nearby spread as another shirtless guy, this one older and a bit more chubby took his seat, ready for painting. "Don't werry!" he added. "It'll come aff in the wash! Wahtah soluble!"

"Eeek, sorry!" I croaked, embarrassed at what had happened. I gave a crooked, mea culpa smile.

"Eh, it's cool," Raz-Ar assured me. "Raz-Ar digs the Phoenix! Except in that shit movie..."

"A-fucking men!" I agreed. "But let's not go there!" I reached back and grabbed my drink from the bleachers by the make-up seat. The artist had re-lit his headlight again, making the dude getting painted wince...and possibly gave him radiation burns as well. "Where the Hell have you been?" I asked Raz-Ar.

"Raz-Ar has been looking for you! Raz-Ar kept walking the Floor all day looking for you! Going to panel rooms, just hanging out hoping to see you! I kept hoping you'd knock on my door!"

He'd slipped again, actually using first person instead of the dissociative third. I noticed his eyes flicker away from me, bouncing around the room with nervous energy. I couldn't help but smile though. He seemed so innocent standing there, just teeming with love.

"I'd hoped you'd knock on my door too," I confessed.

"Raz-Ar would have, but didn't know your room number!" Raz-Ar explained. "I even waited in the lobby yesterday for a while waiting to see you!"

"Yesterday was a bad day," I observed. "Be glad you didn't see me in a bad mood."

"Raz-Ar is just glad he found you today." He reached out

and curled his left index finger over my right pinky, giving a flirtatious tug toward him. I pursed my lips, trying not to smile, averting my eyes, shy. He tugged again, a bit harder, snickering as he did. I looked up at him and submitted to the flattery. I took a deep breath, and sighed.

"Fuck it," I blurted, just as I grabbed his gorgeous geek face and smushed it together with my own. I could feel his body twitch with giggles as we both relaxed and he wrapped his arms around my waist. Our lips parted, and we lingered together a minute, nuzzling our noses together in an Eskimo kiss.

"Cute!" An older man, his white Perry Ellis silk shirt unbuttoned to his navel, bald head shining in the colored lights, patted us both on the back with an approving nod. Raz-Ar and I exchanged a look of *do you know this guy*, and apparently, neither of us did. The Old Gay nodded and flashed a denture smile, resting his hands on his hips as he surveyed us. "I really hope you two make it!"

We both giggled again, and Raz-Ar tightened his grip around my waist, pulling me closer. I watched the Old Gay disappear into the crowd, until a soft kiss on the cheek wrested my attention back to Raz-Ar. I bowed my head, resting my forehead against his, trying to relax into the moment.

"Life's so weird," I uttered. Raz-Ar nodded, his forehead rolling against mine. "It's even weirder than I am," I realized. Raz-Ar kissed me on the cheek.

"Think how bored you'd get if it weren't," Raz-Ar urged me. Just then, a roar came from the next room as the song changed, an abrupt transition from the techno-house beat into the retro-electrical whirr of synthesized organs.

"No fucking way!" I waited a moment, just to be sure that yes, I knew the song. "EJO! It's the ELO!"

"That's a lot of letters," Raz-Ar observed.

I grabbed Raz-Ar by the hand and yanked him through the crowd into the next room. More vibrant gels colored the heads of the crowd packed on the dancefloor as confetti and the fog of dry ice blasted the cheering patrons, their hands and glasses lifted to the air. A drag queen dressed as Poison Ivy, painted green head-to-toe presided over the chaos, a dozen gogo dancers dressed in only skimpy dick-lift underwear writhed and sparkled, their bodies gleaming with glitter and sweat, their silhouettes writhing in the mist.

"Isn't this song like, really old?" Raz-Ar asked me as I towed him to the dance floor.

"It's from *Xanadu!*" I squealed. "It's called *All Over the World!*" I started to bump and grind against Raz-Ar, who danced like a rusty C3PO. Well, I wasn't the best dancer either, so why would I judge him? We were having fun, we were *strange*, we were cool with that...so why complain?

"This is so corny," Raz-Ar laughed.

"The movie is awful, I know," I allowed. "But the soundtrack is fun in a...corny way." Raz-Ar leaned in and kissed me again. By that time, an enormous, joyful, toothy, smile of bliss has taken up full residence on my face, and I decided not to fight it or ruminate on all the troubles that awaited me as soon as it faded into the next song. I'd had a miserable fucking weekend, so I figured I'd earned a few minutes of levity.

"Jesus Christ!" Raz-Ar blurted. I froze in place, alarmed. He pointed across the room to a table, where two men danced beneath the dry ice fog. I could make out their silhouettes: a sprightly, tiny dancer, upright with his hands in the air, his hips thrusting forward and back in perfect sync with the music. In front of him, a rounder man pumped his backside on all fours, like a dog having a seizure.

"Those guys are having fun," I grumbled. "But you know what? More power to 'em! Seize the day!" I laughed and started to dance again, this time with more abandon. As the fog cleared, the sparkle of some reflection caught my eye...something shiny in the churning light of the room. I narrowed my eyes, squinting to try and see through the haze of carbon dioxide. I froze again, not able to believe my eyes.

"Oh dear God," I gasped. "That's..."

I recognized Brigham spring to his feet atop the table, moving in sync with the almost-naked body of the gogo boy, his coke-bottle glasses flickering in the disco light. The two of them kissed with sumptuous passion, their hips rolling and churning a moment as the table began to teeter. I reached out my arm, trying to somehow span the length of the room in a split second, realizing what was about to happen, but of course, I could do nothing. I watched with helpless awe as the table tipped and Brigham slipped, the gogo dancer grabbing him to try and correct his balance. Instead, they both lost theirs, flipping sideways, the dancer leashed to Brigham's arms, yanking him from the table to the floor. I saw Brigham's legs go spread eagle as he belly flopped to the ground.

I darted through the crowd as fast as I could, rushing to my literally fallen comrade, finding him face down atop the dancer, Raz-Ar chasing after me to help.

"Brigham!" I shouted as the song faded out. Brigham rolled over onto his back and off the poor dancer, who wiggled about in a daze. Brigs sat up, his glasses crooked on his nose, looking up at me in confusion. "Oh God are you ok?" I took Brigham by the hands, helping him to his feet. I kept watching for a pack of vicious bouncers to descend on us and beat all of us to a pulp before hurling us out onto University Blvd., but for the moment, we seemed safe.

"I think it's the future of *city living*!" Brigham exclaimed with a grunt. He frowned, nursing a bruised hip with his right hand, but otherwise miraculously unharmed. He looked down at the crumpled gogo dancer and fell to his knees, helping the tiny guy to his feet.

"Ay dios mio!" the dancer moaned, stretching his arms, trying to work through his pain.

"Gizmo!" Brigham exclaimed, embracing the dancer.

"Gizmo?!" I repeated in disbelief. I took a step closer to the beleaguered couple, scanning the dancer's face. "Travis!?" I exclaimed.

"Hey Lik-Ween!" the pocket gay greeted me. He winced holding his backside. "I hurt my ass, Brigham!"

"You can hurt mine later!" Brigham promised, throwing his arms around Travis's tiny body.

"Did Raz-Ar miss something?" Raz-Ar said into my ear.

"Raz-Ar, this is Travis," I introduced.

"Gizmo!" Brigham chirped, interrupting me. I cleared my throat.

"Travis also goes by Gizmo. He's Brigham's ex-boyfriend," I clarified.

"Hola!" Travis greeted Raz-Ar with a wave.

"Gizmo!" Brigham tweeted again, before devouring Travis's face with a massive wet kiss.

"Ex?" Raz-Ar questioned. We stood there watching Travis and Brigham make out like horny teenagers, Brigham's hands slipped beneath the thin fabric of Travis's gogo undies. Travis, for his part, burrowed his own hands under Brigham's beltline, his eyes locked with his fiery passion.

"Well," I mused. "They are rebooting *everything* these days!"

We left Travis and Brigham to have their intimate reunion, adjourning to the smoker's patio, taking up a small corner against the guard railing. Raz-Ar rested his arm around me as I explained how Brigham and Travis had met at Con years before when the latter was our Front Desk clerk at our hotel. We'd had a pool party in the hotel hot tub that had gone a bit awry when Brigham knocked a potted palm into the water, which somehow lead to me getting locked out of my hotel room while Brigham and his *Gizmo* fornicated for hours. They'd had a torrid affair, dating for six months before the distance between Los Angeles and San Diego coupled with Brigham's insane work schedule pulled them apart. I'd not seen Travis in more than a year, and last I'd heard, he'd gone back to University to study nursing.

"At least we know he can pay for his student loans," Raz-Ar joked. "Well, kinda."

"Travis is a good guy," I declared. "And quite resilient despite his pocket size." I shook my head in ironic amusement. "I suppose Brigs won't be home tonight."

"Does that mean..." Raz-Ar trailed off. "You know...could,

um, we…"

"Kate and Windsor will be there," I told him. "Because otherwise, believe me, I'd love to." I didn't feel a need to ruin the moment by talking about the side effects of the Wonder Twin Drugs, how they deflated my wang. A gentle wind blew across the patio, and Raz-Ar hugged me close for warmth. The flowing air fluffed the curls of his air, and I smiled again at the natural cuteness, like a newborn puppy.

"There is one other idea," Raz-Ar said, a distant look in his eyes.

"Your place?" I asked, my nerves fluttering.

"Naw, can't go there. Roommates. Too many of us anyway." Raz-Ar bit his lower lip and gave me a long, thoughtful look. "There is someplace else, but…Raz-Ar isn't sure you want to go *there*."

"Where?" I pressed him, intrigued.

"Down the street," Raz-Ar began with a deliberate pace. "It's sketchy, though."

I turned my head to face him with a slow, deliberate roll of the neck for dramatic effect. I looked him up and down, ran my tongue over my lower teeth, and smacked my lips.

"Is it a bath house, Raz-Ar?" I inquired with buried fear. Raz-Ar shrugged, a timid, almost apologetic smile on his face.

"They call it a spa," Raz-Ar clarified. I slammed my forehead into my palm, exasperated. "Right!" Raz-Ar backpedaled. "Stupid idea. Raz-Ar's stupid. We could always, um…" He trailed off, trying to think of some alternative.

"Am I going to get athlete's foot?" I whined. "Because I had that once in Junior High and it sucked ass. Lord knows what kind of Comic-Con athlete's foot would be living in there." Raz-Ar smiled.

"Let Raz-Ar get his bag," Raz-Ar pleaded, leading me across the patio and back into Rich's. "Raz-Ar had to check leave it at the front when he came in."

"I should check in with Brigham," I realized, pulling out my phone. I followed Raz-Ar through the club, tethered to his arm, looking down at my smartphone screen. Brigham had already messaged me that he and Gizmo were, as he put it, "eating after midnight." I felt glad that they'd reconciled, and that Brigham was getting some Con love. But beyond that, I did not want to know who was eating what.

Raz-Ar collected his bag from the front office, and the two of us spilled out onto University Blvd., both of us swaggering with a near skip of enthusiasm. The sky above had cleared, and the once-gray heavens, opaque with clouds, had given birth to a peppering of glimmering stars. I felt a wave of inner serenity well in my chest, my muscles loosening and back cracking from a weekend of despairing posture. A block away from Rich's, a peaceful silence had set in over the street, broken only by the occasional car zooming by. I could hear the sound of our footsteps echoing against the Hillcrest storefronts. It all felt like such a relief.

Raz-Ar led me to a nondescript building of simple brick, painted roof to pavement with dark black paint, a single door the only portal to the interior. He stopped and looked at me, the blue of his eyes sparkling, but his expression one of hesitation.

"You sure you can handle this?" Raz-Ar asked one more time. "It's pretty intense."

"As long as I don't have to show my wang, I'll be fine," I promised him. "And as long as you stay with me."

Raz-Ar nodded and ushered me through the door into a long, shadowy hallway lit with 45-watt red lightbulbs overhead. Cinder blocks walled the hall into a barren passage, painted as black as the outdoor portion. The air felt thick and wet, reeking of far off chlorine and bleach. At the far end, a burly attendant with a long, ginger beard and a pair of strapping arms covered in tattooing sat reading a copy of *Tales of the City*. He wore a black tank top and a kilt—at least, I guess that's what you'd call it—of black canvas, covered in utility pockets and stainless steel rivets. He looked like Paddington Bear by way of a biker gang. I froze in place as Raz-Ar entered the building behind me, stepping aside to let him lead.

"In or out!" Paddington ordered us. I rushed to keep up with Raz-Ar, deferring to his wisdom.

"Two," Raz-Ar said, getting out his wallet. "One room."

"IDs," Paddington requested. We passed our licenses over to the attendant who waved them under a black light—probably the only black light the place had ever known—and scanned them in a digital reader. "Fifty," he charged, ringing up a sale on an old-style cash register missing several keys. Raz-Ar paid him in cash, and before I could argue to at least pay my own way, Biker Paddington had a few other instructions. "Rules are: no clothes, no drugs, no fucking the staff. Gotta be out by 8am." He tossed us a set of keys on a curly plastic chord.

"Got it," Raz-Ar assured him, taking my hand and pulling me through a black vinyl curtain. We'd entered a locker room just like something out of gym class. A trident of robin's egg blue lockers divided the room which seemed made of bone tile, with two oblong wooden benches situated between each forking. The air felt humid and warm—much warmer than outside, and I could smell the amplifying odor of chlorine with each breath. At the far end, next to a glass door on a pneumatic arm, a stainless steel rack covered in white bath towels stood ready to accept new patrons. Ahead, I could hear the distorted echoes of sounds bouncing off water, just like entering a YMCA, which I somehow found appropriate.

"I'm suddenly very nervous," I blurted to Raz-Ar. I could already see the droplets of sweat beading together at his hairline. He had to roast in that sweater...

"It's cool," Raz-Ar assured me. "Here." He threw open a locker door, unlocked with the key given to us by Paddington, and right away started stripping off his clothes. I watched him, fascinated. "You put your stuff in here too! Grab a towel!" Raz-Ar undressed down to nothing, though by the time he'd unfastened his pants, modesty had me turn away from him, just as it did anytime I entered a locker room—a holdover from years of sexual insecurity in gym class, no doubt. I snatched up two towels and held one out to him, my eyes averted. He took it, and

I wrapped the other around my waist before slipping out of my shirt. Behind me, Raz-Ar went through his bag, snickering.

"What?" I whined, kicking off my shoes. I fiddled with my belt with one hand as I tried to hold the towel tight around my hips. I still couldn't bring myself to look at Raz-Ar, who lay a hand on my shoulder. I jumped in alarm.

"Calm down," Raz-Ar chuckled. "Raz-Ar will protect you."

"Look away!" I ordered. I glanced back over my shoulder to make sure Raz-Ar turned his back, before slipping out of my jeans & boxers. I'd feared that I might drop the towel, and give him a shot of my moon with a fruit basket. "Sorry," I apologized. "I had a religious upbringing. Naked is bad."

"Sounds familiar," Raz-Ar said. He helped me wad up my clothes and stuff them, along with my backpack, into the locker. He locked the latch, and with his own bag over his shoulder, took me again by the hand. "Come on."

The bathhouse of Hillcrest—did it have a name? I didn't know. The bathhouse reminded me of something out of *Hellraiser*: a labyrinth of darkened passages, hidden doors and erotic grunting. Every lightbulb had dim wattage and a colored hue, mostly red and blue. Somewhere, I could hear the sound of running water and splashing echoing against tile. Raz-Ar lead me through the maze of narrow corridors and ambient steam to a tiny stall equipped with low lighting and a cot covered in a latex sheet, no doubt for easy wash-off. He locked the door behind us and put his bag on the floor, squatting down and digging through the contents. I sat down on the cot and watched him, my eyes centered on his legs as they pressed against the worn terrycloth of his towel, bulging through the fabric.

"Here!" Raz-Ar announced, holding out a lighter and tiny one-hitter pipe.

"Careful!" I gasped. "They might have cameras in here! And that bear guy said no drugs!"

"It's illegal for them to have cameras," Raz-Ar assured me. "And the door dude just meant no meth. Nobody gives a damn about weed." He lit the hitter and took a deep inhale, holding his breath a long time as he passed the pipe over to me. I took a hit, coughing as the smoke filled my lungs, feeling like needles on my alveoli.

"Damn," I said, my face going numb. I leaned back on the bed, feeling the latex adhere to my back in a hermetic seal. Raz-Ar chuckled and slithered up next to me, the sheet sticking to his skin making a raspberry sound as he slid over the surface. He averted my gaze a moment, ruffling his spiky hair with his fingers, then biting at his thumb nail. I caressed the side of his arm with my left hand, my thumb studying the tactile sensations of his skin contours, feeling all the bumps from the scarring.

"I really want to touch you again," I murmured. Raz-Ar's head snapped back to attention, a devious grin on his face, as he snatched me up in his arms, burying his head in my bare chest and squeezing me tight. I grunted as the pressure of his embrace forced the air from my lungs, coughing again at the remnant of the weed.

"This feels nice," Raz-Ar uttered against my breastbone. He sounded like he had a mouth full of pudding, his enunciation warped from the pressure with which he grasped my body.

I wanted to grab him, throw him down, and ravage his body right there, doing anything and everything I could to express physical affection. I wanted to go at it for hours, to make him sweat and shudder and moan so loud he'd drown out the sound of the other bathhouse boys. If our room had been on the stage of Hall H, I'd have made love to him before the flashbulbs and cheers of thousands of people—I didn't care who saw or who judged. Holding him, even in that uncomfortable position, just felt so right and like a triumph. Raz-Ar was one of the strangest people I'd ever met in a lifetime of meeting bizarre people, but he was also one of the most beautiful. And most important of all: he saw past my insecurity, my awkwardness, my sickness. He saw into my soul and, maybe, the souls of everyone else he met with perfect clarity and he still *liked what he saw* in me. He didn't care about my career, or my nutjob tendencies, or my flaccid wiener side effects from the Wonder Twin drugs. He just *liked* me.

And I liked him, and respected him and admired him so much, that I knew I wasn't good enough.

"Wait a sec," I whispered to him. He climbed up next to me on the cot as we stretched out lengthwise into a more comfortable position. He moved his face an inch from my own and planted a tiny peck of a kiss on the tip of my nose. I snickered.

"Listen Raz-Ar," I started. "I love being here with you, and I really want to do this, but..." I paused, searching my soul for courage. "But I'm not sure we should."

I looked up into Raz-Ar's face, and saw the crystal blue of his eyes flooded by fear and hurt. I started to panic, as he no doubt did too, trying to explain.

"I really do want to do this and it has nothing to do with you!" I blurted. "But, you gotta understand, it's been ages for me."

"And you don't want to?" Raz-Ar begged.

"I do, but I can't! The drugs I'm on fuck with my system. I haven't been able to get hard in months!" I pulled away from him and rolled onto my side, staring at the wall, my back to his face. I couldn't look at him, so ashamed of my very existence. I didn't know what else to say, so I just whispered, "I'm sorry."

I closed my eyes, waiting to see how Raz-Ar would react. He didn't say anything for a long time, but he didn't get up and storm out either, which is what I feared would happen—what so many other guys had done to me. *So many* guys...they'd hurl insults. They'd laugh. They'd tell me how fucking ugly and useless I was and ask why I didn't have stock in Viagra or something. They'd tell me how if they were in my position, they'd just kill themselves, because what's the point of living as a man if you can't act like one? What's the point of fucking having a useless dick? Even the polite guys, after a couple of great dates...when they'd find out about my side effects, they'd just nod with solemn reverence and get up and leave and never return my calls or my texts again. It only shows how little I'm worth to anyone.

Nobody cares.

We sat there as the minutes past, hearing the distant orgasmic moans of other men having orgies or smoking meth or some anonymous hook-up. I started to wonder if Raz-Ar might have fallen asleep, bored at my confession or just too high from the weed and exhausted from the Con. At last I felt a creek of the bed as he stood up. I didn't turn to watch him at first, still wallowing in my own shame. I heard the rattle of his backpack as it slid across the floor, rummaging through it, no doubt to get ready to leave.

I closed my eyes to prepare myself for the total loser humiliation my body had wrought once again. I gritted my teeth and took a shallow breath, then rolled over.

"I'm sorry," I breathed as I opened my eyes. Raz-Ar sat against the far wall—not that far; the stall was fucking narrow —his sketch pad balanced on his raised knees. He just sat there, watching me, not saying anything. I opened my mouth to speak, but had no idea what to say. Raz-Ar had managed to leave the windbag writer speechless.

"Stand up," Raz-Ar ordered me. I started to shake and quiver, balling up my fists and folding my arms over my waist. I couldn't take this, not from him, not after losing the script. Not after a shitty Con. Not after getting humiliated by Ragnar.

Perhaps sensing the total and utter collapse of my spirit, Raz-Ar put his sketch pad aside and stood up to his full height instead, staring through me all the while. He reached down and undid his towel from his waist, letting me see his full body in the dull light. As he folded his towel, I marveled at his physique —so lean, every tendon and muscle marked by a ripple in the contours of his skin.

"Stand up," Raz-Ar said again, this time with delicate enunciation. I did as he told me, not resisting as he undid the towel from my own waist, letting it fall to the floor in a heap. He knelt down, kissing my lower abdomen on either side where it joined with my hips, before sitting back down and taking up his sketch pad and pen again. He watched me a long time, and I looked back at him waiting for some great revelation. But he said nothing, instead scribbling with furious vigor at the page in front of him.

I opened my lips to ask him what the Hell he wanted, but before I could, he answered me.

"Just stay there," Raz-Ar instructed, his eyes flicking from the sketch pad up to face me and back again. "I just want to see you."

"What?" I asked, resisting the instinct to cover my genitals with my hands like some embarrassed child.

"You're so fucking beautiful, Liquin. I've wanted this since we met. Just stand there, please, and let me draw you. So I can remember. Then if you want to go…"

"No!" I exclaimed, not at all sure how to feel. "I want to be with you." Well, he'd already seen my body naked, so why not be naked with my intentions too…

"Ok then," Raz-Ar smiled. "Then let's be together. Just let me draw!"

I couldn't help but giggle. What the Hell!?

"What, just like this?" I squeaked, my giggles turning into more boisterous chuckles.

"Just like that. You're so hot."

I laughed again, one of those rare laughs where I felt no hesitation, no inhibition, no shame. I just flowed out of me like air from my lungs or tears from my eyes. I felt a rush of energy charge up my back and into my shoulders, wide awake, tingly, and alive.

I fell down to my knees grinning, and pushed the pad away from Raz-Ar.

"Hey! Hold still!" he protested through squeaking giggles. I leaned in and kissed him on the mouth, my heart pumping like the engine of an Aston-Martin, my cheek muscles pinched and sore from smiling so hard. I pulled away after a moment of bliss, then planted one last peck on Raz-Ar's lips before I stood up again. He snickered.

Raz-Ar smacked his lips and widened his eyes as he pulled the sketch pad back up to his knees and resumed his drawing.

"That was pretty...awesome," he confessed. I shrugged and sighed, tilting my head back and rolling my eyes.

"I'm still the best at what I do."

SUNDAY

The Phoenix Saga

That night I dreamed of all the stars in the sky over San Diego; tiny rhinestones, Swarovski crystals drizzled over a canvas of black silk—pure, perfect, transcendent. How man has ruminated and reflected on those countless points of light keeping their silent vigil over us, imagining they are gods or the souls of the dead. How we do aspire to rank amongst their heavenly glory—to be a star, of rock, film, television, literature…something to rank among the ages; someone who commands respect and reverence and the attention of all those who would aspire to greatness. How the stars memorialize the people we lose, how they signify our dreams. So many men and women fantasize that the stars and their celestial neighbors have power over the events of our lives, over are dreams, when it is we that have power over the stars and their significance. Twinkle, twinkle…

Courtney Love wrote about them to memorialize her husband, her love for him, and the rage of his betrayal in abandoning her and their child. *Named a star for your eyes…*

It's better to rise than fade away. Rise, just like a star.

I hummed the song "Reasons to Be Beautiful" as Raz-Ar and I collected a breakfast of coffee and scones from a small beanery in Hillcrest the next morning. I found it fitting, given that fate—

the stars?—had brought us together in a coffee shop days before. I watched him, his goofy posture and bubbling enthusiasm that made him nod like a feeding woodpecker. Every one of his quirks endeared him more to me. And his eyes...two perfect stars glowing from within his soul. He may have housed madness away in his core too, but perhaps that only contributed to the beauty and baroque perfection of who he was.

He'd drawn me more times than I could remember in that tiny bathhouse stall, before we kissed and snogged for hours. We'd fallen asleep in each other's arms, and wouldn't let each other go the rest of the night, intertwined and woven together like threads in an ornate rug. Every now and then I'd wake up to shift my weight in the night, and lean over and kiss his neck or on the arm. Every now and then I'd wake up to feel him do the same. I hadn't slept so well in ages.

We woke up and showered together in the morning. By that hour, the other patrons had deserted the baths, and so we enjoyed each other's immodest company. I'd half a mind to drag Raz-Ar back through the maze to find a whirlpool or sauna, and just lay together relaxing in the soothing heat. Alas though, time required us to get back to the Con, or at least out of the bathhouse lest Paddington Biker Bear come after us. We did, however, enjoy one last perk. For whatever reason —the atmosphere, the emotional agitation, sleeping curled up together, or maybe just because God/Fate/The Universe granted us a reprieve from its usual sadism, we'd both awoken in the throes of firm arousal.

And I mean *firm*! I felt like a fifteen year old in the throes of his first crush, awakening after some wet dream fantasy. We sized the moment, and indulged in full enjoyment of our bodies. Raz-Ar tasted incredible, like ambrosia to a bee. We'd left one another sticky like honey, anyway, hence the immediate need for a shower.

Raz-Ar flagged a cab and we headed to the DoubleTree so Raz-Ar could collect his belongings—his Con badge chief among them—and his medication. I, as much as anyone, understood the need for maintaining an existing regimen. From there, we proceeded to the Bayfront, so I could do the same. We arrived to find the room deserted—no Brigham, no Kate or Windsor, though the car keys of the latter waited for us on the nightstand. Brigham's belongings still littered the room, while those of Starbuck and Straightness had vanished.

I stopped off in the bathroom to attend to my hygiene—we were still at Comic-Con after all, and I'd be damned before I contributed to the odor of the Gink—and to take my own medication. I downed my Claratin and the Wonder Twin drugs dry, then spruced my hair a bit and shaved. I figured I had nobody to impress, so going casual didn't bother me. I emerged from the bathroom to find Raz-Ar sprawled with his sketch pad on one of the beds. I smiled at him and went about packing the rest of my things, donning an *Infinity Gauntlet* t-shirt and a *Harry Potter* hat, cast in red and gold, the colors of my house, Gryffindor.

"You have a great body," Raz-Ar said as I stuffed my suitcase.

"Bull," I spat, not looking up from my work. I heard the rustle of paper and the *plop* of Raz-Ar tossing his pen aside before I looked up to see him standing over me. He tackled me to the floor right there, kissing me on the neck and rubbing his stubble over my soft skin. I writhed and squirmed at the scratchy feeling, giggling at the affection.

"You do!" Raz-Ar chided me. "You do! You're hot! You do!"

"Stop!" I squealed between laughs. "I'll kick your ass!"

"Hot!" Raz-Ar cheered, grinding the word with his vocal chords. "Hot!"

Just then there came a knock on the door. Raz-Ar and I looked at one another in surprise. I kissed him on the forehead and shoved him off of me, as I rose to answer the call.

I threw open the door to reveal Roxanne, the Admiral, her eyes red and face puffy, her hair messed as if she'd walked through a cyclone to get to the room. She shuffled past me into the room dragging her roll-away suitcase behind her, dropping it to the ground with indifference as she crossed the threshold, before she plunged face down into the empty bed.

"Admiral?" I chimed, following her into the room. Raz-Ar climbed to his feet and stood beside me. "You ok?"

"I hit the wall!" Roxanne moaned, burying her face in a pillow. "I hit the wall!"

"What wall?" Raz-Ar asked, confused.

"Roxanne, you remember Raz-Ar..." I reminded her. She didn't look up, just raising her thumb upwards, waving it over her head a couple of times, before letting her arm go limp and drop beside her.

"What happened to you?" I pressed her, sitting beside her on the bed.

"Fox people are nuts," Roxanne grumbled, rolling over to look at me for a moment, then burying her face in the pillow again.

"Good nuts or bad nuts?" Raz-Ar questioned further.

"Nuts!" the Admiral exclaimed again, this time through the pillow. "Nuts!"

I looked back at Raz-Ar who extended his palms, as if expecting me to clarify her answer. I shrugged.

"So what happened to you?" I asked. Roxanne lifted her head, peering at me through her mess of ebony hair.

"You know that *Family Feud* clip where some idiot says that a gun can kill a party?" Roxanne croaked. "Turns out he was right. Leave it at that." Raz-Ar and I looked at each other, both of us widening our eyes at her observation. I shook my head, not knowing what else to say.

"Sweetheart," I broached at last, "we have a couple hours before we need to be out of here. Maybe you should rest..."

"Fucking right," Roxanne moaned. She rolled over onto her back. "Wait, my phone's dead!" I rolled my eyes.

"Where is it?" I grumbled. She pointed at her purse, which I opened and dug through to produce her drained phone and charger. "This explains why we couldn't get a hold of you last night..."

"Yeah, sorry," Roxanne sighed. "You and everyone else." She rolled onto her side to watch me as I plugged her phone into a power outlet on the desk. I went about packing up the remnant of the First Aid Kit, as Roxanne scuttled to the other bed, noticing Raz-Ar's sketchbook.

"You're really good, you know that?" Roxanne said, suddenly alert. "You really capture Liquin's dick."

"Dear God!" I grunted, snatching the sketchbook away from her. "Gimme that!"

"You have no idea," Raz-Ar chuckled. I gave him a stern look. He grabbed me by the waist and kissed my shoulder.

"Ok, we're going to the Con," I told the Admiral. "We need to be out of here by one, so we'll go find Kate, Windsor and Brigham. And maybe shop a bit."

Roxanne nestled herself into the bed, raising her thumb again. By the time I'd donned my Con Badge and we'd left the room a few minutes later, I could hear her snoring.

"She's cool," Raz-Ar said, taking my hand. I could feel the sweat on his palms, signaling that he's anxiety with meeting new people hadn't subsided in the past forty eight hours. Still, he'd coped well.

We descended the elevator to the lobby, where we met with the also-familiar face of Brigham, also accompanied by the diminutive Travis, both of them also looking haggard.

"Did anyone sleep last night?" I uttered as we approached Travis and Brigham, who walked hand in hand. Brigham wore his same clothes from the night before, along with his anonymity sunglasses. Travis had changed from his gogo thong into less revealing attire; a Lady Gaga t-shirt and fitted designer jeans. I glanced down at his tiny body, noticing he still wore the same granny ballet slippers that he had when we'd met him years before.

"Morning!" Travis greeted us through his Latin lisp. "Did you boys have fun last night?"

"Fuck yeah!" Raz-Ar spouted before I could answer. I took him by the hand again, giving his palm a squeeze.

"It was an eventful night," I answered. "Did you guys have fun?"

"Honey, Gizmo and I are making gremlins!" Brigham said, swatting the air with one hand, resting the other at his imaginary pearls.

"I so don't want to know what that means," I grumbled. Travis giggled, kicking one leg up over his head like a ballerina. Raz-Ar fluttered his eyes at the sight.

"Roxanne's napping in the room," I explained. "We're gonna hit the floor and find Kate. Be ready to go by one."

"Didn't she text you?" Brigham asked, his tone grave.

"No..." I trailed off, expectant. "What happened?" Brigham bit his lower lip, glancing at Travis a second. He took a deep breath and held it.

"I'll let her explain," Brigham told me. "But def find her."

Before my anxiety could kick in over Kate's state of mind, a peculiar sight captured my attention: a group of six men and one woman, in full dress and make up as the cast of the original *Planet of the Apes.* I marveled as they strode through the lobby, excited Con attendees rushing to pull out their camera phones and snap a picture. They must have had their make-up professionally applied—it looked incredible!

"Check it out!" Raz-Ar exclaimed. Travis turned and gasped with glee. Brigham looked too, and I saw the color drain from his face...

"ARRRGAHHHH!" Brigham let out a thundering scream, his palms held to the side of his face, vibrating with fear. "A GORILLA!" Brigham screamed again, pointing across the room. The ape dressed as Dr. Zaius waved at us, smacking his orangutan lips as he did.

"NO!" Brigham screamed in terror. "NO!" Across the room, Dr. Zaius nudged to his ape companions, all of whom noticed my Illustrious panicked friend. Leading the pack along, Dr. Zaius rushed toward us, his arms curled into hooks like some sneaking *Scooby-Doo* character.

Brigham howled in panic again, his anonymity glasses bouncing on his nose as he took off running for the elevator, letting out Shelly Duvall screams again the whole way. Travis rushed after him, trying to calm him to no avail. Brigham screamed and screamed pounding the elevator button as the apes rushed closer. One of the shaft doors parted, and Brigham jumped aboard, tethering Travis by the hand. As they both disappeared aboard, a family of screaming children, guided by their also screaming mother, ran from the elevator into the bay. I could see Brigham's hands shoving them off. The poor woman screamed in competition with Brigham, her own panic shutting out any sense of reality.

The apes stopped at the elevator door, grouping together and waving at Brigham as the doors closed. I heard Brigham scream again—blood curdling as ever—as the poor woman from the elevator heaved for breath and cupped her three terrified children.

"Comic-Con!" I hissed with joy, watching the scene conclude. I took Raz-Ar by the hand and lead him over the white polished marble of the lobby floor to the exit, back out to the courtyard and headed for the bustling Convention Center.

"Is he going to be ok?" Raz-Ar asked me as we left.

"Fabulous!" I uttered with glee.

Outside, the sun had finally chased the clouds away, bathing the Convention below in summer light. The air had warmed too, drying the pavement but for a few small puddles of lingering moisture, and forced the attendees to shed their extra layers. Con looked like Con again, even if the sun could not extinguish the memory of a dreadful weekend.

But even the joy of the great weather withered compared to what we saw as we approached the front of the Convention Center: the anti-gay protesters still coagulated into a clump of bigotry, their nasty signs waving over their heads. But surrounding them like Sherman encircling Atlanta, a counter protest comprised of three times the number of protesters cheered and reveled in the sunlight. And they were geeks! I could see the Con badges draped around most of their necks as they cheered and shouted over the hate-speech of the protesters. The counterprotesters waved signs of their own design, prompting passers by to join them in cheering or just plain applaud: "Superman died for your sins!" "Spock has risen!" "Batman hates hate!" "What would God want with a starship?"

"Holy shit," I uttered. Raz-Ar squeezed my hand.

"There are always possibilities," Raz-Ar observed, leading me into the Convention Center lobby with a grin.

Inside the Exhibit Hall, Raz-Ar and I wandered Artist's Alley, a sort of cabal of up-and-coming or veteran comic artists trying to show off their work. Comic-Con had once been *the* place for an artist to get notice, but since the pop culture/Hollywood explosion, the Con had granted them less and less space each year. That did offer one advantage—with most of the attendees distracted by the major booths from the toy, comic and Hollywood exhibitors, Raz-Ar and I had a fine amount of space to mosey at our leisure. I could tell how much Raz-Ar loved walking the area, stopping every so often to examine a portfolio or show off some of his own work. For the record, he didn't show off any drawings of me naked. That brought me a bit of relief.

"There's Jerry Robinson," Raz-Ar pointed out as we passed an elderly man drawing at a folding table.

"The guy who created The Joker?!" I gasped, staring at the old man. He sat there all by himself, no escort, no fans. "How can he sit there in anonymity!? He's a legend! One of the most important comic icons ever!"

"Comic-Con has changed," Raz-Ar reminded me, a hint of sadness in his voice. I nodded in agreement.

"Let's go say hi," I suggested, just before a familiar voice captured my attention.

"Liquin!" I turned to see Monty Doyle mosey up to me with his hot-shot agent swagger, in a pair of khaki pants and blue cabana shirt. He smiled at me, holding out his arms as if to give me an imaginary embrace.

"Monty!" I gasped, trying to pull myself together. "Oh God, I look like Hell!"

"Relax," Monty instructed me. "It's fucking the last day of fuckin' Comic-Con. Who gives a shit!"

"That's what Raz-Ar keeps telling him!" Raz-Ar injected. I introduced him to Monty, who gave me a perplexed look, no doubt because Raz-Ar had referred to himself in third person again.

"Liquin, I gotta tell you something," Monty declared. Without thinking, I grabbed Raz-Ar's hand as I felt my stomach churn and hopes plummet.

"Oh?" I asked, trying to sound casual.

"Yeah, look, I read your script," Monty explained. "It's a fucking brutal jungle in Hollywood right now. Nobody with any fuckin' confidence. Shit for brains."

"Wait...wait a sec," I stammered. "You *read* my script?!"

"Yeah. You can write," Monty complimented me.

"How did you get my script!?" I exclaimed. "I didn't send it out yet!" Monty looked at me, confused.

"I got it on Wednesday night," Monty explained. "You sent it to me." He took out his Blackberry and started scrolling through his Inbox. "Unless I'm losing my fuckin' mind again, which could be..." I scanned his face, hopeful.

"Right here!" Monty declared. "*Leopard Messiah*, yeah. That's right, ain't it?"

"Well yeah, but..." I tried to wrap my head around the situation. "But...you didn't say anything at dinner!"

"Naw, well, I hadn't read it yet and didn't want to bring it up then. Didn't want to stress you." I felt my knees go slack. Raz-Ar wrapped his arm around my waist to steady me, captivated by our every word.

"Stress...me..." I murmured in shock. "So, um, what...what did you think!?"

"Listen kid," Monty said, hands outstretched as if to give me some package. "You're a fine fuckin' writer, but we're all still smartin' from that fuckin' shit writer's strike a couple years ago. I got a backlog bigger than my ex-wife's ass!"

"M-Monty," I stuttered. "Could you send me a copy of that file?" I did my best to keep calm, but my heartbeat thundered and my pulse raced. I wanted to scream and laugh and cry and break stuff and plant a big fucking wet kiss on Raz-Ar's lips all at once. I wanted to kiss Monty too, but didn't want to entertain that idea *too* much.

"Sure kid," Monty chortled. He pecked away at the keys of his Blackberry. Monty smirked, amused by something on the screen. "Stick it in?!" Monty exclaimed. "You put that in an email?!"

"What?" I asked, dumbfounded.

"Monty dude," Monty quoted. "Stick it in! Enjoy my script. Get me money. I'll get you money. And we'll all be happy dude." He chuckled again. "Then it says 'Love Liquin, the Lizard Queen.' And at the bottom you wrote 'stick it in' again in parentheses.

"Oh," I said, my voice high-pitched with stress. "Yeah, I did... I..." I trailed off shaking my head, not knowing what else to say or how to explain that I had *no idea* when I sent the file or why or anything else.

"There," Monty declared. "Forwarded ya the file. You ought to make sure you have it backed up!"

"Yeah right," I said, my voice airy. "So..."

"You got a fuckin' great sense of humor, kid," Monty complimented me. "But I can't rep your script, not right now. I got too much shit to do." I nodded as I stared at him, my face blank. "Work on it though. Write somethin' else. I'm happy to look at it when you do!"

"Thank...thank you Monty," I managed to say though my mouth had gone dry and my face numb. I stood there, stupefied.

"Keep up with the dream, kid," Monty encouraged, nudging me on the shoulder with his fist.

"I feel like the dream is dreaming me," I confessed without thinking.

"Yeah? I get the same way after four martinis!" Monty laughed and nudged my shoulder again, nodding at Raz-Ar in courtesy. "See ya around, kid!"

As Monty strode off into the aisles of the Exhibit Hall, disappearing into the crowd, Raz-Ar just stared at me waiting for some reaction. I stood there, numb, dumbfounded and perplexed.

"What just happened?" Raz-Ar asked me after a long pause.

"I got it back," I mumbled. "I got my script back! And Monty won't rep me!" I felt such confused emotion, I didn't know what to do.

"The Adrenachrome!" I realized. "Stick it in…Lizard Queen… Roxanne and I must have sent him the file in a drugged stupor on Wednesday!" I felt the blood drain from my face. "Oh God, did I just get lucky…"

"Happens to everybody sometime!" Raz-Ar observed. I rolled my eyes to face him, then planted a huge kiss on his lips, clutching his face with both of my hands.

"C'mon," I ordered, pulling out my phone. "It's noon already. We gotta find Kate!"

I dialed Kate on my cell phone as I led Raz-Ar from the Exhibit Hall and back out to the curb. Attendees crowded the curbside waiting for shuttle buses back to their hotel, as I weaved around the clumps of people, my finger to my ear trying to hear Kate.

"I'm by the Bay where we shot last night," Kate said, sounding tired. I told her I'd meet her there, and charged off with Raz-Ar in tow to find her. I had to tell her everything that had happened, and I knew she'd be so happy for what had happened…

Then, when we arrived at the cabana bar, I spotted Kate down at the waterfront talking to Ragnar. I froze in place, Raz-Ar poised behind me, trying to assess the situation. Kate just slumped over the guard rail, looking out over the water. Ragnar stood at his full height, his red hair and scarlet trench coat rippling in the warm breeze. He puffed on his cigarette, saying something to Kate that I couldn't quite make out. Before we could approach them, Ragnar glanced over and noticed Raz-Ar and I, firing off a wicked smile in our direction.

I watched as Ragnar uttered something to Kate, who gave a slight nod. He turned and walked up the pathway past the deserted cabana bar toward the hotel. As he met us, he stopped, looking both Raz-Ar and I up and down with judgment. He smirked again, tossing his cigarette butt aside and emitting a thick plume of tobacco smoke from his lips.

"This doesn't change anything," Ragnar declared to me.

"No, it doesn't," I replied, my voice cold and low, cool as the ring of a cathedral bell. Ragnar's smile cracked a bit wider, and I could tell by his tiny eye movements he scanned my face for some weakness, some hesitation. I wouldn't fucking show him any.

"I'll see you again, Liquin. It's your destiny." Ragnar turned to leave, when I took a step to block his escape.

"That's your destiny too," I observed. "The dreamer becomes the dream, Ragnar. A man becomes his reflection. His negative."

For a moment—just a split second—I saw a spark of fear glimmer in Ragnar's eyes. Then, it vanished and he smiled again.

"Meanwhile," he purred, disappearing back into the hotel.

"Who was that?" Raz-Ar asked, sounding agitated.

"A reflection," I mumbled, turning to rush to Kate's side.

I found her watching the tiny pulses and waves of the bay, the occasional white cap of foam appearing as the undercurrent collided with the underwater shoreline. She drank long swigs from a Starbucks cup, looking exhausted and forlorn. Before I could even ask, she explained without greeting me.

"He's gone," Kate told me. "He left on the train this morning."

Raz-Ar ran up beside us, trying to catch up with the conversation. Kate shot him an off-hand grin.

"We broke up," Kate declared. "I guess it was bound to happen sooner or later." My jaw went slack at the admission. I tried to offer some comfort as I wrapped my head around this development, but didn't even know where to begin.

"Christ Starbuck," I whispered.

"Whatever, right?" Kate dismissed. "It happens. I just need to get home and finish my short film with Puck, and I can go on from there."

"Kate," I protested.

"I can do whatever I want," Kate said, more to assure herself, I expect. "I'm not tied to one person. I can follow my dream. My

Northern Star. Whatever…you taught me that, right?!"

"He…" I started to say, but didn't know how to finish. "He left his car keys," I told her at last.

"Yeah, I know. I loaded up the equipment early this morning. It, um… Last night wasn't pretty."

"No, not for any of us," I conceded.

"You sure?" Kate glanced back and forth between Raz-Ar and I, and I realized, it was the first time she looked at me since finding her that day. She seemed so distant, so soulless. I'd never seen Starbuck so defeated, not ever.

"I want to go home," Starbuck declared. Kate raised her sparkling blue eyes, looking past me and into my soul again. The edges of her lips curled a bit in a faux-smile, trying to elicit some reaction from me. I didn't know how to feel.

I nodded to Kate, and followed her back into the hotel. Not long after, the five of us—Kate, Brigham, Roxanne, Raz-Ar, and I—stood outside the Bayfront at the valet, loading the last of our luggage into Windsor's SUV. Nobody said much, all of us either too tired or too emotionally drained to find any excitement in the end of the Con. I think we all needed time to reflect, and at that moment, all I wanted to do was to get Kate home to bed, and Raz-Ar home to my own to think. I knew I'd want to be held like a baby as soon as I got back to my apartment, and I knew Kate would want the same thing, though she wouldn't have anyone to hold her. Even if one of us offered, I knew she would decline.

"Got everything?" Kate asked as we loaded the last of our bags into the back of the SUV. I nodded, and Kate shut the door. "I gotta pee," she declared.

"Good idea!" Brigham chimed, following Kate back into the lobby. I looked at Roxanne who stood on the curb. She nodded, intimating my request. She followed Kate into the lobby toward the ladies' room, just to keep an eye on her.

Raz-Ar motioned that he was going to do the same, and I waved to him. Finding myself alone, I rubbed my weary face with my hands, walking the length of the curb, out from under the awning of the hotel to a sunny corner, where the sidewalk ended. I sighed, not even noticing the dude in black jeans and a red t-shirt, the words "Magneto was Right" printed under a picture of the supervillain, mugging like Che Guevera.

I gazed out over the bay, my line of sight scanning from the water circling behind the hotel to the Convention Center and the knoll beside it, where the scant remains of the shanty down undergoing disassembly provided a memorial to the chaos of the weekend.

"Thank God the sun is back!" The stranger in the Magneto shirt lounged over the edge of the guard rail of the curb, his face basking in the sun. He looked at me through a pair of cyberpunk sunglasses, and grinned. "Isn't Con so much better with the sun and the heat?"

"Yeah," I agreed, not paying much attention. The stranger rose to his erect posture, running a hand through his dark, spiky hair.

"I shouldn't be in the sun too much," the stranger confessed. "My pasty skin." He had a point: his skin was so pale, it almost seemed translucent. I could see the blue of his veins snaking up under the thin skin of his arms.

"I have that problem" I confessed.

"We've met before," the stranger told me.

"We have?" The stranger had wrested my attention from my pining over the pain of the weekend back to the present.

"Yeah, just in passing," he said. "Couple years ago, here at Con. Just in passing. I'm Davy."

The name did ring a bell.

"Liquin," I introduced myself. "You having a good time?"

"Are you, is the real question," Davy offered. "Con's gotten hard to take."

"That's a fucking understatement," I agreed. "Where do you suppose it's headed? Will they move it to a different city? Restrict the attendance?"

"Who can say," Davy muttered. "What will happen to any of us?" I sighed, taking a step toward the Convention Center, still far off ahead.

"It used to be a dream to come here," I confessed. "I came here to follow my dreams. My imagination. It was like all those superheroes and aliens and monsters and God knows what else was real here. I could reach out and touch my dreams. Talk to them. And I'd always find more." I sighed. "And that gave me hope."

"And what's changed?" Davy asked.

"The dream is dreaming me...*us* now. And this place that I loved, this haven for beautiful, wonderful strange people, is dying."

"Is it?" Davy posed. I shrugged. "Maybe the dream always was dreaming us. Or maybe we need each other." Over by the SUV, I saw Raz-Ar and Brigham emerge from the Bayfront. I knew Kate and the Admiral wouldn't be far behind.

"And maybe," Davy added, "we just need to find what and *who* it was that made us love Comic-Con in the first place. Maybe we don't need a Convention for that at all."

"Yeah," I whispered. "I need to get going," I started to say.

"Right," Davy waved, signaling his understanding. "Remember who it is you love. Maybe I'll see you again in another two years." He gave me a cryptic smile, as I rushed to join my friends at the car.

I climbed into the front passenger seat as Kate took the place at the wheel. In the backseat, Roxanne and Brigham already dozed with Raz-Ar between them, each with a head tilted on his shoulder. I looked back and he smiled at me as he drew on his sketchpad.

"You know," Kate said as she started the engine. "What if he's right?"

"Who?" I asked, fastening my seatbelt. "Windsor?" Kate shook her head. I didn't have to ask who she meant to know.

"Ragnar," I uttered.

"What if all those things he said were true? Right now..." her voice faltered, and reached my left hand out in instinct to clasp her right arm. She frowned, her lower lip quivering. She shifted in her seat, steadying herself.

"In my dark moments, I think Ragnar might be right about a lot of things," Kate admitted. She threw the SUV into gear, and started to pull out of the cul-du-sac, and out to Harbor Blvd.

"He is right about one thing, Kate," I realized. "I will have to do things...terrible things...to conquer life. This planet of geeks." We halted, waiting for a stop light, and Kate looked at me, her blue eyes shimmering like sunlight off the bay. She looked as beautiful as I'd ever seen her. "Yesterday I wanted to die. Now I just want to see Ragnar die, or at least keep going long enough to make sure he doesn't have an easy win."

"One day soon, the moment will come," I confessed. "It will be me or Ragnar." I gave a pensive nod.

"And in that moment...no forgiveness in this world."

EPILOGUE

Reasons to be Beautiful

The sun had risen over the cracked sidewalks of the North Hollywood Arts District, as I helped Windsor force the Dutch door of his SUV closed. We'd piled almost his every belonging into the back of that damn car, and I had no idea how he would see out the back window, as every bit of clothing, artwork, and countless action figures stacked up from the floor mats to the ceiling light. He and I exchanged weak smiles as we joined Kate, Brigham, Raz-Ar and Roxanne back on the curb.

A gentle breeze rustled the great oak tree laves above, and in the distance we could hear the hum of the freeway as the morning traffic started to fill its lanes.

"I'd better get going," Windsor said with solemn voice. I nodded to him. "It's a long way to Ohio," he continued, the tic under his eye twitching just a bit.

"You have some good listening material?" Roxanne asked.

"Kate got me the collected works of Ray Bradbury as read by George Takei," Straightness said, avoiding Kate's gaze.

"Careful that doesn't put you to sleep!" the Admiral chided, exchanging a brief hug with Straightness. He and Brigham hugged too.

"She has a point!" Brigham clucked. "You be careful Professor Animator Straightness!"

"Thanks Brigham," Windsor smiled.

Raz-Ar extended his palm and shook hands with Windsor, a perfunctory farewell that felt uncomfortable to both of them, I could tell. But then, the two had a lot in common, so maybe what I perceived as discomfort was actually strange camaraderie.

"Take care of this one," Straightness nodded to me.

"Raz-Ar will," Raz-Ar nodded.

I couldn't bring myself to look Straightness in the eye, and I knew he didn't want to do the same to me, either. His under eye pulsed with the speed and fury of a hummingbird's wings. Instead, we just exchanged a silent embrace, neither of us pulling away from each other. I could feel the sorrow exploding in my chest, and I patted Windsor on the back in hopes that he wouldn't notice my body start to quiver. I closed my eyes and took a deep breath, smelling the odor of cigarette smoke emanating from his body, concealed beneath a spritzer of cheap cologne.

"Go find your dream," I managed to whisper. Windsor patted me on the back before pulling away from me.

"I will chief. You better do the same!" I nodded.

Though none of us wanted to be obvious, we all watched as Kate and Windsor hugged for the last time. I wanted to cry so bad...my surrogate family of geeks fragmented before my very eyes and there was not a fucking thing in the entire fucking world I could do about it. I just watched, helpless, as my real inspiration dissolved before me.

Kate wore plain clothes—jeans and a black t-shirt, same as Windsor—no make-up, and her hair just brushed. I could tell she hadn't slept the night before. Yet she stood there a pillar of resolve and strength, hugging Windsor, her eyes shut. I didn't have to see Straightness's face to know he'd shut his eyes too, both of them terrified of breaking down in front of us. I knew they wanted to kiss too, but they didn't, instead just brushing their cheeks against one another, a soft caress to say all they couldn't say. Kate pursed her lips, wincing.

Straightness released Kate, stepping backward, scowling back his emotions. He made eye contact with her one last time, his tic flinching, before he turned and walked toward the driver's seat.

"I love you," Kate blurted, voice trembling.

"I know," Straightness replied, almost turning back to her, but hesitating. He clenched his fists, walked to the SUV, climbed in, and started the engine.

Kate pressed her right hand to her lips, watching as the brake lights flashed and Windsor put the car into gear. I took a step toward her, wrapping my arm around her, resting my right hand on her shoulder. She moved her own quaking hand to my own, and our fingers interlaced that I might steady her. Raz-Ar took my free hand in his own, and I squeezed his palm for strength.

"Nothing really ends, Liquin," Raz-Ar whispered in my ear. "Not really."

We all watched as Windsor drove off down the street, through the shadows of the trees and fingers of light pouring from the morning sun, until he turned onto a main thoroughfare and into traffic, vanishing into the world.

"I had a dream," I murmured, "but now that dream is gone from me."

ACKNOWLEDGEMENT

My eternal thanks to Rasheed, Tyler, Jim, Derek, Lucky & Jody for their continued encouragement;

Vaunceil Strassenburg-Kruse and Barry Sandler for their gifts I continue to employ;

To all the readers of *Sex, Drugs & Superheroes*,

And to you, for sticking around with me this long.

ABOUT THE AUTHOR

David Reddish

Internationally read and revered author David Reddish continues to earn a loyal readership around the world. His novels include the cult works Sex, Drugs & Superheroes and its sequel Conquest of the Planet of the Geeks, as well as the Lambda Literary Award-nominated The Passion of Sergius & Bacchus.

As a journalist, he has made worldwide headlines, penning articles for such publications as Wealth of Geeks, MovieWeb, Queerty, ScreenRant and Playboy. He lives in Los Angeles. A native of Chicago, Illinois, Mr. Reddish graduated with a degree in Film from the University of Central Florida. He currently resides in Studio City, California.

BOOKS BY THIS AUTHOR

Sex Drugs & Superheroes

It's July 2008, and uber-geek Liquin Sonos journeys back to the one place on Earth where he feels normal: the San Diego Comic-Con.

Accompanied by first-time attendee Kate, socially inept would-be animator Windsor, and the flamboyant talent agent Brigham, Liquin delves further into the sex- and drug-fueled parties that underscore the convention and his mind and spirit wear down, he must confront his own creative ambition and loneliness to discover his life direction as the ultimate outsider.

Sex, Drugs & Superheroes is the hereto untold story of the famed San Diego Comic-Con. From a stark look at the camaraderie, rivalries, vernacular language, and traditions of Comic-Con, to the love-hate relationship with the Hollywood establishment that feeds it, never before has a book covered the nature of the American geek subculture.

The first in an open-ended book cycle following the adventures of Liquin and his friends as they follow their dreams, Sex, Drugs & Superheroes speaks to anyone with a love of all things geeky, or to anyone who has ever had a creative dream.

The Passion Of Sergius & Bacchus

In 357 A.D. Engulfed in turmoil, the Roman Empire had divided itself in two: the West, overrun by barbarian marauders, and the East, prosperous, encroaching toward the orient, its borders extending and contracting with battles against Persians. Julian, aged only twenty-three, became Caesar of the West, custodian of Rome against the pillaging tribes. An academic at heart, no one in the Empire believed he stood a chance leading the armies of Rome, until one day in Gaul, a great battle altered the course of Julian's career, and changed the lives of two soldiers destined to make history...

Here is the untold history of Christianity, of two soldiers in love, of Rome's last Pagan emperor, and of a world teetering on the brink of transformation.

Sex, Drugs & Superheroes 3: The Wrath Of Comic-Con

In the year 2012, Liquin Sonos and his friends return to the San Diego Comic-Con in a last bid to achieve their Hollywood dreams. But the bonds of friendship strain under the pressure to succeed, and Liquin fears the emergence of his nemesis, Ragnar Wortham, signals his doom.

In the year 2047, Ashlyn, a freedom-fighting refugee, struggles to survive among plague, poverty and factional warfare. But a frightening revelation into her past offers a way to end the bloodshed once and for all, and the death of Liquin Sonos is the key.

The Wrath of Comic-Con brings the Sex, Drugs & Superheroes trilogy to an exciting close, exploring the ever-changing Comic-Con subculture and the struggles of creative frustration. The third in author David Reddish's Comic-Con Chronicles, the mistakes of the past, choices of the present and shadows of the future all collide in a shocking, science fiction climax.

www.ingramcontent.com/pod-product-compliance
Lightning Source LLC
Chambersburg PA
CBHW051643260626
47170CB00004B/1299